My One and Only

An Ardent Springs Novel

My One and Only

An Ardent Springs Novel

Terri Osburn

Text copyright © 2016 Terri Osburn
All rights reserved.

Published by Montlake Romance, Seattle

www.apub.com

Amazon, the Amazon logo, and Montlake Romance are trademarks of Amazon.com, Inc., or its affiliates.

ISBN-13: 9781503935037
ISBN-10: 1503935035

Cover design by Michael Rehder

Printed in the United States of America

For Lynnette

Chapter 1

"We've got action in room four."

The coffee Haleigh Mitchner had been pouring when Nurse Dottie Parish burst through the break room door splashed onto the counter. She resisted the urge to slurp the black fuel off the Formica.

"We've had three false alarms in the last six hours," Haleigh said, dropping paper towels onto the mess. "At this rate, I might as well change careers from delivering babies to delivering pizzas. At least that would be a sure thing."

And oh, how such a career downgrade would drive my mother bonkers.

False alarms came with the job description, as Haleigh knew well, but they made for a boring shift. County General served at least four towns in the surrounding area, which meant lots of babies took their first breath beneath its roof. Tonight, lots of babies were preferring to stay right where they were.

"You're a laugh riot, doc," the nurse said, holding the break room door open. "This one is not a drill. Now forget that mess and let's go."

"What do we have?" Haleigh asked, following the nurse into the hall.

"Jessi Rogers. Nineteen years old. BP 140 over 85. First pregnancy and it doesn't sound like she's had much prenatal care." Dottie gave Haleigh a skeptical side-eye look. "She *thinks* she's thirty-eight weeks. Fully dilated, we've had her pushing for fifteen minutes and she's progressing fast."

Adrenaline lit through Haleigh's system. "Is the OB kit ready?" she asked. Even after bringing hundreds of babies into the world, the exhilaration never ebbed.

"All set up with a box of six and a half gloves, thanks to those false alarms."

"Is she by herself?" Haleigh asked. Childbirth was scary in the best of situations. Being a petrified teenager with no support only made it more so.

"Not alone," Dottie said. "She's got a vise grip on a guy who looks about as scared as she does. Serves him right for messing with a girl so young."

Haleigh ignored the censure in the nurse's tone. During her four-year residency in Memphis, she'd seen enough unlikely pairings to know lust didn't discriminate or encourage high standards. A muffled scream echoed from behind the next door down.

Picking up her pace, Haleigh said, "Time to go to work."

Dottie charged through the door first with Haleigh close behind. Two steps into the room, she stopped cold.

"Cooper?"

What in the world was Cooper Ridgeway, the most upstanding guy Haleigh had ever met, doing with a pregnant teenager? Surely her best friend, Abby, would have mentioned if her own brother were on the verge of parenthood.

"Jessi, is it?" she asked, catching the mixture of panic and surprise that crossed Cooper's chiseled features. Haleigh hadn't seen much of her former classmate since returning to town six months before. Though the pictures around the house she shared with Abby revealed a man larger than the boy she'd known in high school, film didn't do the mechanic justice.

Between the greasy ball cap, bulging biceps, and tattered Carhartt jeans, Cooper Ridgeway looked like a redneck body builder. A mute one if his current drowning fish impersonation was any indication.

"Jessi, I'm Dr. Mitchner, and I'm going to help you meet your little one." Sliding on the gloves Dottie passed her way, Haleigh eased onto the stool at the end of the exam table. "I need to see where we stand. You're going to feel some pressure."

Dottie's report had been accurate. This baby was coming fast.

"Is everything okay?" her patient asked, speaking for the first time. The accent wasn't local. Contrary to what many assumed, there were countless variations on the Southern accent, and as a lifelong Tennessee native, Haleigh knew immediately that Jessi was not from the Volunteer State.

"All good." Haleigh shared a reassuring smile. "We should be meeting this little one in no time at all."

"Wait," Cooper said. "I'm not—"

Jessi bore down with a growl, and Dottie said, "That's right, honey. Chin to your chest and push through it. Don't forget to count for her, coach."

"Count?" Cooper asked. The green eyes that cut to Haleigh silently begged for rescue.

Haleigh ignored him. She didn't know how he'd landed in this particular mess, but she couldn't resist letting him see this mission through. Cooper had a knack for playing the white knight role. He'd certainly done so for her once upon a time. And in a somewhat similar circumstance.

"Up to ten." Dottie barked at Cooper, lack of patience heavy in her tone. "You've got to step up for your girl here. Let's go."

"But she isn't—"

"Tell me this is almost over." Jessi threw her head back on the pillow propped behind her while a drop of sweat rolled down her temple. "I knew it would hurt, but I thought I'd get some good drugs. Why can't I have drugs?"

"You're too far along for an epidural," Haleigh said, focusing on the task at hand. "The baby is crowning now. You're doing great, but we need a few more pushes." Casting a furtive glance Cooper's way, Haleigh said, "You want to have a look?"

"What?" Green eyes went wide. "Heck no."

Haleigh struggled not to laugh. Abby was going to love this one.

"Here it comes again," Jessi cried and curled forward.

"Grab that knee," Dottie said to Cooper, who reluctantly followed the nurse's order. "You can do it, Jessi. Get that baby out here."

As Jessi pushed for all she was worth, two newcomers entered the room.

"Looks like we're just in time." Edgar Lauden, the pediatrician on duty, stepped into Haleigh's peripheral vision. "Nurse Felicia and I almost missed the little guy's entrance."

"It's a girl," Jessi corrected through clenched teeth.

Haleigh looked to Dottie as she asked the patient, "Did an ultrasound show that?"

Jessi shook her head. "I had a dream. She's a girl, I know it."

Not the answer Haleigh wanted to hear. "Did you ever have an ultrasound?" she asked.

The young girl shook her head no, her body still clenched in half.

Haleigh nodded toward her fellow doctor, giving a silent warning to get ready. "A couple more pushes," she said. "That's all we need."

Two minutes later, Haleigh held Jessi's screaming baby girl in the crook of her arm. As Dottie slid the clamps into place, Haleigh met Cooper's eye. "Are you ready to cut the cord?" she asked.

The mechanic's face went sheet white as he shook his head. "I'm not cutting anything," he said. "I don't even know this girl."

❧

Haleigh Mitchner was more beautiful than ever. And downright evil.

When she'd walked into the tiny exam room, Cooper had nearly forgotten that his hand was locked in the bone-crushing grip of a total stranger, who was in the process of trying to evict another human being out of her body. One look into Haleigh's dancing brown eyes and he knew she'd guessed right—that he didn't belong in that room.

But had she saved him? Hell no. She always did have a wicked sense of humor.

No amount of brain bleach was ever going to get those images out of his head. Women were right. If men had to give birth, the human species would die off quick. And to think, his mother had given birth to two at the same time. No wonder he and Abby didn't have younger siblings.

This was not the way he wanted to run into his high school crush.

Before she became Dr. Mitchner, Haleigh had been the prettiest girl at Ardent High—smart, ambitious, and out of Cooper's league. A gearhead with grease-stained hands, who couldn't spell *calculus* let alone pass it, didn't stand a chance with a girl like Hal. But that never stopped him from wanting her.

"Are you pursuing a second career as a birthing coach or is this a one-time deal?" Haleigh asked as she joined Cooper in the hall.

Her golden-blonde hair, pulled tight into a ponytail, still mimicked the flecks of gold in her expressive brown eyes, while the grin that showed off perfect teeth and a full bottom lip still hit him in the solar plexus. Though her face had defied aging, this wasn't the girl he'd pined for as a young man. Haleigh the MD was sleek, professional, and even more out of Cooper's reach than ever.

"I didn't mean to be in there," he said. "I tried to tell you."

Hugging her white lab coat tight over her chest, Haleigh smiled. "I assume you *aren't* the father?"

"Come on," he answered, shocked that she'd make such an assumption. "She's a kid. You know I wouldn't be knocking up some teenage girl."

"I was joking, Cooper," she said. "If anyone knows your penchant for stepping in for lesser men in situations like this one, it's me."

Neither of them had ever talked about what happened that summer after senior year when Haleigh had gotten herself into a delicate condition and Cooper had attempted to play the white knight. In response to his marriage proposal, she'd jerked him out of fantasy land with a flip, "Don't be ridiculous." As far as he knew, Cooper was still the only person aware of how Haleigh had dealt with the situation.

"Two times in thirteen years doesn't make it a habit," he corrected. "And this isn't exactly the same thing."

"You're right. This one is very different." The laughter went out of her eyes as Haleigh dropped her hands into her lab coat pockets. "So why were you in there?"

Excellent question. One Cooper had been asking himself for the last half hour.

"Because somebody had to be, I guess." Which was true. No one should have to go through that alone, especially not a frightened teenager.

"But you say you don't know her."

"I don't. I found her in the storage building behind my garage. Spence and I fixed a hole in the roof last week and I wanted to make sure it was holding up in the rain. That's when I found Jessi huddled against my old Thunderbird. I thought she was hurt at first. When I realized she was in labor, I rushed her here."

"And you stayed." Haleigh pressed.

What was she getting at?

"She was scared and alone, so I stuck around. But I never meant to be in there for the whole show." And Haleigh was at least partly to blame for him having to witness that. "Thanks again for the assist there. You could have helped me get out."

The grin returned. "Where would be the fun in that?" She followed that teasing statement by poking him in the chest, and then looked surprised when he didn't budge. "Seriously. Do you fix cars or toss them for sport?"

The look of female appreciation as she tested his biceps threatened to short-circuit his brain. "I work out." Now he sounded like a caveman.

"That's obvious." She snorted. "It's hard to believe you're the same lanky guy who sat behind me in World History."

The only class Cooper ever looked forward to in his entire high school career. He'd even passed it, thanks to Haleigh's tutoring.

"Still me, just bigger," he said. "You're as tiny as ever."

"I only look tiny because you're so tall." Haleigh had a point. He had her by nearly a foot in height. "So what do you know about this girl?" she asked.

"Not much," he said, replaying what little the new mother had shared. "On the way here, I offered to let her use my phone, but she turned me down. I suppose the panting would have made talking difficult."

"I'm sure she'll want to call someone now." Haleigh reached for the handle to Jessi's room, but Cooper needed to know something before they went back in.

"Did everything really go okay in there? I saw a lot of blood on my way out."

"What you saw was normal."

Normal? That shit was not normal.

"You can't be serious. That's how it always goes?"

"Well, not always that smoothly. Jessi got lucky that her little girl was in a hurry. I don't know how long she suffered in your storage building, but first births can take anywhere from four to twenty-four hours. Sometimes longer."

"You're shittin' me."

The response earned him a giggle. "You're right," she said, shaking her head. "You're still the same old Cooper."

His ego prickled at the comment. She made him sound like a hound dog to be scratched behind the ear.

"But bigger," Cooper reminded, wanting her to see him as something more. Even if only physically.

"Oh yes," she agreed. "The bigger part is hard to miss." As the hidden innuendo floated between them, Haleigh blushed. "That sounded way more innocent in my head."

"Innocent is overrated," Cooper replied, surrounding her with an arm braced on each side of the door frame. "And you're still pretty when you're flustered."

Brown eyes narrowed as he loomed above her. "Are you flirting with me?"

With one brow raised, he pressed his luck. "Maybe."

Haleigh crossed her arms as she relaxed against the door. "I'd be flattered if I didn't know that you could flirt with furniture." She poked him in a particularly ticklish spot on his side, making him drop his arms. "Save your moves for a more susceptible female. One who never saw you in your underwear at age fourteen."

She'd only caught him in his skivvies because he'd been trying to catch Haleigh in hers. By high school he'd learned to hate her floor-length pink bathrobe. Was a bare ankle too much to ask for?

8

As she reached once again for the doorknob, he said, "I look a lot different in my underwear now."

Her husky laugh shot straight to his groin. "I bet you do. Too bad we don't have sleepovers anymore so I can see for myself."

Cooper would let her see a lot more than his underwear if she'd only take him seriously for once. Disheartened but not defeated, he said, "You're never too old for a sleepover."

"I'll keep that in mind," she replied before spinning away to become the doctor in charge once again.

Chapter 2

Heaven help her but the man was hot. If Cooper Ridgeway had been harmless back in high school, at this moment, he was anything but. Not that he hadn't always been a flirt—he'd simply never turned his talents in her direction. And even if he had, she'd have laughed him off, same as she'd done just now.

A few extra muscles didn't change who he was. As much time as she'd spent in the Ridgeway household, they might as have well have been brother and sister. Not that she felt very sisterly toward him today, but that was nothing more than hormones. As a doctor, Haleigh knew better than anyone that women were preprogrammed to respond to the kind of physique that Cooper clearly worked hard to maintain.

Very hard. He could have stepped right out of a mechanic-of-the-month calendar.

And she'd been going solo in the bedroom for more than six months, which meant her libido was on high alert. If he were anyone else, she might take him up on that sleepover offer, but they shared too much history for her to use Cooper to scratch an itch. He deserved a nice girl-next-door who would give him a comfy home and a pack of dimpled, green-eyed babies.

In fact, she couldn't help but wonder why he was still single. Surely there was a girl in Ardent Springs who knew a solid catch when she saw one.

"How are we doing?" Haleigh asked Jessi, who was staring at her infant with a combination of shock and awe.

"I can't believe she's finally here," the young girl said. "She's so beautiful."

Black hair streaked with bright red highlights hung over the right side of Jessi's face, while the left side had been buzz cut, giving her an edgy, punk rock look. Smudged black makeup outlined bright blue eyes that didn't carry near enough age or experience to deal with the responsibility in her arms.

"What's her name?" Cooper asked, stepping close enough to look down on the little cherub sleeping against her mother's chest.

"Emma," Jessi said softly. "Emma Rose Rogers."

"A pretty name for a pretty little thing." Cooper ran one finger gently over the baby's head, and a pulse beat rocked Haleigh's womb.

What the hell was that? In more than four years of delivering babies, she'd never felt the slightest urge to have one. In fact, thirteen years ago, she'd taken extreme measures to avoid being in Jessi's current situation.

But one glimpse of Cooper Ridgeway going all soft over a newborn and her maternal clock wakes from dormancy?

No freaking way.

Clearing her throat, she attempted to move this scene along. "Jessi, I need to know who to contact to let them know you and the baby are here."

The new mother's smile faded. "There's no one to call."

"What about your parents?" Haleigh asked. "I'm sure they want to meet their new granddaughter."

Jessi shook her head as she pulled the sleeping baby tighter against her chest. "No."

What did she mean *no*? The girl hadn't fallen out of the sky. And she surely hadn't gotten *herself* pregnant.

"What about the baby's father? Don't you want to call him?"

"Bobby doesn't want anything to do with me and Emma," she said with a tight jaw. "He says he has plans and he isn't giving them up for a kid. When I refused to get an abortion, he got pissed and took off." Tucking the blanket around her daughter, she added, "Doesn't matter anyway. We don't need him."

This scenario sounded way too familiar, except back in the day, Haleigh had been the one with the plans. Having a baby would have ruined everything. She couldn't have gone to college with a baby in tow. And she sure as heck couldn't tell her staunchly Catholic mother that not only had her daughter had sex before marriage, she'd been stupid enough to get pregnant.

Haleigh gave herself a mental shake. Jessi's story wasn't remotely the same as hers.

"Real men don't walk away from responsibility," Cooper stated, repeating the words he'd once spoken to Haleigh. "Tell me where to find him and I'll teach the little pecker a lesson."

He'd made a similar threat thirteen years ago, but then he hadn't been much of a threat to the class jock, and Haleigh hadn't wanted to see him get hurt on her behalf. Today, she had no doubt Cooper could beat the stuffing out of anyone stupid enough to take him on. She almost wished she knew where to find David Stapleton now.

"Let's stay rational here," she said, speaking as much to herself as to Cooper. "Are you sure there isn't anyone we can call? Where are you staying here in town?"

"I didn't make it far enough to find a place to stay before I went into labor," Jessi said. "That's why Cooper found me where he did. It was pouring rain when the pains hit, so I ducked into the first dry place I could find. I thought they'd go away, and then once it stopped raining, I'd move on."

"Move on to where?" Did the girl realize that you didn't tuck a baby into your purse and wander off to parts unknown?

Jessi shrugged. "A motel, I guess. I had a couple weeks to go. I thought I had more time to figure this stuff out before she got here."

"Figure what stuff out?" Haleigh asked. "Jessi, what are you doing in Ardent Springs if you don't know anyone here?"

The teen toyed with the end of the sheet. With her eyes locked on the foot of the bed, she said, "I'm here to find my father."

"Great," Cooper said. "Give us his number and we'll call him."

The stubborn chin jutted out again. "I can't. I haven't found him yet."

The mystery of Jessi Rogers grew more complicated by the second.

"I'm confused." Haleigh propped a hip on the foot of the bed. "What do you mean you haven't found him yet? Do you have an address?"

"All I have is a name. Well," Jessi hedged, "initials. Mama said he went by J.T. and that he was from Ardent Springs, Tennessee."

Cooper leaned a hand on the bed rail. "You mean you've never met your father?"

Bright red locks swung as Jessi shook her head. "I always thought Calvin was my dad. He was married to Mama when I was a little girl, and it wasn't until I got pregnant that she told me the truth. She didn't remember much about my real father, except for the J.T. part, where he was from, and that he was older and had a family already before getting Mama pregnant."

"How old was your mother when she had you?" Haleigh asked.

"Eighteen."

Great. To an eighteen-year-old, twenty-five was ancient. This mystery father could be anywhere from forty to seventy by now. Whoever he was, they weren't going to locate him before Jessi and the baby were released, and Haleigh was not about to let this girl leave the hospital without having a safe, stable place to stay.

Haleigh contemplated solutions. There were no shelters for miles, and a newborn couldn't be exposed to the germs present in a group home anyway. Haleigh caught a glimpse of Cooper in her peripheral vision and an idea formed. He'd put himself in the hero role once this evening. It was time to see how heroic he was willing to be.

"Cooper, I need to see you in the hall," she said, motioning for him to follow.

"Where are you going?" Jessi asked.

"This will only take a minute," Haleigh answered, pulling the door closed after Cooper stepped into the hall. When she turned to once again find him looming above her, she took a step back. "We can't let that girl leave this hospital without someplace to go."

"Agreed," Cooper said, carrying none of the flirtatious nature of a few minutes ago. "I doubt she has enough money to afford more than a night or two at a motel."

"She can't take a newborn to a motel."

"Then where else can she go?" he asked.

Here went nothing. Haleigh took a steadying breath and said, "You need to take Jessi and the baby home with you."

He could not have heard her right. "Are you crazy?"

Haleigh didn't flinch at the outburst. "You found her. You helped her give birth. And you're apparently the only person she knows in this town."

"Well," Cooper said, floundering. "She knows you, too."

"Don't be ridiculous. You know I can't take her home with me."

"And I can't take her home with me."

"Why not?"

"How about because I'm a grown man and that's a young girl? And that doesn't even touch the fact that she comes with a newborn baby."

"You're being unreasonable," Haleigh said, sounding as if she were suggesting he take home a plant instead of two vulnerable females. "There's no other option. We can't let her leave this hospital without making sure she has a safe place to go."

Cooper whipped the ball cap off his head to jam a hand through his thick curls. He couldn't argue that Jessi needed someplace to land, but he'd stepped up enough for one night. Other than the fact that she was a kid, he didn't have space for the high-maintenance pair. Spending time with Carrie Farmer and her four-month-old had taught Cooper how much crap the little buggers required. Crap he didn't have room for.

And then inspiration struck. Someone he knew well had plenty of room.

"I've got an idea," he said, slamming the hat back on his head. Without waiting for a response, Cooper charged off toward the elevator.

Haleigh yelled after him. "Where are you going?"

"I thought of another option," he yelled back, and then stepped into an open elevator before she could demand more details.

Less than a minute later, the elevator opened to the neurology unit, and by a stroke of luck, Cooper found his target at the nurses' station.

"Abby, I need your help," Cooper said, giving his twin sister a pleading look.

"What are you doing here, Cooper? Did something happen to Mama?" Abby was out of her chair and rounding the desk before he could answer.

"Mama's fine," Cooper hurried to clarify. "I said *I* need your help."

Abby's black ponytail swung as she tilted her head, concern replaced with curiosity. "What did you do now?"

"A good deed. And it's coming around to bite me in the ass, as usual."

"Betty, I'll be back in twenty minutes," his sister told a fellow nurse as she motioned Cooper back to the bank of elevators. "Start at the beginning and don't leave anything out."

On their way to the cafeteria, Cooper brought Abby up to speed on the Jessi situation. As they stepped off, he stated the obvious. "You have to agree that I can't take the pair home."

"That *would* be weird," she said. "But what do you want me to do?"

While attending nursing school at Austin Peay University in Clarksville, Abby had met a soldier six years her senior stationed at Fort Campbell and fallen hard for the army infantryman. Kyle Williams had been a nice enough guy, though a little too hard-core for Cooper's tastes. Still, he made Abby happy, so the family accepted him.

Seven months ago, while serving in Afghanistan, Kyle had taken an extra duty shift, and with it a roadside bomb. Abby was devastated by his death and immediately withdrew from life. She worked her shifts at the hospital and volunteered with veterans' organizations, but the rest of her world seemed to have stopped the day she'd gotten the news.

No one expected her to finish grieving at some designated time, but that didn't mean people weren't worried about her. Last week their mother had suggested that Abby needed something else to focus on. A project to get her out of the past and moving forward again. Jessi and the baby could be that project.

"Let her stay with you."

His sister froze in place. "What?"

"You agree that I can't take them home, but I can't drop them at the edge of town and drive off either. You have that big four-bedroom house—there's plenty of room for both Jessi and the baby."

"Oh no." Abby shook her head as she marched toward the coffee machines. "You are not putting some strange girl in my house. She could rob me blind. Or worse, leave the baby and take off for good."

"She wouldn't do that." Cooper may not know the teenager well, but the protective way she'd held the bundle to her chest told him she'd never leave her little girl. "She's on some mission to find her birth father and thinks he might live here in town. Based on what she told us, I highly doubt he's still here, if he ever was, which means she'll be moving on in no time. Probably won't stay for more than a week."

Abby remained silent as she poured three helpings of hazelnut creamer into her cup.

"Please, Abby. You know I wouldn't ask you to do this if I could think of any other way."

Tossing her stirrer in the trash, she continued to hold her tongue. Abby always did need an extra minute to process things, and he could practically see the wheels turning in her head. He just hoped they were turning in his direction.

"You *do* remember that I have one boarder already, right?"

He sure did. And that boarder was not going to be happy about his solution.

"You still have two other bedrooms," he reminded her. "Help me out here."

"I'll need to meet her before I agree."

Relief washed through him, and Cooper thanked his lucky stars that the sucker gene ran in the family.

"She's still down in the ER. You can come meet her right now."

With a glance at her watch, Abby sighed. "I can't believe I'm even considering this."

"It'll be good for you to have someone else to focus on."

Giving him the evil eye, his sister said, "Now you sound like Mama. Did she put you up to this?"

17

"Abbs, this all happened in the last hour," Cooper said. "I haven't had time to talk to Mama."

"Right. Sorry." After a brief hesitation, she asked, "Is the baby cute?"

"She's beautiful. And I think Jessi has a good heart. She was staring at little Emma as if she were the eighth wonder of the world."

His sister shook her head. "Why can't you stick to saving lost dogs and random barnyard animals?"

Repeating Haleigh's words, he slung an arm over Abby's shoulders. "Where would be the fun in that?"

Chapter 3

"So how long have you and Cooper been a thing?"

Haleigh looked up from Jessi's chart. "Excuse me?"

"Is no one supposed to know?" the youngster asked. "Are y'all just having an affair or something?"

For a kid reluctant to share her own personal details, Jessi sure didn't mind prying into other people's lives. Flipping the chart closed, Haleigh hugged it to her chest. "Cooper and I went to high school together, and his twin sister is my best friend. What makes you think we're having an affair, as you put it?"

Pencil-line brows shot up a wrinkle-free forehead. "I'm not stupid. You look at him like I used to look at Bobby. Like you want to rip his clothes off and take a ride on the Cooper train."

That was absurd. He may be big, but Cooper was a man not a locomotive. Though he did have a nice caboose. And a man who worked out probably had impressive endurance.

"See?" Jessi said. "That look is what got me Emma."

Glancing down at Emma's cherubic face, Haleigh couldn't help but wonder what a little version of Cooper would look like. Dark hair most likely. Happy and long-limbed.

Haleigh gave herself a mental shake. Had someone laced her coffee with extra estrogen or something?

Anxious to change the subject, Haleigh said, "Dottie should be in with your room assignment any minute, and then we'll get you both settled upstairs for the night."

Refusing to cooperate, Jessi said, "So where did lover-boy go?"

Offering a counterstrike, Haleigh asked, "So why won't you call your mother?"

Blue eyes narrowed, conveying a clear eff-you, but she didn't hurl the insult. "I don't know where she is, okay?"

"You said she told you about your father. How could she do that if you don't know where she is?"

With a nonchalant shrug that did little to hide her true feelings, Jessi replied, "A week after sharing the biggest news of my life, she picked up a trucker and skipped town. Her cell stopped working a few days later."

Haleigh's heart ached for this young girl fighting to be strong while her world spiraled out of control. Who could abandon her daughter like that? Especially when that daughter was about to have a child of her own? The violent urge to find Jessi's mother and shake some sense into her vibrated down Haleigh's spine.

"What about grandparents?"

"Don't you think if there was anyone to call, I'd do it?" Jessi asked, showing a sudden burst of anger. Something she had every right to feel. "I'm not stupid. Emma deserves a home and a family."

"So do you," Haleigh pointed out. She was all for selfless parenting, but this girl needed a dose of self-preservation.

"I have Emma now." Her stubborn chin jutted forward. "She's all the family I need."

"And yet you're here looking for your father."

The fight went out of the teenager, and she stayed quiet long enough that Haleigh considered apologizing for prying into something that wasn't any of her business.

Breaking her silence, Jessi asked, "Do you have a good mom?"

Talk about a loaded question. The word *no* nearly escaped before Haleigh chose a more diplomatic answer. "My mother and I don't always agree on how I should live my life. She has high standards and expects me to live up to them. But she loves me." *In her own way,* she added, keeping the disloyal sentiment to herself.

"What about your dad?"

A slightly less chilly feeling filled her chest. "Daddy was different. Where Mother pushed, he encouraged. He offered unflinching support instead of constant judgment."

"That sounds nice," Jessi said with wistful longing.

Haleigh took a mournful breath. "He died when I was sixteen. A truck driver fell asleep at the wheel. Daddy never saw it coming."

"Wow," Jessi whispered. "That sucks."

"Yeah," Haleigh agreed. "Big time."

Lost in her memories, Haleigh startled when the door to Jessi's room swung open. A tall brunette followed Cooper into the room, and his newfound solution became instantly clear.

"You cannot be serious," Haleigh said, cutting off the introduction Cooper was about to make.

"Relax, Haleigh Rae," the newcomer said. "I haven't agreed to anything yet."

In her youth, Haleigh had gone by both her first and middle names, but dropped the Rae during college. Unfortunately, few people in her past ever adapted to the change.

"Who is *she*?" Jessi asked, the rebel teen back in full force. "Are you my new nurse or something?"

"Or something," Abigail said. "I'm Cooper's sister. You can call me Abby."

"Why would I call you anything?"

Gesturing toward the patient, Abby turned on Cooper. "This is the child you want me to take home?"

"What?" Jessi bristled. "I am *not* a child."

Cooper ignored the outburst. "Abby has a big house with plenty of room for you and Emma."

"But I don't even know her."

"You don't know me, either," Cooper pointed out.

Haleigh couldn't believe that Cooper would ask this of his sister. The woman was still mourning her husband. Still reeling from having her entire future pulled out from under her. Didn't he understand how badly Abby wanted a baby? Having Emma around would be a constant reminder of what she'd lost.

Abigail Ridgeway and Haleigh had been best friends since the first day of third grade when Abby had saved a scared little blonde girl from the clutches of Constance Beauregard, the class bully. From her father's death to Haleigh's downward spiral in her college years, Abby had been her rock. Watching her grieve for Kyle these last six months had been heartbreaking, made even more frustrating by the fact there was nothing Haleigh could do to help.

And now Cooper wanted to make things worse.

"Do you have a family of your own?" Jessi asked, making Haleigh want to slap everyone in the room, especially Cooper.

A shadow fell over Abby's face. "No, I don't."

"Back in the hall!" Haleigh barked, stomping toward the door.

"What?" Abby asked.

"This is their thing," Jessi said. "Every time the doc needs a Cooper fix, she drags him into the hall."

Abby snorted. "A Cooper fix? What have I been missing?"

Haleigh didn't stop to correct the teenager or explain to Abby. Instead, she grabbed Cooper by the arm and said, "We'll be back."

Haleigh spun on him the moment the door clicked shut. "How could you do this to your sister?"

"Do what?" Cooper asked. "Jessi needs a place to go. Abby has plenty of room, a doctor in the house, being you, obviously, and it's only temporary anyway. This is the perfect solution."

"For you, maybe," she hissed. "You know what Abby has been through."

"It's been seven months, Hal, and she's been stuck ever since. Having Jessi and the baby around is exactly what she needs to get unstuck."

"Wrong," Haleigh snapped. "Having a baby around will be a constant reminder of what she lost."

Abby didn't lose a baby, she lost a husband. "What are you talking about?"

"Their plan was to get pregnant during Kyle's next leave. That would have been mere weeks after he was killed. Which means that right now your sister should be preparing for her own baby, not some stranger's." Haleigh motioned to the narrow window in the exam room door. "Look at her, Cooper. She's practically crying just looking at Emma."

He'd had no idea. It wasn't as if his sister talked to him about this stuff. Abby had been a mess after Kyle died, but any woman would be. If he'd known about the baby plans . . .

"She never told me," he said. Cooper would rather take a tire iron to the knee than hurt his sister. "I didn't know."

Haleigh continued the guilt trip. "What's going to happen when she gets attached to Emma, and then Jessi takes her away?"

"What do you want me to say?" Cooper asked, throwing his hands in the air. "I said I didn't know, but there isn't much I can do about it now. I mean, what other choice do we have? There's nowhere to put them at my place, and you live with Abby."

With a frustrated sigh, Haleigh pinched the bridge of her nose. "I know, I know." She glanced through the small window. "Maybe it won't be so bad. She's been so obsessed with Kyle's death that a new life in the house might not be such a bad thing. But we need to find this girl's father or prove he isn't around before Abby gets too attached."

The collective *we* caught his attention. "I'll start asking around tomorrow. Might as well start with our moms. One of them might remember the guy, if he really did live here."

"It's a place to start." Tucking a loose strand of hair behind her ear, Haleigh gave him a weak smile. "I need to finish up some paperwork. Tell Abby I'll see her later, okay?"

"Will do."

Before turning to leave, she said, "You really came through for that girl tonight, Cooper. Not many guys would have done that. Especially for a stranger."

"I didn't do anything special," he replied. "You and Jessi handled the hard part."

"You always did sell yourself short. Face it, Cooper, you're a good guy."

Without awaiting a response, Haleigh left him staring after her. "And good guys never get the girl," he mumbled.

Insomnia was a bitch.

Haleigh couldn't remember the last time she'd been this tired, yet her brain wouldn't shut down. And every time she closed her eyes, she saw Cooper's flirtatious grin and those inviting green eyes. She'd never considered anything about Cooper to be inviting before. He'd always been sweet and funny, and good for forgotten lunch money or an oil change, but there had never been any attraction between them.

That had certainly changed tonight.

Since returning to town six months ago, Haleigh had practically lived at the hospital, while using a room at Abby's house to store her meager belongings and catch the occasional nap. She had her own reasons for avoiding social interactions, especially in places that served alcohol. The only interactions she couldn't avoid were the mandatory dinners with her mother. Not that Meredith Mitchner ever used the word *mandatory*, but she'd presented the weekly meal idea as more of an edict than an invite.

In truth, Haleigh's mother was an intimidating figure who rarely took no for an answer. Especially not from her daughter.

Preferring images of Cooper to those of her disapproving parent, Haleigh let her mind wander back a few hours. Though she would never admit as much aloud, that sleepover suggestion had merit. A casual romp would do her body good, and she could replace the image of fourteen-year-old Cooper in tighty-whities with the new and improved version.

But, alas, that was a no-trespassing zone. Haleigh had a less-than-stellar history with men and would not add Cooper Ridgeway to her long list of failures. He deserved better, for one, and for two, Abby would never forgive her for breaking her brother's heart.

The subtle chirp of the cell phone on her nightstand snapped Haleigh from her thoughts. The clock read 12:30 a.m. Who would call so late? Checking the screen, she couldn't believe her eyes.

Marcus Appleton—plastic surgeon with delusions of grandeur and Haleigh's ex-fiancé.

Speaking of her long list of failures.

She considered ignoring the call, but since she hadn't heard from him in months, curiosity won out. "Hello?"

"Hey there, beautiful."

Why had she ever thought that greeting romantic? Sadly, he'd picked her up in a bar with that line. A bar she never should have been in considering her proclivities. But sadly, she couldn't even use being drunk as an excuse for talking to the arrogant doctor, since she'd been nursing nothing more than a glass of water that night.

"What do you want, Marcus?"

"Try not to sound so happy to hear my voice."

"It's after midnight," she pointed out. As if she'd been sleeping like a normal person would be.

"Oh, that's right. I forgot about the time difference. It's barely after ten out here on the coast."

He didn't forget. He was too stuck in his own world to consider that the rest of the planet didn't operate on his schedule.

"Why are you calling?" she asked.

"Because I miss you, baby."

Of all the . . .

"I'm not your baby anymore, Marcus. Remember? Staying with me would have meant wasting your skill and talent in a backwoods town. Or did you forget that, too?"

Not that Haleigh was bitter or anything.

"I was mad," he defended. "You sprung that move on me without any warning." Music blared in the background and then faded. "You weren't even willing to talk about it." The music blared again, this time accompanied by a car horn. The man was standing outside a nightclub on the streets of LA claiming to miss her. Jerk.

"You always knew I intended to move back home once my residency was over. And I reminded you of the fact the night you proposed."

In a muted tone, he replied, "I thought you'd change your mind. I mean, this is Los Angeles we're talking about."

"What's the matter, Marcus? Are the women out there not as susceptible as the ones in Memphis? I suppose plastic surgeons *are* a dime a dozen in celebrity-land."

"You're deflecting because you know you were in the wrong," he said, using the psychobabble that drove her nuts. "We should have decided where to move together."

The man never listened.

"This is my home, Marcus. If you'd have loved me, you would have made it work."

"I'm a thirty-five-year-old plastic surgeon on the rise. Moving to Archer Springs would have meant taking a step back in my career."

"It's Ardent, Marcus. *Ardent* Springs." What had she ever seen in this self-centered man-child? "But there's no point in arguing. You're in LA. I'm here. We both got what we wanted."

"I wanted you *and* LA," he whined. "I can't believe you can be so callous about this."

No matter what Haleigh said, the petulant child on the other end of the line was never going to see things any differently than he wanted to. Which meant getting angry would get her nowhere.

"I'm not being callous. I'm being realistic. We ended as friends who want two very different things." Pressing the button she knew would get his attention, she added, "Better now than after the wedding. California *is* a community property state, after all." No one came between Marcus and his money. "You need to move on with your life."

Marcus's voice dropped. "Is that what you're doing? Have you already found someone else?"

Cooper's green eyes flashed to mind. "No," she said more emphatically than necessary. "I'm not interested in finding someone else right now."

"So you *do* miss me."

Saints alive, the man's ego knew no bounds.

"Goodnight, Marcus," she said. "It's late and I have to work tomorrow. I suggest you go back into whatever club you were in and buy a pretty girl a drink."

"Drinks out here are expensive," she heard him say before she ended the call. Haleigh rolled her eyes as she tossed the phone back on the nightstand. Flopping onto her back, she stared at the ceiling, pondering her long-standing pattern of dating self-centered, shallow men. The habit went all the way back to high school. You'd think after David had dumped her, leaving her to deal with the pregnancy by herself, she'd have learned a lesson.

She'd been so scared that summer, but just as he'd done for Jessi, Cooper had stepped up to take another man's place. David should have been the one shelling out money and holding her hand in the clinic waiting room. Gah! She really could pick them. Well, no more. Men were off-limits until Haleigh's judgment improved. With her luck, that would be never, but better to be alone than married to a man like Marcus Appleton.

Haleigh shivered at the thought.

Chapter 4

Cooper spent his Tuesday lunch break filling the back of his truck with cargo he never thought he'd be hauling. After Haleigh made her exit, he'd returned to Abby and Jessi to find them building a sizable list of baby items. To his dismay, they'd expected him to fill the order as if he knew anything about drool cloths or suction bulbs.

He didn't even want to know what they planned to do with a suction bulb.

"I couldn't find the name-brand powder, so I grabbed the generic," Lorelei said, tossing several white plastic bags into the bed of the truck.

Lorelei Pratchett, another former schoolmate, spent twelve years chasing a Hollywood dream before returning to her senses and coming back to Ardent Springs. To hear Cooper's best friend, Spencer, tell it, she came back for him, but then Spencer liked to make his fiancée laugh. She'd guffawed at this version of the story on more than one occasion.

To Cooper's great relief, when Lorelei learned of his mission, she'd volunteered to come along.

The plastic bags joined a bassinet, rocker, changing table, and car seat—all used but for the car seat, as no one was willing to compromise on safety in that area—in the back of the truck. Blankets and clothes had been donated by Carrie Farmer, his best friend Spencer's ex-wife, who had a four-month-old girl of her own.

Carrie's husband had been killed in a bar fight while she was still pregnant, so the entire gang had stepped up to make sure the munchkin wanted for nothing, especially not attention. Baby Molly had stolen Cooper's heart the first second he saw her, and she loved nothing more than to bend him to her will. Which most of the time meant holding court atop his shoulders while drooling into his hair.

"I think that's everything," Cooper said, checking the last items off the list. "Now we have to set it all up."

Glancing to the back of the truck, Lorelei said, "Didn't you say this is a temporary situation? We've collected a lot of stuff for this girl to stay with your sister only a week or two."

"That's why it's all used or borrowed," he answered, ignoring the niggling concern in the back of his mind. He'd called his mother first thing that morning about the J.T. person, but she'd never heard of him. His mother then called several friends, who'd reported the same.

This mystery was not going to be solved as quickly as he'd hoped.

"Okay, then. I'm ready if you are." Lorelei drummed the seat like a two-year-old on a sugar high. "Let's go."

Cooper had noted Lorelei's higher-than-usual level of enthusiasm as she'd flitted around Snow's Curiosity Shop, the secondhand store that had served as his baby furniture supplier and happened to be where Lorelei sold her homemade desserts.

As he climbed behind the wheel, Cooper said, "You're in a good mood today."

Lorelei gave a noncommittal shrug. "It's a good day."

Cooper narrowed his eyes. "Spill," he said.

Biting her lip, she looked torn. "If I tell you, Spencer might get mad."

"Now I'm really curious. What's so important that Spencer wouldn't want me to know?"

"Oh, he wouldn't be mad that you *know*," she said. "He'd be mad that I told you instead of letting him tell you."

The woman was talking in circles.

"Well then you'd better not—"

"We set a date!" she gushed, bouncing up and down in her seat. "We're getting married in October. I've got a million things to plan, and it's going to be insane trying to do it all in only six months, but I don't care. We're getting married and it's going to be the most fabulous wedding ever!"

Of that, Cooper had no doubt. Lorelei did everything with flair and drama, and Spencer would doubtless smile and endure any off-the-wall idea she came up with. The two had been high school sweethearts before Lorelei's West Coast detour, and the road back to their current status of sickeningly-in-love had been paved with numerous speed bumps and potholes.

If two people had ever deserved a happy ending it was Spencer and Lorelei.

"I'm happy for you," Cooper said as the engine turned over. "And I'll do my best to act surprised when he gets around to telling me."

"I hope your acting skills are better than mine," she laughed. "In my defense, we didn't know I'd see you before he did."

"And I didn't know I'd be setting up a nursery for a girl I found in my storage building less than twenty-four hours ago. Life is full of surprises." Pulling onto Main Street, Cooper said, "I appreciate you helping me out. Abby is working and there's no way I could have done this on my own."

Lorelei spun in her seat, giving Cooper a poke in the arm. "Has anyone told you lately how good a guy you are?"

"That seems to be coming up a lot lately," he said, checking the side streets before pulling out of the four-way. "A lot of good it does me."

"That doesn't sound like the chipper Cooper that I know. Who put a dent in your fender, my friend? I'll set her straight for you."

Cooper had never made a habit of discussing his unrequited love for Haleigh Rae Mitchner, and he wasn't about to start now.

"I appreciate a little hair-pulling cat fight as much as the next guy," he said with a wink, "but you can put the claws away. These particular dents are nothing new."

"She's an idiot, if you ask me," Lorelei said.

He glanced over to catch his passenger's indignant expression as he asked, "Who's an idiot?"

"Haleigh Rae. She delivered the baby last night, didn't she?"

This conversation was quickly heading in a direction Cooper didn't like. "Haleigh was the doc on call, sure. But how—"

"She'd be lucky to have you," Lorelei interrupted. "Any girl would."

"What makes you think I want Haleigh Rae?"

Lorelei lifted one brow. "That night at Brubaker's last year when Spencer pretended that he'd seen Haleigh. You reacted as if he'd announced Henry Ford himself was standing behind you."

"You read more into that than there was."

"Oh, come on, Cooper. I'd have figured it out even if Spencer hadn't told me."

Fighting the urge to hunt Spencer down and sew his lips shut, he said, "How do you figure?"

"I caught you watching her at the hospital back when Carrie had Molly. The way you looked at Haleigh is how every girl wishes a guy would look at her. Like she's the most beautiful, amazing woman on the planet."

"You got all that out of one glimpse down a hallway?"

The corner of her mouth tilted up. "The fact that you know the exact moment I'm talking about says a lot, don't you think?"

Dammit, he'd just nailed his own tail to a tree.

"How I feel about Haleigh doesn't matter," he said. "That's a dead-end road."

"Does she have any idea?"

What would be the point of telling her? Haleigh would take it as a joke just like she had his flirting last night. And his marriage proposal thirteen years ago.

"Like I said, dead-end road."

"But if—"

"Lorelei," Cooper barked louder than intended and felt instant regret when she jerked in her seat. He hated the rare times his anger got the best of him. Mostly because he sounded like his father in those moments, which was not a good thing. "I'm sorry," he said. "Just drop it, okay?"

"I shouldn't have stuck my nose in," she mumbled, keeping her gaze on the passing buildings.

"Hey." He tapped her with his elbow. "I know you mean well. Really. Someday I'll find the right girl, and maybe I'll be half as lucky as Spencer."

Blue eyes met his as glossy lips curled into a smile. "I hope you're luckier, Coop. You deserve a girl way better than me."

"Nah," he said. "They don't come any better than you, Lor. Though I won't mind if she's a little less high-maintenance."

"Oh!" Lorelei squawked. "That's so mean!" But she laughed through the protest. "Just for that, I'm insisting that every guy in the wedding wear a tux. With a tight bow tie!"

Haleigh arrived home shortly after five, dog-tired and bone-weary. She'd been scheduled from eight to four, but babies didn't abide by schedules and she'd been called in by six for a difficult delivery. Never a pleasant way to start the day, but baby and mother had pulled through and were doing well.

Speaking of mother and child, before leaving the hospital, Haleigh had signed off on Jessi's release papers, which meant Cooper would arrive any minute with her new roommates in tow. The lonely child desperate for a father had been nowhere in sight when Haleigh had checked on her patient earlier in the day, though Jessi looked even younger without the heavy eye makeup. The change in appearance had taken Haleigh by surprise, but the teenager had been too distracted by her newborn to notice.

Desperate for a shower and a nap, Haleigh trekked down the hall, drawing up short at the doorway to the room before hers. Someone had set up a nursery. The furnishings were sparse, but appeared well cared for. A white bassinet trimmed with three layers of ruffles graced the left wall, while a changing table rested beneath the window. Bunnies and baby chicks frolicked across the curtains, anxiously awaiting the new child they were about to meet. The shelves of the changing table were filled with diapers, wipes, blankets, and even a pink bin of booties and bibs.

Abby had been at work all day, which meant only one person could have done this.

Cooper.

"How did he find all this stuff?" Haleigh asked aloud as she drifted toward the most appealing piece in the room—a cherrywood rocking chair. Heavy and finely carved, the rocker had clearly undergone a recent update with its polished gleam and bright, butter-yellow cushion. Thankfully, the restorer had resisted the urge to even out the faded areas along the arms, evidence of loving use over many years. Solid and welcoming, the chair all but oozed motherly love.

The man was a force to be reckoned with. A virtual paragon of his gender. And then a stray thought crept in.

Would he have done the same for my baby thirteen years ago?

The question cut like a scalpel to the throat, and Haleigh backed out of the room as if the curtains had burst into flames. Sure, Cooper had offered to marry her, but they both knew that had been no more than misplaced chivalry. Neither of them had been prepared to be a parent. And the baby hadn't even been his to begin with, which had made the suggestion all the more ridiculous.

Darting from the room, Haleigh sought an escape. A long drive would settle her mind. So would a good stiff drink. Smacking the wall, she took a deep breath and corrected that thought. She did not need a drink, regardless of the urge gnawing at her gut. An uncomfortable memory wasn't anything she couldn't handle. She'd sure as heck handled worse in the past.

Purse and keys still in hand, Haleigh rushed through the house and out the front door only to run headlong into Cooper's chest.

Cooper struggled to keep both Haleigh and the infant-filled car seat in his left hand from hitting the ground.

"Whoa," he said. "Slow down."

Haleigh jerked out of his grasp. The woman was spooked about something.

"Hal, what's going on? Is someone in the house?"

"No." She twisted the strap of her purse as she shoved a loose lock behind her ear. "Of course not. Don't be silly. I just have an errand to run."

"Dr. Mitchner?" Jessi said from behind Cooper. "What are you doing here?"

"I live here," Haleigh replied, her eyes landing everywhere but on Cooper's face. "I was on my way out."

"Are you sure you're okay?" Cooper could see the panic clawing at her. "Come inside and sit down."

"No," she said again. "I told you, I have somewhere to be."

"I'm confused," Jessi said. "I thought this was Abby's house."

Haleigh stepped around them both, saying, "I rent a room from Abby. We're friends."

"Why is a doctor renting a room from anyone? Shouldn't you have the biggest house in town?"

Ignoring the question, Haleigh increased her pace. "I really have to go," she said over her shoulder.

Cooper took a step after her before realizing he was still carrying the baby. "Well, hell," he said, rushing into the house and setting the seat gently inside the foyer. To Jessi he said, "Close the door to keep her out of the wind and I'll be back in a second." He reached the gray Ford Fusion as Haleigh dropped into the driver's seat. "Wait," he said, blocking the door with his body. "Come inside and calm down. The errand can wait."

She tugged on the car door. "Get out of the way, Cooper."

He squatted down to see her face. "Come on, Hal. Let me get Jessi settled and then I'll drive you wherever you need to go."

She shook her head like a stubborn child. "I'm fine. Let me go."

"I can't do that," he said, and had never meant anything so much in his life. "Whatever it is, let me fix it."

"No," she said, finally looking him in the eye. "Stop trying to be the hero, Cooper. You can't fix everything."

He dropped back on his heels, feeling the weight of her words like a punch. "I'm trying to be a friend," he said, managing to keep his anger in check. Barely. "You want to get yourself killed, who am I to stop you?" Rising to his full height, Cooper stepped away from the car. "Just try not to take anyone else out when you do."

Brown eyes closed tight as Haleigh sat frozen, her hand on the door but not moving. "That's a mean thing to say," she whispered through clenched teeth.

"Yeah, well," Cooper replied, "maybe I'm not such a good guy after all."

Giving her what she wanted took every ounce of willpower Cooper possessed, but he walked away. Before he reached the front door, Haleigh drove off.

On autopilot, Haleigh's mind paid little attention to the road, too busy wallowing in guilt and regret to focus on incidentals like speed limits and turn signals. She shouldn't have been so mean to Cooper. He didn't deserve her insults or her anger. Those were reserved exclusively for herself, but Cooper always seemed to get caught in the crosshairs.

As rows of hickory trees raced by, the past bubbled to the surface. David Stapleton, all-around star athlete and the boy voted most likely to succeed, had cooed all the things Haleigh's teenage heart wanted to hear. He'd fed her nothing but empty promises, and she'd fallen for every lie that rolled off his tongue up to the moment he'd dumped her outside their senior prom.

I can't be tied down, Haleigh Rae. I'm going off to State, and I'm gonna be the next great quarterback to come out of Tennessee. A guy like me has to keep his options open.

A guy like him needed to be castrated, Haleigh lamented. He'd even had the nerve to throw the classic cliché in her face.

How do I even know the kid is mine? You gave it up pretty easy, so who knows how many guys there's been.

Looking back, she couldn't believe she hadn't scratched his eyes out in that moment. Especially when he *knew* she'd been a virgin. And there was nothing *pretty easy* about her. David had coaxed and sweet-talked for months before she'd agreed to go all the way. The guilt had nearly suffocated her, and Haleigh hadn't been able to look at her mother for a week.

She'd been so pathetic in her prom dress, crying behind a dumpster, certain that her life was over. But then Cooper had appeared out of nowhere, offering a handkerchief to dry her eyes. In her weakened state, Haleigh had confessed everything, declaring herself worthless and stupid and leaving a disgusting puddle of snot on Cooper's rented tuxedo jacket. And he'd known just what to say to make her feel better.

David the Dipshit was never good enough for you, Haleigh Rae. You're the prettiest and smartest girl at this school. Heck, in the whole county.

She'd laughed through her tears, but couldn't bear the humiliation of walking back into the dance. After making sure his date was taken care of, Cooper had driven her home, assuring her the whole way that everything would work out. Haleigh didn't see how that was possible, since her mother was going to kill her when she found out about the baby.

That's when Cooper had attempted to fall on his sword. The proposal had taken Haleigh by complete surprise. The whole thing was so ridiculous that she couldn't help but laugh it off, certain that he'd been more than a little relieved by her refusal. Two weeks later, he'd driven her to Nashville, paid more than half of the abortion fee, which he'd insisted on doing regardless of her protests, and driven her back home. All without judgment or condemnation.

When they'd reached her house, Haleigh had once again cried on Cooper's shoulder. Whether the tears came from sorrow or relief, she'd never figured out—she'd been hit by waves of both. And in his typical way, Cooper had been ready with the handkerchief.

Bright lights snapped Haleigh back to the present. A horn blared as she swerved to the right and skidded to a halt on the shoulder of the road. Heart racing, she looked for markers in order to determine where she was. The sign for Mount Hope Cemetery put her on Tucker Road, several miles outside of town.

Adrenaline pumping, her forehead dropped to the center of the wheel.

Her first thought was, *Thank God I'm alive.* Her second was that she owed Cooper Ridgeway an apology.

Chapter 5

Though he'd been lifting weights for more than an hour, Cooper's adrenaline continued to run on full throttle. He couldn't stop picturing Haleigh's car wrapped around a tree, and the fear that his phone would ring with the sheriff calling for a wrecker kept him on edge.

Why had he gone and said something so stupid? As if he wouldn't give a rat's ass if she got hurt. He should have gone after her right away, but by the time he'd finished nursing his injured pride, it was anybody's guess where she'd gone.

Not that he could have left Jessi and the baby alone anyway. The girl was still technically a stranger in Abby's house. He'd stayed until Abby arrived home from work to take over settling in her new tenants.

Finishing another twenty reps, Cooper shook the fog from his brain. Haleigh had peeled out hours ago, and he hadn't gotten a call or heard any accident reports over the scanner. She was fine. She didn't need his help. And he needed to get a freaking grip.

Maybe Haleigh was right. The hero act needed to stop. Not that Cooper went out of his way looking for opportunities to save people. Or that he did it all that often. He sure as heck hadn't been looking for a pregnant teenager when he'd found Jessi. And that birth thing was not an experience he wanted to repeat. Horror flicks had nothing on that mess.

So how did he stop something that he wasn't intentionally doing? And did he really *want* to stop? If someone was in trouble, the right thing to do was to help. That's how his mother had raised him. His father's philosophy had been to look out for himself and to hell with everyone else. Thankfully, his mother's influence had won out.

So was he supposed to carry Jessi out of the storage building and drop her at the bus station? Looking out for people was in his DNA, and Cooper wasn't about to change who he was. Not even for Haleigh Rae Mitchner.

Lost in his own mental pep talk, Cooper barely heard the knock on his front door over the Jason Aldean tune blaring from his speakers. Dropping the thirty-pounders at his feet, he cut the radio on his way to the front door.

"Who the—" he said as he swung the door open to find the last person he expected. "Haleigh Rae?" Cooper's gut hit the floor as she stared at him with an expression most women reserved for desserts and shoes. Her mouth moved, but nothing came out while brown eyes ogled his bare chest.

"Are you lost?" he asked, proud of himself for not begging her to come in. Though if she kept looking at him like that he'd be tempted to invite her upstairs for a different kind of workout.

"No. Um . . . You're wet," she finally managed. "And shirtless."

"I'm working out and I was hot."

"Yes. Yes, you are." The woman looked ready to jump his bones. "I mean, of course you are. Were," she quickly corrected. "You *were* obviously working out. And I'm sorry to disturb you, but this will only take a minute."

She hadn't wanted to talk earlier, so why should he want to talk now?

"It's already late and I still need a shower. Maybe some other time."

"Please," she pressed. "Give me two minutes. That's all I'm asking."

Against his better judgment, Cooper granted the request. "Fine," he said, stepping aside for her to pass.

She looked relieved but nervous as she fidgeted at the end of his couch. Cooper resisted the urge to clean up. He shouldn't care what Haleigh thought of his place.

Cooper closed the door and said, "Your two minutes starts now."

"Right." Her eyes dropped to the floor as she rubbed the back of her neck. Shifting from foot to foot, she surprised him by asking, "Could you put on a shirt?"

"A shirt?" He had to dirty another shirt for a two-minute conversation?

"It's just . . ." She waved a finger in front of him. "That's a lot of . . . And your shorts are riding kind of . . ." This conversation was going to take more than two minutes if she couldn't finish a sentence. "Please just put on a shirt."

Haleigh was clearly uncomfortable, and not because his looks offended her. The temptation to test her restraint tickled at the back of his brain. Dismiss him all she wanted, but Haleigh Rae was not immune to good old Cooper. At least not his body.

"You don't look like you want me to put on a shirt," he said, stepping closer.

"No woman in her right mind would *want* you to put on a shirt," she argued, stepping back. "I'm asking you to do it anyway."

The compliment made him generous. "All right. I'll be right back."

When he returned wearing a plain gray tee, he said, "Better?"

"A bit, yes." Haleigh took a deep breath and squared her shoulders. "Now. I'm here because I owe you an apology."

Not what he expected. "An apology for what?"

"For a lot of things, but most of all for taking advantage of you thirteen years ago. And for insulting you earlier tonight. You didn't deserve that."

He latched onto the first part. "You took advantage of me?"

"Yes," Haleigh said. "I'm a crappy person, and my track record goes back pretty far. I doubt I can find the boy I made fun of for flunking first grade, or the transfer student I said horrible things to in third, but I have to start somewhere."

This had to be a joke. "Hal, you are not a crappy person."

"But I am," she argued. "I never should have dumped my problems on you that night at the prom. And I definitely shouldn't have taken your money."

"Where is this coming from?" he asked. "You didn't dump anything, and I didn't give you a choice about the money. What were you going to do, get it from your mom? I'd have beaten it out of Stapleton, but you wouldn't let me."

"He outweighed you by fifty pounds."

"Ever heard of a tire iron? It's a great equalizer."

"Are you crazy?" she squawked. "You could have jeopardized his football scholarship."

"Please," Cooper said. "That dipshit drank himself out of school in the first year. He never played in a game, and now he's selling cars in Chattanooga."

Haleigh looked less appalled. "Really? I knew he hadn't become the next great quarterback, but I never bothered to find out what actually happened to him."

"You dodged a bullet," he said. "You never told Abby about that summer, did you?"

Haleigh shook her head. "She'd been talking about being a mom since sophomore year. She'd also warned me about David, and I hadn't listened. I was stupid and weak and I couldn't bring myself to confess. She'd have been so disappointed in me. As the years went on I committed enough *other* sins that keeping this one to myself got easier."

Knowing his sister and the bond that she and Haleigh had, Cooper said, "You weren't stupid, you were young. We all were. But she'd have been there for you."

"I know. But I don't want to talk about the past anymore." She ran a hand through her hair. "I shouldn't have been so mean to you today. Something else was bothering me, and I took it out on you."

Cooper nearly asked what that something was, but forced himself to stay out of her business. That didn't mean if the circumstance happened again, he'd let her go a second time.

"Okay then," he said with a nod. "Apology accepted."

Haleigh wasn't sure she'd heard right. "Really?" she asked. "Just like that?"

"Sure," he said. "Just like that. I'm getting a beer. You want one?"

Cooper really was a breed all his own. Few men would so readily forgive, and though he'd flashed a hint of temper that had surprised her, in the end, the good guy won out. Haleigh once again lamented her poor taste in men. Whatever girl ended up with Cooper Ridgeway was going to be a very lucky woman.

"I'd better not," she said, loading up her go-to refusal line. "I'm not a fan of alcohol." Which couldn't be more true. Being addicted to the stuff didn't mean she liked it. Quite the opposite, in fact. "And I've bothered you long enough anyway."

"You don't have to go," Cooper said. "I was just being a dick about the two-minute thing."

Haleigh shook her head. "You couldn't be a dick if you tried, Cooper. Trust me. I'm an expert on the breed."

"So what's that about anyway?" he asked as he loomed above her, practically blocking the light from the lamp behind him.

She still couldn't believe he was so . . . big. His shoulders seemed to go on forever, and that had definitely been a solid six-pack that had greeted her at the door. She'd never been one to melt at the sight of a hot body, but then she'd rarely encountered a body like Cooper's. Odd to think that she'd occasionally slept one wall away from him during their high school days, but back then he hadn't looked anything like the man standing before her now.

"I don't know," she said. And she really didn't. David had been the first in a long line of guys who'd fallen squarely into the bad boyfriend category. "If I dig deep enough, I'm sure it has to do with like attracting like."

Cooper strolled into an adjoining room that Haleigh assumed to be the kitchen, giving her a prime shot of his killer ass. "What's that supposed to mean?" he asked over his shoulder before returning with a sweating longneck and a bottle of water that he passed her way. "If you're going back to that crappy person thing, I'm calling bullshit."

"Do you know why I became a doctor?" she asked him.

"Nope," he said, taking a draw off his beer. The action drew attention to his full lips pressed against the mouth of the bottle.

She wondered what they'd feel like pressed to her.

Sensation prickled up her neck at the images flashing through her mind. Vivid, detailed images that sent heat pulsing to her core.

What the hell was wrong with her today? She'd just apologized for using the man thirteen years ago, and here she was, treating him like a side of beef in her mind.

"I am so messed up," she said.

"You became a doctor because you're messed up?"

"Um . . ." she hedged. "No. I just . . . My mind wandered for a minute." Haleigh cleared her throat to buy time. "I became a doctor because my mother had high expectations and I was determined to meet them. Med school was my version of go big or go home. I liked the prestige of the occupation and thought for once I could make my mother happy."

Cooper studied her with a tilt of his head as if searching for some deeper motivation at the back of her skull. She hated to tell him, but there was nothing deep about it. Simply put, Haleigh was a shallow people-pleaser. And a sucky one at that.

"I don't believe it," he said.

"I'm not surprised, but facts are facts. The act of becoming a doctor was nothing more than me chasing the shiniest brass ring I could find."

The confession, something she'd long feared but never spoken aloud, scraped another layer off her fragile ego, making Haleigh feel as if her skin had been flipped inside out, leaving her exposed and raw. Though uncomfortable, the experience was also oddly liberating.

"No way," Cooper said, dropping into the chair he'd been standing next to. "I watched you deliver that baby last night. Nothing that happened in that room was about some brass ring."

Haleigh took a seat on the black leather couch.

"Just because I had selfish motivations for becoming a doctor doesn't mean I'm not good at my job. I bring babies into the world, making sure they and their mothers come through the ordeal healthy and happy. The point is that what I do doesn't change who I am."

"Wrong," he argued. "If you were a crappy person, healthy and happy patients wouldn't be a priority."

"Believe what you want." She spun the top off the water bottle. "I think I know me better than you do."

"Could you make more money doing your job someplace else?" he asked.

That one was easy. "Of course I could."

"Do you know your patients' names?"

"Do you know how long it takes to grow a baby? I spend months getting to know them, Cooper. I couldn't *not* know their names."

"So they aren't just a means to an end? There to give you something to do that makes you feel better about yourself?"

These rapid-fire questions proved nothing.

"What's your point?"

"You, Haleigh Rae, are a good person," he said, pointing the beer bottle at her chest. "In fact, you're a better person than I am. A superhero almost."

Now he'd gone way off the deep end. "You're being ridiculous."

"I'm right on this one," he said with a wide grin that deepened the dimple in his chin. "Who refused to let Jessi leave the hospital without a safe place to go?"

"She's a homeless girl with a new baby to take care of."

"And you took care of both of them," he pointed out. "You made sure she got the applications she needed to get insurance for both of them, and even when you figured out that they might be invading your life, you were more concerned about Abby's feelings than your own. Does that sound like a horrible person to you?"

Though she hated to admit as much, the man had a point. Her actions did *appear* to be those of a somewhat generous person.

"Maybe I'm just trying to make up for being such a crummy person all these years," she mumbled.

Cooper leaned forward, resting his elbows on his knees. "You keep telling yourself that, doc. And I'll keep setting you straight."

Cooper whistled an upbeat tune as he perused the Mamacita's menu.

"Someone has his happy panties on today," Spencer said over his menu. "What's up with the whistling?"

"Nothing," Cooper said. "Can't a guy whistle when he wants to?"

"Not when he's whistling a show tune."

Cooper's mother had conned him into watching *Oklahoma* with her the week before, and the surrey with the fringe on top song had been stuck in his head ever since. "How do you know it's a show tune?" he asked his friend.

"Everybody knows the surrey with the fringe on top song," Caleb McGraw said, drawing the attention of both his lunch mates. "What can I say?" He shrugged. "The McGraws are big supporters of the arts."

The McGraws were one of the richest families in Louisiana, owners of a giant media conglomerate that would one day belong solely to Caleb. Which made the fact that the heir to a fortune held down a steady gig selling ads for their local paper, the *Ardent Advocate*, even more bizarre. Cooper hadn't known the younger man for long, seeing as he'd only arrived in town the previous winter.

Caleb was married to Snow of the Curiosity Shop, though exactly how they'd gotten together remained a mystery to Cooper. The guy had just shown up one day, claiming to have been in a long-distance relationship with Snow, and on New Year's Eve, the pair tied the knot.

Though not a mechanic, Caleb shared Cooper's appreciation for old cars, and the two had become fast friends from the first time they met, haggling over a '56 Ford pickup at an auction.

"Can we get on with ordering lunch before you two burst into song?" Spencer asked.

"Sure," Caleb said, giving Cooper a sideways look. The melody started again, this time as a chipper hum.

Seconds later, Spencer joined in. They'd just finished describing the fancy ride when the waitress approached and they all cut the tune.

The young girl with the swinging black ponytail looked perplexed. "Were you guys singing?"

Spencer shook his head. "No. No singing going on here."

By sheer willpower, Cooper and Caleb kept straight faces as she took their orders and disappeared into the kitchen.

"You two are a bad influence," Spencer said. And just like that, the revival ended. "How's the fundraiser looking?"

In just over four weeks the first classic car rally fundraiser benefiting the Ruby Restoration Committee, a citizen group trying to save the local theater, would kick off in the Ruby Theater parking lot. A few months back, Cooper agreed to plan the event, even though at the time he wasn't on the committee.

"Good." Cooper nodded. "The Cars for Sale slots, which as you know are the higher moneymakers, are selling steadily. We picked up two from Clarksville last week. Lorelei has a handle on the food vendors, and Kickin' 96.5 will be on site from noon to two doing live broadcasts from the event." Bringing in the local country station had been his best idea by far, and Cooper mentally patted himself on the back for the rare stroke of genius. "The block at the Ridgetop Inn is going quick, so I'm looking at the Deerfield on Highway 11 as a lodging backup."

Conversation paused as the waitress returned with two bowls of nachos. "Your food should be up any second," she said.

"Much appreciated," Cooper replied with a wink. The waitress blushed and nearly tripped over another server as she backed away from the table.

Caleb shook his head. "Snow's right. You could flirt with a tree stump."

"I think he dated one once," Spencer said, dipping a chip into salsa. "She left him for a squirrel with bigger nuts."

"You're just jealous that your nuts are about to be in a sling till death do you part."

"That's right," Caleb said. "I hear you've got six months left to live."

Cooper remembered his promise to Lorelei and cringed. So much for acting surprised. Evidently, she'd told Snow the good news as well. Who'd passed the secret on to her husband.

"Is there anyone that woman hasn't told yet?" Spencer asked on a sigh. "Did she take out an ad in the *Advocate*?"

"I directed her to Brenda Jo, who handles the public announcements." That Caleb managed to say this with a straight face amazed Cooper.

Spencer threw his hands up, but the smile gave him away. No matter what she did, and Lorelei had done some bone-headed things, her intended groom would always forgive her. The thought made Cooper think of Haleigh. Half the town considered Lorelei Pratchett irredeemable, when she hid a heart of gold. At the same time, Haleigh Rae was looked upon as a shining example of all that was good, while condemning herself for being a terrible person.

He still couldn't believe she'd said that. So her motives weren't always selfless. That didn't make her a bad person any more than going to church every week made someone a good person. Actions were what mattered.

"So what do you say?" Spencer said, jerking Cooper from his wayward thoughts. "You up for playing best man?"

"Hell yeah," Cooper said, proud to be asked for the second time around. "Tux me up. I'm ready."

The groom turned his attention to Caleb. "Lor says I have to drag two guys up there with me. You willing to be my number two?"

Dark brows shot up Caleb's forehead. "You serious?"

"Sure."

"Well, then count me in," Caleb replied. "I'd be honored."

"Good," Spencer exhaled. "That means my part of the planning is done."

As the waitress returned with their food, Cooper raised his beer bottle for a toast. "Here's to many years of wedded bliss."

His plate hit the table in front of him with a thud. "You're engaged?" the young girl cried.

"Not me," Cooper said and pointed the bottle at Spencer. "Him."

"Oh." Dark lashes fluttered as the other two plates landed in front of their owners. "That's good," she said, dropping the large tray to her side. "You let me know if you need anything else." With a long look at Cooper, she added, "Anything at all."

Once the girl was out of earshot, Spencer burst out laughing. "Anything at all, big boy," he feigned in a girlish voice.

Cooper had no intention of taking the pretty little thing up on her offer, but that didn't mean he wouldn't goad his friend. "It isn't my fault I'm the only one left to handle all the pretty girls."

"Right," Spencer answered. "If by *handle* you mean date until they start talking commitment and then running like hell. We both know that you're holding out for one particular woman."

"About that." Cooper rested his elbows on the edge of the table. "Looks like Lorelei isn't the only one who has trouble keeping secrets around here."

"Are we talking about that OB doctor?" Caleb asked, earning the attention of his table mates.

"Who told you?" Cooper asked.

Caleb sliced into his enchilada. "Carrie."

Spencer's ex-wife. Odd how all sources led back to one person.

Cooper zeroed in on the groom. "And how would she know, Spencer?"

"Dude, you can blame me all you want, but every thought you have shows up on that ugly mug of yours. You haven't fooled anyone about your feelings for Haleigh Rae since middle school." If Spencer was right, then how had Haleigh managed not to notice? "She's back now," Spencer continued. "You need to make your move, buddy."

He'd been toying with the idea since Haleigh left his house the night before. She was definitely attracted to him, so he had an advantage there. If he'd known buffing up would do the trick, Cooper would have spent his teen years lifting weights instead of tearing apart carburetors. But he wanted something more than physical from Haleigh, and short of a drastic career change on his part, didn't see how they could ever match up on any other level.

She dealt with life and death. He dealt with nuts and bolts. She was educated and refined. He was countrified and clumsy. Ironically enough, the only thing Cooper really had going for him was a total lack of resemblance to the guys she typically dated.

"I know what you're doing," Cooper said, preferring to keep his thoughts on Haleigh to himself. "Married guys trying to recruit one more into the fold." He tucked his napkin into his shirt collar. "You're not getting me, buddy. Go hunt up some other poor sucker."

Spencer gave Caleb a bored look. "Twenty bucks says he's married within a year."

With a nod, Caleb said, "I give him six months." He grinned. "The big ones always fall the hardest."

"Keep it up, fellas." Cooper picked up a taco. "I'll prove you both wrong."

Chapter 6

Haleigh needed coffee, and she needed it now.

After her conscience-cleansing visit with Cooper she'd returned home exhausted and ready to sleep for possibly the first time in days. Too bad the universe had other ideas. A late-night call pulled her back to the hospital shortly after two for a difficult delivery that ended with a C-section at four in the morning.

Though she was home by six, adrenaline had kept her going for another forty-five minutes before she'd crashed just as the sun peeked through her curtains. But her peaceful sleep had been invaded by a very vivid dream. One in which a bare-chested mechanic with devastating green eyes and a mouthwatering body put Haleigh through a highly pleasurable workout.

The sensations had been so real that she'd awoken with a gasp, sweaty, aching, and wanting more.

"My brain hates me," she mumbled, shoving tangled waves away from her face. "Stupid libido."

Ten minutes later, she used the kitchen counter for support while waiting for Abby's Keurig machine to do its magic. The smell of caffeine helped open her eyes, but it was the piercing cry that brought Haleigh to full alert.

"What the—"

Rounding the corner into the hallway, she met Jessi coming out of her room with Emma in her arms. "I don't know what's wrong," she said. "I've changed her and tried to feed her, but she won't latch on. She did it great before we left the hospital, but now it's like she can't figure it out." Wide brown eyes bored into Haleigh as if she had all the answers. "I'm doing it wrong, aren't I? I'm doing something wrong!"

Nursing wasn't really Haleigh's territory and, oddly enough considering her line of work, neither were babies. That's what nurses and pediatricians were for. Haleigh dealt with the mothers, got the babies out, and then handed them off to a person qualified to handle them.

"We can figure this out," she said, hoping beyond reason that she could find a solution despite her brain feeling like mush. "The hospital sent home bottles, right? Those little premade ones they give to newborns?"

Jessi vigorously shook her head. "The nurse was adamant that I breastfeed. It's the best thing for her."

"Not feeding her at all would be worse." Haleigh charged into the baby's room, half looking for bottles and half trying to outrun the headache-inducing screams. "Here we go," she said, finding the bottles in a box beneath the changing table. "Try this."

The young mother hesitated. "Are you sure?"

"Of course I'm sure," Haleigh answered. "I'm a doctor."

Not a pediatrician, but Jessi didn't need to think about that.

"Right. But don't we need to warm it up? Do that test on the wrist thing?"

If Jessi already knew so much, why was she asking Haleigh? Taking the bottle back, she said, "Let's run it under hot water. In the meantime, have you tried a pacifier?"

"Of course I have," Jessi snapped. So Haleigh wasn't the only person who needed a nap.

Without another word, Haleigh marched into the kitchen with Jessi close behind—heaven forbid she spare anyone else's eardrums— and flipped on the hot water. "How long should it take?" she asked.

Jessi stopped her shushing long enough to say, "You're the doctor. Shouldn't you know?"

"My experience with babies happens while they're still *inside* their mothers. Warming bottles doesn't come up much at that point in the process."

"You're more clueless than I am," Jessi accused. "Here." She rolled Emma into Haleigh's arms. "Let me do it."

Shocked to find the angry bundle in her care, Haleigh followed her instincts and began swaying from side to side. Desperate to stop the screaming, she slid a knuckle between the baby's quivering lips. Emma quieted instantly.

"How did you do that?" Jessi asked.

An excellent question. "I don't know."

Emma continued to nuzzle for several seconds before showing signs of a returning fit. "I can't fool her much longer," Haleigh said.

"Almost there." Jessi drizzled three drops on her wrist, then looked to Haleigh. "I think it's good."

"Here." Haleigh extended her free arm. "Let me check." The formula felt more room temperature than warm, but at least it wasn't cold. "Feels okay to me."

"Take your knuckle out and let's see."

Haleigh did as ordered, and Jessi dipped the small nipple into the baby's mouth. The hungry little thing began eating like a champ.

"It's working," Jessi said, doing a happy dance on her toes. "She's taking it."

"She is." Chubby cheeks sucked in and out as a little hand wrapped around Haleigh's thumb. The newborn might as well have thrown a lasso around Haleigh's heart and tugged it out of her chest. "So precious," she whispered.

"I should probably take her back now," the mother said, reminding Haleigh that they were standing nose to nose in the middle of the kitchen.

"Of course," she said, fighting the urge to keep the child close. It wasn't as if Haleigh didn't hold babies every day. They were just usually bright red and covered in bodily fluids.

Jessi mimicked the swaying motion Haleigh had used to calm the child and smiled at the doctor. "Thank you for helping. I panicked for a minute there."

"I'm sure every new mother panics at first." Haleigh certainly would if she were in Jessi's position. And then she remembered that she almost *had* been in Jessi's position. Somehow the memory didn't feel as raw today. She took that as a positive sign. "There's a learning curve, but you'll figure things out."

"We didn't keep you up last night, did we?" Jessi asked. "You look like you haven't had much sleep."

Ah, the honesty of youth.

"I spent most of the night at the hospital. Which is why, as you point out, I look like roadkill this morning."

"I didn't say that," Jessi corrected. "I'm probably the one who looks like roadkill." She punctuated the assertion with a yawn. "Maybe she'll sleep after this bottle and I can pass out."

A pushy voice niggled at the back of Haleigh's brain, and it sounded an awful lot like Cooper.

You're a good person, Hal. You know you want to help the girl out and let her get some sleep.

She *could* volunteer to babysit. For once, she had the day off and wasn't on call again until after midnight.

"Where is this angel I've heard so much about?" echoed a high-pitched voice from the front hall. Abby and Cooper's mother blew into the kitchen, heading straight for Jessi.

"Hello, Mrs. Ridgeway," Haleigh said, stepping between the older woman and the retreating teen to give her second—and possibly favorite—mom a hug. "Linda Ridgeway, this is Jessi and baby Emma. I'm afraid the new little angel kept her mother up last night, so Jessi and I were working on getting her to sleep."

"You poor thing." Linda gave Jessi a sympathetic frown. "Though it's been decades, of course, I still remember those first days of having them home."

"She slept a little," Jessi said, defending her baby's behavior. "An hour here and there."

"You must be exhausted." The newcomer cupped Jessi's cheek. "No need to worry now. I'm here."

Brown eyes caught Haleigh's over a puff of gray curls. "You are?"

Haleigh mouthed the words *Go with it* then said, "I'm sure Jessi doesn't want to put you out, Mrs. Ridgeway."

"Don't be silly," the woman said, taking the bait as Haleigh knew she would. "You need your strength to take care of a baby. Especially in the beginning. Don't fret one minute more. I'll take care of the little one while you crawl right back into bed. And then, when you wake up, I'll make you something to eat."

"Um," Jessi hesitated. "Okay?" She passed Emma into Linda's impatient arms, eliciting a loud belch from the baby.

"Very good, little one," Linda said, shooing the other two women out of the room. "Go on now. I have everything under control."

"If you're sure," Haleigh said, pushing Jessi out of the kitchen from behind. Linda didn't answer but continued to hum to the bundle in her arms.

"Am I dreaming?" Jessi asked, standing outside her bedroom.

"Linda has been hoping for a grandchild for nearly a decade. Emma is in capable hands, and if you're smart, you'll sleep as long as she'll let you."

"I don't know. It feels kind of weird to hand my baby over to a total stranger."

"You're living with strangers, Jessi. How much weirder could it get?" Haleigh blamed that zinger on lack of sleep. "Sorry," she said. "I've known Abby and Cooper's mom my whole life. I promise that Emma will be fine."

Jessi tugged on the hem of her faded black T-shirt. "I *am* really tired."

"You and me both," Haleigh said, and disappeared into her own room with a casual wave. As her head hit the pillow, she sent her brain a cease and desist order on dreams about Cooper Ridgeway. Unfortunately, her brain had other ideas. All of them X-rated.

Within an hour, she gave up and faced the day.

Lunch had ended and the three men were lingering outside Mamacita's when Cooper remembered to ask about Jessi's father. "Spencer, do you remember anyone in town going by the initials J.T.?"

"Doesn't sound familiar. Why?"

"That girl I found in my storage building the other night is looking for her biological father, and all she knows is that he's supposedly from here and gave her mother the initials J.T."

"Did her mother meet him here?" Caleb asked.

"No. Up in Bowling Green," Cooper answered. "Her mom was eighteen at the time and recently told Jessi that the man was older and already had a family."

"Sounds like an upstanding guy," Spencer observed. "Why is she looking for him now? Not that I don't get wanting to meet your father, but does she have a reason?"

Spencer grew up not knowing so much as his father's name, and only learned the facts last year, shortly after the man had passed away.

"I'm not sure." Cooper hadn't thought to ask what Jessi intended to do if she found this mystery man. Was she going to hit him up for money? Break up his family? Expect to move in with him? Or did she simply want to get to know him?

"Gerald would know," Caleb said.

"Gerald Nichols?" Spencer asked.

"Yeah. He's lived here all his life except for a few years spent in Korea during the war. If someone named J.T. lived in Ardent Springs, he'd be the man to ask."

"I should have thought of old Mr. Nichols," Cooper said. "He might be the last of his generation around here. Could you ask him for me?"

Caleb grimaced. "I would, but he and his wife are over in Napa Valley for the rest of the month. The poor man thought retirement would give him a chance to sit still, but Dolly's kept him on the road since a week after his goodbye party. Says she's waited their entire marriage for it to be her turn and she's taking it."

"Can't blame her for that, I guess." So much for solving the mystery on the first try. Jessi's one- to two-week stay with Abby was starting to look like a month, at least. "I'll keep asking around, and if we don't find an answer before he gets back, I'd appreciate it if you could see what Nichols knows."

"Consider it done," Caleb said. "Are we all still on for Brubaker's after the meeting on Friday?"

Spencer pressed the key fob to unlock his truck. "Lorelei has reminded me twice, so I'm guessing yes." Turning to Cooper, he pressed his hand to his forehead to block the sun. "You should bring Haleigh Rae."

Not back to this again. "I don't think so." If he convinced Haleigh to go out on a date, Cooper wasn't going to drag her to the loudest, most obnoxious place in town.

"I admit," Spencer said, "your terrible dancing could run her off before you make the first move, but maybe she'll feel bad and take pity on you."

"I'm not bringing Haleigh to Brubaker's," Cooper argued. "She's too good for that place."

Caleb and Spencer both looked offended.

"We take our women there all the time," Spencer said. "What are you trying to say?"

"Come on, guys. You know what I mean."

"I don't think we do," Caleb said, crossing his arms as he squared his stance. "Explain it to us."

Shit fire. Cooper hadn't meant to insult Lorelei and Snow. And he sure didn't mean to piss off their other halves.

"I'm not saying that Haleigh is better than Snow or Lorelei. She's just . . . different." The tick in Spencer's jaw proved Cooper was digging himself a deeper hole. "Forget the too-good-for stuff," he said. "If I take Haleigh out on a date, I want to be able to talk to her without yelling over loud music, okay?"

The explanation seemed to do the trick as each man visibly relaxed. Caleb turned to Spencer. "Should we let him off the hook?"

Spencer grinned. "I don't know. I like seeing him squirm."

Cooper flipped them off as he turned toward his truck an aisle over. "You guys suck," he said, ignoring the laughter behind him.

"Come on, buddy," Spencer yelled after him. "You make it so easy."

This was the crap he got for being a nice guy. "Screw you!" he hollered back. "I've got work to do."

Chapter 7

Since sleep wasn't in the cards, and Haleigh felt in the way with Abby's mom and the baby, she ventured downtown in search of artwork for her bedroom wall.

This was an unusual occurrence to say the least.

When she'd moved in, Abby had suggested that Haleigh personalize her room. Make it her own. And in six months, she'd failed to add so much as an accent pillow. In her own defense, the idea of decorating anything intimidated her.

She'd apparently been absent the day they passed out the decorator gene, which was likely the same day they'd distributed non-addictive personalities and the ability to pick a suitable partner. The go-to excuse of her long hours at the hospital grew thin when Abby pointed out that other doctors managed to have full lives.

Even ventured into polite society on occasion.

If only socializing wasn't so . . . dangerous. In her drinking days, Haleigh had been the life of the party. Once sober, she realized she hated small talk and sucked at mingling. Pretending to have a good time was the worst when all she wanted to do was escape. Marcus had been the king of the dinner parties, always looking for new connections and encouraging Haleigh to do the same. *Networking*, he'd called it.

Torture was her preferred term.

Marcus had known about her addiction, but as he'd never seen her fall off the wagon, he assumed being in the presence of alcohol bore no challenge for her. Raquel, Haleigh's longtime sponsor, had suggested she correct this assumption, but for some reason she never did. Heaven forbid she not bend over backward to please her fiancé.

Which reminded her, she needed to call Raquel with an update. The sweet older woman had recently found the love of her life—again— and was blissfully planning her third wedding, this one hopefully the proverbial charm. Haleigh couldn't bring herself to interrupt the cheerful time. And in truth, she was handling things on her own just fine.

Mostly.

Ardent Springs didn't offer anything as convenient as a mall, but the downtown area had developed quite a bit since she'd left for college. Her mother had dragged her to a cute little store on the corner of Fourth and Main last summer, so Haleigh pointed her car in that direction.

The first person Haleigh spotted inside the store was Lorelei Pratchett, more an acquaintance than a friend during high school. Lorelei's penchant for drama and rebellion had led Haleigh to keep a comfortable distance between herself and the bold blonde. Haleigh had yet to find her rebellious side in those days.

As she considered spinning on her heel to beat a hasty retreat, Lorelei caught sight of her. "Hey there, Haleigh Rae," she called, her voice carrying without the necessity of a megaphone. "Welcome to Snow's Curiosity Shop."

Sliding past inviting displays of old suitcases and funky bookends, Haleigh joined Lorelei near the center of the store.

"Hello," she said. "I'm doing some overdue shopping today."

"Then you're in the right place." Lorelei's genuine smile went a long way in helping Haleigh to relax. As the store owner approached, Lorelei said, "Have you met Snow?"

"We met briefly last summer when I came in with my mother, and then again when Carrie delivered," Haleigh replied as she accepted the petite woman's nod of greeting. "The place is as quaint as I remember."

Unlike the flea markets and consignment shops Haleigh had visited in the past, Snow's place was organized while maintaining a relaxed and cozy feel. In lieu of junk in piles, themed displays surrounded them, each with an eclectic mix of items that should have clashed but somehow meshed in an inexplicable shabby-chic sort of way.

The store's owner had clearly implemented her own style into the business. Her necklace should not have gone with her earrings, and the sweater, which reached the back of her knees, would typically be a no-go on such a petite person. Yet, Snow looked stylish. Like one of those women who could drag three random items from her closet and make them look like something off a runway.

In addition to missing the decorator gene, Haleigh also lacked in the fashion department. Thankfully, scrubs and a lab coat didn't require Fifth Avenue know-how.

"Thanks," Snow said. "It's always a work in progress, but I like it. Are you looking for anything specific, or just browsing today?"

"I'm looking for artwork, actually."

"Can you be more specific?"

"Afraid not," Haleigh said, embarrassed that she couldn't offer a better answer. "I have a bare, dark blue bedroom wall to fill, but no idea what to put on it. If you'll point me in the right direction, maybe something will catch my eye."

"Of course," Snow said. "There are a couple of areas to check out, but I'd suggest starting along the left wall over here."

"Do you want any help?" Lorelei asked.

"No, thank you," Haleigh said quicker than necessary. She'd rather skip the humiliation of anyone realizing how inept she truly was at this decorating thing. "But I'll call if that changes."

Unbelievable. Haleigh could handle bringing tiny humans into the world on a daily basis, but found two stylish women inordinately intimidating. What a proud moment.

Flipping through a small stack of still-lifes, Haleigh gave each an immediate pass. Being greeted every morning by a bowl of fruit didn't seem very inspiring. The piece needed to be beautiful, of course, but uplifting, too. Something that would tell a story and maybe even make her think.

This was what happened when you sent a bookworm to do a decorator's job.

Sifting through the next stack, she found three unicorn paintings, two of frolicking cats, and the classic dogs playing poker reimagined with visor-wearing pigs. Definite nos.

"That's the one you should buy," Lorelei said, popping up out of nowhere. Following the direction Lorelei pointed, Haleigh located the suggested image.

A half-naked woman, with light hair piled carelessly atop her head, sprawled elegantly across a stool. The man kneeling in the shadows at her feet looked both mesmerized and forlorn, as if he'd give her anything if only she'd ask.

With a tilt of her head, Haleigh said, "I don't know." The picture was beautiful enough, and certainly told a story. But maybe not the story Haleigh was prepared to live with.

"What's not to love?" Lorelei asked. "The woman is gorgeous, clearly in a position of power, and the man at her feet shows she's desirable."

Haleigh examined the painting closer, focusing on the woman's eyes. "She looks lonely," she observed. "Like she'd rather the man sweep her off her feet than worship at them."

"Huh," Lorelei said. "How apt." Before Haleigh could ask what that comment meant, Lorelei reached for the painting. "I'll help you get her down."

"But I haven't agreed to buy it yet," she said, rushing to catch the opposite side of the painting as it leaned precariously forward. "I might like something else better."

Lorelei ignored the protest. "Nope. This one is perfect."

Reminding herself that she wasn't the expert here, Haleigh conceded and allowed Lorelei to carry her soon-to-be newest possession to the register. Preferring not to display a mostly naked woman on the streets of Ardent Springs, she said, "Can you wrap it up for me? I don't want it to get damaged on the way home."

Right. Potential damage was the issue and not the delicate sensibilities of the local church ladies. All of whom would report back to Haleigh's mother.

"Not a problem." Leaning the canvas on the wall behind the counter, Lorelei stepped to the register. "What are you doing Friday night?"

An odd and unexpected question. "I'm on duty at the hospital until six. And then I'm having dinner with my mother. Why?"

"A bunch of us are going to Brubaker's after the Ruby committee meeting. You should come along."

"Brubaker's?" Haleigh's mouth went dry. "The dance hall?"

"That's the one," Lorelei said as she tapped the screen of what Haleigh realized was an iPad. "Spencer and I are taking Carrie out for the first time since she had Molly and she's nervous about leaving her. You could reassure her that one night of dancing does not make her a bad mother." Without waiting for a reply, she added, "That's seventy-one fifty-two."

Crap. Haleigh hadn't intended to spend that much on a wall decoration. Quickly debating her options, she decided to avoid the embarrassment of balking at the price and whipped out her credit card. To her surprise, Lorelei twirled the iPad to face her.

Sliding her card through the reader, she said, "That's kind of nifty."

Lorelei's voice dropped to a whisper. "You should see the old biddies jump back when I do the flip thing. They act like I pulled a python out of my pocket and told them to kiss it."

Since Haleigh had nearly jumped back herself, she couldn't blame the older women. "It is a bit of a shock when it spins around like that. A warning might be helpful."

Minutes later, Lorelei passed the painting, now wrapped in brown paper, across the counter. "See you Friday night," she said with a nod.

Haleigh had hoped the invitation would be forgotten. "I never actually agreed to go," she clarified.

Lorelei stared at her over the painting. "What else do you have to do after the dinner with your mom?"

Her reasons for declining were none of Lorelei's business. "I don't have to be busy to say no," she defended.

"How long has it been since you had a night out?" the blonde pressed, making Haleigh regret this spontaneous shopping excursion. Why hadn't she ordered something online? All the cool kids were doing it.

Haleigh dragged the painting off the counter as she resisted the urge to explain that it was impolite to invite an alcoholic to a bar and to freaking take no for an answer already. Not that Lorelei knew she was an alcoholic. Or that Haleigh intended to tell her so.

"I'll think about it." A noncommittal answer that put Haleigh under no obligation to show up at the dance hall.

"Good," Lorelei said, looking very happy with herself. "We'll be there between eight-thirty and nine. I'll save you a stool."

That didn't sound like a graceful acceptance of Haleigh's round-about refusal. Regardless of her efforts, Lorelei was not going to guilt Haleigh into doing something she did not want to do. And on the off chance that she ran into Lorelei again after Friday and was asked why she didn't show, Haleigh could remind the pushy blonde that she'd never given a definitive yes.

Dammit.

Considering a call to Raquel on the way home, Haleigh left Snow's Curiosity Shop with a troubled conscience but firm in the knowledge that she would not be visiting Brubaker's dance hall anytime soon.

Cooper hadn't laid eyes on Haleigh in three days, though not for lack of trying. Each evening he checked on Jessi, making sure she had what she needed and reporting his findings on her J.T. mystery man. Unfortunately, there wasn't much to report. No one Cooper had talked to had ever heard of anyone in Ardent Springs going by those initials.

On Wednesday evening, he'd been surprised to find his mother keeping watch over the new pair, but her presence had allowed the three of them—Cooper, his mom, and Jessi—to brainstorm the situation. The Ridgeway matriarch couldn't think of anyone in town who'd ever gone by the initials J.T. And while Jessi had offered details on the kind of men her mother typically dated, her input hadn't helped them narrow the search.

Understandably frustrated, Jessi remained convinced that someone had to know him. Cooper admired her determination, but the girl was chasing a ghost. If her father had ever lived in their little town, he hadn't left much of an impression with the locals.

At least the young girl wasn't relying on the rest of them to do everything. She'd completed the paperwork to get Emma into CoverKids, the Tennessee state aid insurance program for children, and during her limited free time when Emma didn't require all of her attention, devoted herself to cleaning Abby's house, regardless of the fact that his sister had assured her this wasn't necessary.

Simply put, Jessi was a hard worker determined to take responsibility for her tiny family. His mother seemed to like her, and to his surprise, so did Cooper. A spunky kid with nerve and a positive attitude, Jessi had slipped into their world with less hassle than expected.

His initial motivation to find her father had been the need to get the young woman out of Abby's house and on her way. After knowing her for five days, Cooper's desire to help had shifted to simply wanting to give the girl the father she so desperately sought.

During his brief visits, Cooper had hoped that Haleigh would either walk through the front door or wander out of her bedroom. Neither wish came true. Short of finding another pregnant woman to rush to the hospital, he wasn't sure how he'd run into her again without enlisting his sister.

Lost in his own thoughts, Cooper nearly missed hearing his name called from the front of the room until Spencer elbowed him in the ribs.

"Mr. Ridgeway," Buford Stallings intoned from behind his faded brown podium. "Are you prepared to update the committee on the car rally or not?"

"Yes, sir," Cooper said, rising to his feet.

Without looking at his notes, he repeated everything he'd told Spencer and Caleb over lunch two days before. When he finished, the group seemed satisfied, but then Mayor Jebediah Winkle raised his hand and Cooper tensed. Winkle was a born obstructionist, and had long been an opponent to the car rally idea.

Before Caleb had suggested they organize a series of rallies as fundraisers, Cooper had tried for two years to put on something similar at the county fairgrounds with the goal of bringing tourist dollars to the town. Every attempt had been unsuccessful thanks in whole to Jebediah's interference. As longtime head of the fair committee, the mayor opposed the use of the fairgrounds on the bogus assumption that old cars meant leaky pieces of junk. The yes-men who made up the rest of the committee bowed to their leader and voted down every proposal Cooper put forward.

"What is it, Jebediah?" asked Stallings, who was less a fan of the mayor than Cooper was, thanks to having been defeated by Winkle in the last election.

"Has anyone considered what this rally will do to traffic in the downtown area?"

Giving the obvious answer, Cooper said, "Traffic will increase around the theater, along Margin Street from Fifth to Third, but that's the whole point. The more people we attract, the more successful the event and the more money we raise."

Jebediah wasn't appeased. "What about the locals who need to get through that area?"

Keeping a tight hold on his patience, Cooper replied, "The rally is on a Saturday. Nearly every business along Margin is a Monday through Friday operation. Meaning no one is going to be late for work because of this event." The mayor opened his mouth, but Cooper didn't give him the chance to fire off another question. "I've talked to nearly every business owner for four blocks and all have offered their support. The ones with freestanding parking lots have given us permission to use their property as needed, and several others have bought ad space in the rally program. Not one has complained, but if you've heard from anyone specifically, let me know and I'll be happy to pay them another visit."

Knowing he'd been beaten, at least for now, Winkle backed down. "I'm just trying to anticipate problems before they arise," he said.

Stallings rolled his eyes as he moved to the next item on the agenda and Cooper returned to his seat. Thirty minutes later, the meeting ended.

"That was impressive," Spencer said, a wide smile splitting his face. "Who knew you had that in you?"

An excellent question. Cooper had even surprised himself. Growing up with a father who'd never believed his son would do anything worthwhile had driven more than a few holes into Cooper's confidence.

"He was fishing for problems," he said, playing down the encounter. "Luckily, I had the answers to shut him up."

"Did you really talk to all those businesses?" Spencer asked.

Cooper grinned. "Most of them. Caleb sold the ads for the program, so I can't take credit for that part."

They followed Caleb, Snow, and Lorelei out of the room. "But you *can* take credit for handing Winkle his ass. That was fun to watch." With a smack on the back, Spencer said, "We'll see you over at Brubaker's. First round's on me."

Cooper never turned down a free beer. "Sounds good."

As his friends walked away, Cooper enjoyed a satisfaction he'd never felt before. Being the person in charge instead of an invisible cog in the wheel was a new experience. And he liked it. Tonight, he'd proven he had more to offer than a tune-up and a tow. Too bad Malcolm Ridgeway hadn't lived long enough to see how far his son had come.

"Never amount to anything, my ass," Cooper muttered on his way through the parking lot.

Chapter 8

"In the name of sweet baby Jesus, please let my mother be in a good mood."

Haleigh had been repeating this prayer before every family dinner for the last six months. So far, the Big Guy upstairs hadn't seen fit to grant her request, but hope did spring eternal.

The house at 429 Rebel Circle loomed over Haleigh like a specter that she couldn't expel. This was where she'd spent most of her childhood. Where she'd disappeared into endless worlds reading by the light of the moon in her blanket-filled bay window. Raced over the hardwood floors giggling with glee as her father chased his little princess from room to room. Teased her little brother as he grew from an annoying shadow into a barrel-chested boy on the cusp of manhood.

And then there was her mother.

Without ringing the doorbell, Haleigh opened the front door and stepped into the foyer of her childhood home. "Mom?" she called, hanging her thin jacket on a hook to her left. "I'm here." The scent of meatloaf and fresh bread filled the air. The Church Street Deli must have been running a special.

Meredith Mitchner wasn't the meatloaf-making, cookie-baking, always-ready-with-a-hug type of woman. At least not behind closed doors. She put on a good act, of course. Stay-at-home mom. Member of the PTA. Soprano in the church choir and leader of the bereavement committee, which meant making sure the refrigerators of the families of newly deceased church members were fully stocked with casseroles and side dishes within twenty-four hours of the passing.

"I'll be down in a minute," her mother yelled from upstairs. A staunch proponent of punctuality, Meredith was never late for an appointment. Dinner with her daughter seemed to be the exception to the rule.

"That's fine," Haleigh assured. "No hurry."

Though she took great pride in her community duties, Meredith did not give the same effort and attention to her daughter. At age ten, Haleigh hadn't understood the cold looks and lack of affection. By fifteen, she'd matured enough to recognize jealousy in another woman's eyes.

Stepping into the living room, Haleigh crossed to her favorite picture on the bookshelf. Her parents beamed with pride and joy as they nestled close, each holding a child. Haleigh had been three and perched on her father's knee showing off a mouthful of baby teeth. Her mother balanced Ryland on her hip. He'd just begun walking and Haleigh could still remember his toddler demands of "Down! Down!"

If only things had stayed that simple.

Richard Mitchner had doted on his daughter, declaring her the most beautiful girl in the world. He'd bragged of her intelligence and determination, telling anyone who would listen that Haleigh was destined to be more than a wife and mother. She would do important things. She would be somebody.

The more he'd bragged, the more Meredith silently seethed.

Haleigh knew Daddy hadn't meant to belittle his wife. He was a progressive thinker, ahead of his time, while cursed with the age-old male trait of obliviousness. He didn't see Meredith's hurt, because the possibility that Haleigh's mother didn't share his pride and hopes for their daughter never entered his mind.

Willful or not, that failure to recognize the consequences of his words had poisoned Haleigh's relationship with her mother. When he'd been killed in the car crash, the situation had only gotten worse. A review of her father's financial dealings revealed a sizable college fund for Haleigh, but no will or even reasonable life insurance policy on himself.

Which meant Haleigh's college dream had remained intact, while Meredith had been left to fend for herself and Ryland. Guilt, even by association, could be a powerful motivator. Guilt had driven her to drink. And guilt was the reason that most of her current income went straight into Meredith's bank account.

At least she didn't have to pay for Ryland's college education since he'd gone into the military. Haleigh had always suspected that he'd signed up to get away from their mother, though he'd never confirmed the fact. Thankfully, he was stationed at an army base in Germany and not in the fray in the Middle East.

Running a finger along the frame, Haleigh lamented the family they could have been. If only things had been different. If only her father had chosen his words differently. If only her mother had spoken up instead of bottling her hurt and anger.

Though the chances were slim, Haleigh held out hope that someday she and her mother could have a better relationship. That, eventually, Meredith would stop holding her father's words against her and give Haleigh the love and approval she so desperately desired.

"I see you couldn't be bothered to change your clothes for your mother," Meredith said from the doorway to the foyer. Critical blue eyes assessed Haleigh's scrubs. "I guess I don't rank high enough for regular clothes."

Without waiting for a response, the older woman spun and disappeared into the kitchen. Clearly, that love and approval would not be granted this evening.

Bracing for the meal ahead, Haleigh cut her eyes back to the picture. "No use dwelling on the past," she said to herself. "When the present is so much more fun."

Her mother wouldn't appreciate the sarcasm, but at least Haleigh was smiling when she entered the kitchen.

"Something smells good," she said, determined to be cheerful. "I can't remember the last time I had a home-cooked meal." Both of them knew this dinner had not been cooked in a home, but the pretense had become habit at this point.

"That explains why you're swimming in those shapeless scrubs. Being a doctor doesn't mean you have to look like one all the time."

They'd had this conversation on more than one occasion. Haleigh didn't like fashion any more than she liked decorating. Scrubs were easy. And thanks to supporting her mother, who refused to sell the house and move into something smaller—meaning cheaper—Haleigh couldn't afford to buy the high-dollar pieces her mother would approve of.

Employing her most successful tactic—deflection—Haleigh asked, "How was your week?"

For the next fifteen minutes, her mother provided uninterrupted commentary on the deteriorating state of the Rotary Club—that tramp Piper Griffin never should have been elected president—predicting that they would be lucky not to lose half their membership by the end of the year. On a roll, she shared her relief in not having to attend any more of those dreadful Ruby Restoration meetings, having left the committee due to an influx of new members with whom she'd rather not associate.

Not that she'd included this reasoning in her resignation. Meredith Mitchner would never allow her predilection for snobbery to show in such a public way. If Haleigh recalled correctly, her mother had used the excuse that other priorities were demanding her time and attention. Because being on call to produce a cluster of casseroles on a moment's notice could be extremely stressful.

When they were finally seated in the dining room, her mother said, "Did I tell you that I've volunteered for Jebediah Winkle's reelection campaign?"

Haleigh struggled to hide her distaste. Jebediah Winkle was a difficult man to like. How he'd managed to win the previous election remained a mystery. Buford Stallings had been mayor for more than a decade, and he'd done a satisfactory job as far as Haleigh knew, before Jebediah had deposed him. Due to being eyeball-deep in her residency at the time of the election, she hadn't paid much attention to the local news, so she wasn't certain how Winkle had pulled off the defeat.

"Why would you want to get involved in politics?" Haleigh asked. Her mother had never shown an interest in such matters before.

Manicured brows nearly met over an aristocratic nose. "A woman doesn't have to go to medical school to be interested in something other than grocery shopping and pressed linens."

As if the woman had ever ironed a sheet in her life.

"I didn't mean to insult you," Haleigh said, knowing better than to touch that nerve. "I'm sure they're happy to have you."

Setting her silverware on the table, Meredith said, "Don't patronize me, Haleigh Rae. I don't appreciate it."

"I'm not patronizing you, Mother. I sincerely believe you'll be an asset to the campaign."

Keeping her eyes on her food, Haleigh maintained a placid expression. Any inkling of irritation would only add fuel to the fire.

"Thank you," her mother said, reclaiming her fork. "I'll expect you to vote for him."

Haleigh jerked upright. "You expect what?"

Unruffled, Meredith said, "To vote for Jebediah. As my daughter, your support is a given."

"I don't think so," she sputtered. "Who I vote for is my business."

"Would it be so much to ask that for once in your life you put my desires first?"

The gall of the question struck Haleigh speechless. Nearly every aspect of her life revolved around her mother's *desires*. Her choice of career. Her surrendered paychecks. Her pointless efforts to atone for someone else's sins.

All for nothing.

"I'm not hungry anymore," Haleigh said, slamming her napkin onto her plate.

"Where do you think you're going?" Meredith demanded. "Dinner isn't over yet."

"Yes," Haleigh said, rising to her feet, "it is. I have someplace else to be."

Following her daughter into the foyer, Meredith said, "What do you mean you have someplace else to be? Having dinner with your mother should be more important than anything else."

After tugging on her jacket, Haleigh spun with her hand on the door. "There are a lot of things that should be in this house, Mother. But at some point we all have to admit the truth."

For the length of a breath, recognition shone in her mother's eyes. She knew exactly what her daughter's words meant. And if Haleigh had caught even a hint of regret in those blue depths, she might have stayed.

"By all means," her mother said, "don't let me keep you."

With her jaw clamped tight, Haleigh dragged the keys from her pocket, willing herself not to cry. After all, this wasn't a new wound. This was her reality. She had to accept it eventually.

Going to Brubaker's didn't have to be a mistake. It wasn't as if Haleigh had never been in the presence of alcohol and maintained complete control over her cravings. She could hang out with friends, chat for an hour or so, and return home feeling less like emotional roadkill.

"Are you sure I don't look like an idiot?" Haleigh's closet didn't contain honky-tonk attire. Jeans would have been good, if she'd been able to find a clean pair. Though her scrubs were washed regularly, the rest of her wardrobe tended to sit in the hamper for weeks on end.

"Would you trust me already?" Jessi said for the third time. "I've got this."

This was a denim jacket thrown over a casual dress that Jessi had found in the back of Haleigh's closet. The periwinkle flowers dotting the simple beige hem played off the jacket, and thankfully, she and her best friend wore the same size shoe as Jessi had snagged a pair of cowboy boots from Abby's closet.

They both stepped back to assess Haleigh's reflection in the full-length mirror.

"Maybe a shorter dress," Jessi suggested.

"This one already hits mid-thigh," Haleigh argued, tugging on the thin material. "If I go any shorter, I'll be arrested for indecent exposure."

Reaching for a polka-dotted pouch, Jessi said, "Sit down on the bed so I can do your makeup."

Haleigh obeyed the order. "I don't see why I can't apply some lipstick and go."

Opening an eye shadow palette of varying shades, Jessi stared down at her canvas with an expression of pity. "I get that you're naturally gorgeous, which is really annoying, by the way, but that doesn't mean you can't make a little effort."

Rolling her eyes, Haleigh said, "I am not naturally gorgeous. I'm too thin, my eyes are too close together, and I have bushy eyebrows."

"Full brows are in," Jessi informed her as she dug in the bottom of the pouch. "Lucky for you, we have the same color eyes so my stuff will work for you, too." Whipping out a small brush, she said, "Now close your eyes."

"Please don't make me look like a clown," Haleigh said.

With a hand on her hip, the teen said, "Are you saying I look like a clown?"

Jessi's look might be considered bold, but she'd never crossed into clown territory. At least not in the few days Haleigh had known her.

"Forget I said that." She closed her eyes. "Make me up."

For several minutes Haleigh followed orders to open wider and look this way or that. When the artist was satisfied with her work, she stepped back and said, "Now you're ready."

Walking to the mirror, Haleigh almost didn't recognize the face staring back. Gold eye shadow made her eyes pop, her cheekbones had been contoured to perfection, and thanks to Jessi's steady hand, Haleigh's eyes were lined with a slight flare at the corners. She looked like a blonder, less-edgy version of her makeup artist.

"That's amazing," she said, turning left and right. "Where did you learn to do this?"

"YouTube," the youngster answered. Of course.

While Haleigh continued to examine her look, Jessi said, "Not that it's any of my business, but based on your lack of club outfits, I'm guessing you don't go out like this very much?"

"I do not." Haleigh spun to make sure the dress covered her bottom.

"Why not?" she asked. "You're single and still kind of young. Why stay cooped up here when you're not at work?"

Ignoring the *kind of young* part, Haleigh answered with a half-truth. "I hit my quota of club hopping a long time ago. At a certain point, you grow up and standing in a room full of rowdy strangers loses its appeal."

"But then why are you going tonight?"

The nosy question should have annoyed her, but Haleigh had grown to like the cheerful teen and that bought the girl a pass.

"Have you ever just wanted to feel normal?" she asked. "To shut down the crap churning through your brain and pretend that your life isn't a bowl of rotten cherries?"

Jessi sat on the bed. "I don't know. I'm not sure I've ever experienced normal."

Haleigh's heart went out to the young woman. It wasn't often she met someone who made her own childhood look like a Rockwell painting.

Settling onto the bed next to her, Haleigh said, "To be honest, I'm not sure I have either, but I've heard good things about it."

"Funny," Jessi said. "I've heard it's pretty boring."

Laughing at the comment, Haleigh shook her head. "Sounds like you have better sources than I do."

"Is Cooper going to be there tonight?"

She hadn't considered the possibility, but knew that he and Spencer were good friends. A fissure of awareness tripped up her spine at the thought of seeing him. Of dancing with him. Yet another temptation she would need to avoid if the offer arose. Close bodily contact with Cooper Ridgeway would only drag her closer to an edge she had no business walking.

"He might be," she replied, rising to her feet. "Thanks for helping me out, Jessi. Are you sure you don't mind being here alone this evening?"

"I have Emma," she said, and as if on cue, the baby's cry echoed down the hall. "Looks like I better get a bottle ready."

As the new mother left the room, Haleigh once again checked her reflection in the mirror. The woman looking back wasn't an alcoholic or a tragic disappointment to her mother. Now all she had to do was walk by the bar without hearing her mother's hateful voice in her ear.

Chapter 9

The Brubaker's crowd was still thin thanks to the early hour, though the place would be wall-to-wall bodies by eleven. Fifteen minutes after they'd arrived, Cooper noticed Lorelei watching the door. She continued to check the entrance as Spencer spun her around the dance floor. When the song ended and the couple returned to the table, the glances continued as the rest of the group was business as usual.

Curious, Cooper leaned close to Lorelei's ear. "Expecting someone?"

She jumped, nearly dousing them both in Budweiser. "What? Me? No. I don't know what you mean."

Right. And a bear didn't shit in the woods. "Is Tillman coming in here tonight?" Cooper asked. "Did you get some inside scoop you're not sharing with the rest of us?"

Wes Tillman, once upon a time one of the most popular voices in country music, enjoyed his semi-retirement while living on the outskirts of their county and making occasional appearances at a local watering hole called the Second Chance Saloon. He'd never visited Brubaker's as far as Cooper knew, but there wasn't anyone else he could think of who would put that stir of anticipation on Lorelei's face.

"How would I have an inside scoop on Wes Tillman?" she asked.

"Let's see." Cooper hedged. "Snow sings with him from time to time. You and Snow are as close as two fleas on a tick's ass. I wonder how you'd know?"

Lorelei's lips pinched. "That's the grossest description I've ever heard."

"Just fess up already."

"No," she answered. "I don't know anything about Wes Tillman coming in here."

"What's up?" Spencer said, likely drawn by the tone of his fiancée's voice. "We all good?"

Cooper shrugged. He'd only been teasing her. And Lorelei *had* been watching the door.

"No freaking way," Lorelei muttered, ignoring the two men beside her. "I can't believe she came."

From his vantage point above most of the crowd, Cooper scanned the area near the entrance. At the end of the bar, he saw her. Blonde hair scattered around her shoulders. Brown eyes searching the crowd as if looking for a familiar face. His heart kicked in his chest.

She was gorgeous. And as skittish as a cornered rabbit.

Spencer spotted her, too. "I thought Haleigh didn't like crowded bars?"

"I don't know what she's doing here," Cooper said, unable to take his eyes off her.

"I invited her," Lorelei said, snagging Cooper's attention. She met his surprised gaze, looking very proud of herself. "Don't just stand there," she added with an elbow to his ribs. "Go get her."

"Right." Cooper set his beer on the table behind him. "I can do that."

If Haleigh didn't spot Lorelei in the next fifteen seconds, she was leaving. Though talking with Jessi had soothed the hurt from earlier, the closer she'd gotten to the club, the tighter her stomach had gotten. Two attempts to call Raquel had landed in voicemail. Hearing the familiar voice on the message had helped a bit, but in the end, Haleigh was standing in a bar facing her demons alone for the first time in several years.

Why in the hell had she thought this was a good idea?

"What can I get you?" asked a pretty brunette wearing the tightest pair of shorts Haleigh had ever seen.

Haleigh hesitated. She didn't need a drink. She wanted one more than her next breath, but she didn't need one. Resolved to stay the course, she said, "Water, please." And then her mother's glacial stare punctured her brain and Haleigh changed her order. "Make that a rum and Coke."

"Coming right up," the waitress replied, strolling to the bar a few feet to Haleigh's left.

No way. She was not going to do this. If she swallowed that drink, not only would her mother win, but Haleigh would blow years of sobriety. And over what? Meredith Mitchner's disdain? Her unreachable standards and failure to see her daughter as anything more than a paycheck and emotional punching bag?

Obviously, this had been a mistake.

If Spencer and Lorelei were there, Haleigh didn't see them. And Carrie was shorter than she was, which meant finding her would be even more difficult. Haleigh took two steps toward the door before someone called her name.

"Haleigh Rae!" came the familiar deep voice. She spun in time to see Cooper barreling down on her, the crowd parting as if Moses himself had demanded it. "Are you okay?" he asked, concern etched in his tone.

"I'm fine," she lied, determined to act as normal as possible. If Cooper so much as sniffed a problem, he'd roll into fix-it mode. "I didn't know you would be here. Is it always this crowded?" she asked.

Cooper's chuckle hit Haleigh like the first bite into a warm brownie and served as a distraction from her mounting panic. "This is nothing compared to what the place will look like in a couple hours." Taking her hand, he said, "Here. Walk in front of me and I'll take you over to the others."

"But I ordered a drink," she said, using the excuse to send him on his way so she could leave without having to explain.

"Dana!" Cooper yelled.

The brunette turned his way. "Heya, Coop." Her smile was friendlier than Haleigh deemed necessary. "What can I do you for?"

"Bring her drink up to the table, would ya?"

With a nod, she said, "Sure. No problem."

Great. Now she would have to explain why she couldn't touch the glass once it arrived. Before she could find another solution, Cooper slid his body behind hers to navigate them through the room. The crowd grew thicker away from the bar, forcing Haleigh to slow down, which put their bodies in constant contact. At this rate, she was going to need a cigarette by the time they reached their destination.

When they finally arrived at a small raised area adjacent to the dance floor, Haleigh spotted Lorelei talking to Snow and Carrie, while Spencer and a man Haleigh didn't recognize conversed behind them.

"You look great," Lorelei said after the greetings had been exchanged. "That outfit is adorable."

Haleigh looked down at her dress. "You think so? I didn't know what to wear." Speaking like a normal person was proving difficult, and not only because of the alcohol around her, as Cooper remained pressed against her back.

"It's perfect," Lorelei assured her. "You know everyone, right?"

In need of space, Haleigh stepped to the side only to have Cooper's hand fall to the small of her back. She had to admit, the touch had a calming effect on her nerves. Unfortunately, Spencer called him over before she could regain total control.

"I'll be close by," Cooper whispered in her ear, as if he knew how much she needed his steady presence. His breath on her neck spiked her temperature, and Haleigh struggled to remember Lorelei's question.

"I don't know the guy talking to Spencer," she answered, proud of her ability to still think. "Should I?" Next to Cooper, the stranger was arguably the hottest guy in the room. Haleigh doubted she'd forget having made his acquaintance.

"That's my husband, Caleb," Snow said, sharing the smile of a happy newlywed. "He was at the hospital when Carrie had Molly, but I'm not sure if you two met."

"You're a lucky girl," Haleigh muttered before she could stop herself. "Wow. That was seriously inappropriate."

Snow laughed. "No worries. Lorelei drools over him on a regular basis. I'm getting used to it."

"How long are we staying?" Carrie cut in, looking even less happy to be there than Haleigh was.

Lorelei nudged the new mother. "We haven't been here an hour yet. Molly is fine. She probably doesn't even know you're gone."

Carrie looked stricken. "That's a horrible thing to say."

Having just left a doting mother, Haleigh had to agree with Carrie. Telling a woman that her child didn't miss her was like kicking a puppy.

Wrapping both arms around Carrie's shoulders, Lorelei grew serious. "Stay with me, girlfriend. You know what I meant. Granny is ecstatic to have Molly all to herself, and I'm sure your little one is being ridiculously spoiled as we speak. You deserve a little spoiling, too. Starting with a night that does not revolve around changing diapers and scheduled feedings."

"Rosie *is* good with her," Carrie conceded. "But it still feels weird."

"Tell her, doc." Lorelei nodded Haleigh's way. "Tell her this is good for her."

Three sets of eyes turned her way as if Haleigh possessed the secrets of the universe. They could not be more wrong.

"Well, I . . ." she floundered. "I mean . . . I'm not really an expert on babies or motherhood. My specialty is more before they emerge."

"I knew it." Carrie pulled away from Lorelei. "I never should have left her."

"I didn't say that!" Haleigh backpedaled. Reaching for a more supportive answer, she said, "It's good for babies to learn a little independence. To experience new social situations and interact with people other than their parents."

"Really?"

Haleigh had no idea since she'd totally made the facts up.

"Yes. Of course. And it's good for you, too. Think of it as recharging your battery. A happy, fulfilled mother means a happier baby." That had to be from a parenting magazine somewhere. "It's been scientifically proven," she added.

The bomb appeared to be defused. "That makes sense, I guess," Carrie mumbled. "Thanks for the reassurance, Dr. Mitchner."

Feeling as if she'd just lied to a child, Haleigh felt the familiar mantle of guilt settle heavily on her shoulders. She prayed the waitress would forget about her drink.

"Where's my dance partner?" Spencer barked as he wrapped his arms around his fiancée. "I came here to dance, woman. It's time to get your pretty little butt on the floor."

"I second that," Caleb said, then corrected himself. "About my woman's butt, of course."

Lorelei rolled her eyes as Spencer pulled her toward the twirling dancers. As if unable to resist, Caleb planted a hot kiss on his wife before all but carrying her to the floor. A task easily accomplished considering his impressive bulk and her diminutive size.

"What do you say?" Cooper asked, nodding after the others. "You up for a spin or two?"

Panic assailed her. If memory served, done correctly dancing could be as arousing as a good bout of foreplay. Haleigh could not handle this much temptation in one night. "I'm not sure I remember how," she said.

"Come on," Carrie encouraged. "It's good for straitlaced doctors to experience new social situations and to interact with people other than their patients."

The gleam in the woman's eye took Haleigh by surprise. "I wasn't born yesterday," the younger woman said. "But I do appreciate your efforts. Now do yourself a favor and give Cooper a dance."

Green eyes met hers and Haleigh knew she couldn't turn him down. At least there was no liquor on the dance floor. She could smell an amaretto sour nearby and the scent was making her mouth water.

"I might step on you," she said.

"So long as I don't step on you we should be all right."

Slipping her hand into his, Haleigh followed Cooper to the floor with a mixture of anxiety and anticipation. Without hesitating, he squeezed between a pair of dancers and had her shuffling backward in a Texas two-step without missing a beat. Running on instinct, Haleigh fit her body against his as her left hand slid up his neck to nestle in the dark curls that tickled his collar. When Cooper pressed her right hand over his heart, she couldn't help but notice the kick in his pulse.

By the time they made a full turn around the floor, Haleigh stopped worrying about her footwork and focused on the man holding her tight. Despite the fact that Haleigh was far from perfect, Cooper still liked her. Thank goodness someone did.

Chapter 10

Cooper had died and gone to heaven. And if Haleigh didn't stop playing with his hair she was going to find herself horizontal by the end of the song. Not that he'd mind the change in position, but the other dancers might take issue with a couple compromising their dance floor.

"What brought you out tonight?" he asked. Certain she'd been on the verge of making a break for it when he'd reached her near the bar, he'd half expected her to make some excuse even after he'd caught her.

"Lorelei invited me."

"Hal," he said, lifting her face with one finger beneath her chin. "You've been back in town for six months and never stepped foot through those doors." As she bit the inside of her cheek, he said, "I saw your face before I called your name. Why don't you tell me what's chasing you."

"It's annoying when you do that," she huffed. If looks could kill, she'd have offed him right there. "I had dinner with my mother tonight. Does that answer your question?"

Haleigh's mother had branded herself the all-American mom, and to most of the town, that's exactly who she was. But Cooper knew better.

"So things are still the same on that front?"

Based on the conversations he'd overheard through the wall between his and Abby's bedrooms back in the day, Mrs. Mitchner treated Haleigh like a disease instead of a daughter. Nothing Haleigh ever did had been good enough, which Cooper never understood. She'd been a model child. Even graduating top in their class hadn't softened the woman.

"I don't know why I bother. Tonight was just another reminder that I'll never measure up."

"Hey," he said, unsettled by the defeat in her voice. "You more than measure up. If she can't see that, it's her loss."

Glancing away, she said, "I don't want to talk about my mother. Let's pick a new topic."

Cooper dodged a spinning couple and moved himself and Haleigh closer to the floor's edge. Delicate fingers massaged his scalp, making it difficult to breathe, let alone carry on a conversation.

"I know Lorelei and Spencer were at one of those Ruby meetings tonight," she said. "What were you up to?"

"Same thing they were," he answered.

She stiffened. "You're on that theater committee?" She sounded as if he'd admitted to smuggling drugs.

"I haven't been on it for long, but yeah. I'm putting together a classic car rally as a fundraiser."

Her hand slid down to his shoulder. "Good for you," she said, sounding less than impressed.

"What do you have against restoring an old theater?" Glossy lips flattened as she shook her head but failed to meet his eye. "Come on, Hal. What gives?"

"It just irks me," she snapped. "Some dilapidated building has become a top priority in this town while real issues are ignored. Women like Jessi have no place to go, but heaven forbid we not save an old theater."

Surprised by the sudden burst of anger, Cooper had no idea how to respond. Lucky for him, the last notes of the song kept him from having to.

"Thanks for the dance," she said, exiting the floor at a full trot.

Cooper didn't like Jessi's lack of options any more than Haleigh did, but he didn't see how restoring a theater added to the problem.

As he stared after Haleigh, the next song started and dancers began shuffling around him. Before he could step off the floor, a hand clasped his arm.

"Hey there, Coop. Long time no see." Heavy-lashed hazel eyes looked up in invitation. "You haven't forgotten about me, have you?"

"Hi, Daisy," he said. "No, I haven't forgotten. I've just been busy."

Cooper had dated Daisy Carmichael for the first couple months of the year, until the day she'd snapped his head off for canceling a date without enough notice. The sweet girl with the ready laugh had revealed her claws and an impressive collection of colorful insults—some he'd never heard before.

Having grown up with a quick-tempered father and bearing witness to the abuse his mother had endured, Cooper had no intention of stepping into a similar situation.

He'd ended the relationship within the week.

In a full-on pout, the curvy redhead trailed a finger down Cooper's forearm as she edged in closer. "You don't look too busy now," she cooed. "You aren't going to leave a girl stranded on the dance floor, are you?"

Reluctant to hurt her feelings, or test her fiery temper, he agreed to one dance. "All right, Daisy. Let's take a spin."

Haleigh returned to the table to find her drink waiting. She reached for the self-talk and affirmations that would keep the glass on the table. Listened for Raquel's voice of reason in her head only to find her mother's glacial tone.

By all means, don't let me keep you.

She proceeded to down the concoction in one swallow.

"Whoa," Carrie said. "You might want to slow down there."

Excellent advice, except one shot was all she'd needed to cross the line. Haleigh caught a passing waitress's eye and raised her glass. "Another rum and Coke when you get a chance." The order was acknowledged with a nod and the waitress melted into the crowd. "I need a beer chaser for that," Haleigh murmured as heat scorched her esophagus. Motioning toward the longneck in front of Carrie, she said, "Are you drinking that?"

"Not anymore," Carrie answered, sliding the bottle Haleigh's way. "You seem to need it more than I do."

"Good observation." After a long draw, Haleigh wiped her mouth on the cuff of her jacket. The beer cooled her throat but did nothing for the heat pumping elsewhere. Not only was she drowning in her mother's disapproval, but her body had developed more than a passing fancy for her hard-bodied dance partner.

She shouldn't have snapped at him like that. Haleigh had been angry at herself. Angry for being there. Angry for wanting him. Angry that a young girl and her baby had some limited resources in a country as wealthy as theirs.

"Are you part of that stupid Ruby Restoration thing with the rest of them?" she asked Carrie.

"Afraid I'm too busy restoring my own life to worry about an old theater," the single mother replied. "But what do you have against restoring the Ruby?"

"Nothing," Haleigh answered. "Everything. I mean, there are a lot of things this area needs. A renovated movie theater should not be at the top of the list, you know?"

Carrie nodded. "I do know. Dr. Mitchner—"

"Stop calling me Dr. Mitchner," Haleigh interrupted. "I just drank your beer, for heaven's sake. Pretty sure that puts us on a first-name basis." Realizing that Cooper hadn't returned to the table with her, she glanced back to the dance floor. "Where did he go?"

Carrie didn't ask who *he* was. "Cooper is dancing with Daisy," she said, pointing toward the far end of the dance floor near the DJ booth.

The moment she spotted them, Haleigh's teeth went on edge. A redhead with centerfold curves looked as if she were trying to climb inside Cooper's clothes. And from the look on her face, she'd achieved the feat before.

"Who the hell is *Daisy*?" she snarled before taking another swig of beer. "And why is he letting her paw him like that?"

"Daisy and Cooper dated a few months ago," Carrie said. "I'm not sure why they broke up, but from the looks of things, she'd like to have him back."

The new rum and Coke appeared out of nowhere, and Haleigh said, "Bless you," to the waitress before once again downing the cocktail like a shot. "Keep 'em coming," she coughed, tipping the beer bottle to her lips. As the waitress spun to leave, Haleigh hollered, "And two more beers while you're at it."

"Are you sure you want to do that?" Carrie asked.

What Haleigh wanted didn't seem to matter tonight. She didn't want to have dinner with her mother, but she did. She didn't want to come to this bar, but she did. And she sure as heck did not want to have these drinks, but if she downed a few more she might forget the fact that her mother hated her.

Haleigh waved away the question. "Do you think Cooper wants her back?"

"You'll have to ask him that question."

Slamming the bottle onto the table, Haleigh turned on her former patient. "I don't need to ask Cooper anything." Gesturing toward the couple in question, who were twirling by not far away, she added, "Look at all those curves. Of course he wants her."

Dragging her arm out of the air, Carrie propelled Haleigh until both their backs were to the dancers. "Have you lost your mind?" she hissed. "I don't know what happened between you and Cooper during that dance, but I'm not about to let you embarrass him or yourself. Let's get you some coffee."

"I don't need coffee," Haleigh argued. "Coffee doesn't make you forget things. I want to forget things tonight, and that means I need another rum and Coke."

"I've got this, Carrie," Cooper said, showing up like the freaking white knight that he was. "Come on, Hal. It's time to go."

"I don't want to go. The waitress is bringing me another drink, and I plan to drink it."

"How many has she had?" he asked Carrie. "She's only been up here for five minutes."

"Don't talk about me like I'm not here." Haleigh hated when people did that. Her father had done it all the time. Talked about her as if she were a new car or kitchen appliance. Bragging to his friends about all the upgrades and fancy features while she kept her mouth shut and looked pretty.

"Two rum and Cokes so far. Plus my beer." Carrie waved the returning waitress away. "We changed our minds, thanks."

"Where's she going with my drink?" Haleigh whined. "I need that."

Cooper leaned so close that their noses nearly bumped. "Haleigh Rae, you have two choices. Get your shit together and walk out of here like a normal person, or go out kicking and screaming over my shoulder. What's it gonna be?"

Haleigh weighed her options. Even with an alcohol-fogged brain, she knew that Cooper would make good on his threat. Sadly, the knowledge that the scene would no doubt reach her mother's ears by lunchtime tomorrow made her surrender. Challenging her mother in private was one thing. Embarrassing her in public was another.

The possibility of damaging her own reputation registered somewhere in the distance, but Haleigh was too caught up in her pity party to focus on self-preservation.

"Fine," she growled through clenched teeth. "I'll walk out."

"That's my girl." Cooper slipped something into Carrie's hand. "Tell the guys I had to go. That's enough to cover the next round."

Keeping her balance required full concentration, but Haleigh was determined to leave the bar under her own power. She made it within ten feet of the exit before the room began to spin. "Carrie was right," she slurred. "I need coffee."

Somehow her feet stayed under her as Cooper swept them both out the door. "What you need is food," he said, lifting her off the ground the moment they reached the parking lot. "When was the last time you ate?"

"I had a bite of meatloaf," she answered, dropping her head onto his strong shoulder. "And some chips for lunch."

"That explains it," he said, stopping next to her car. "Where are your keys?"

Haleigh's head popped up. "Am I driving?" she asked.

"*I'm* driving. Now where are your keys?"

Struggling against Cooper's wall-like chest, she squirmed to get her hand into her pocket. "This would be easier if you'd put me down."

Not that she wanted him to put her down. Ever.

"Unlock the doors and I'll put you down in the car." She did as ordered, and Cooper did as promised, going so far as to buckle her in.

Toying with the dimple in his chin, Haleigh whispered, "What about Daisy?"

He caught her wrist as she traced the outline of his bottom lip. "Daisy can take care of herself."

They stared at each other for several seconds until Haleigh nearly dragged his mouth to hers. Before she had the chance, Cooper pulled away. "We'd better get you home," he said, then closed her door.

As she watched him cross in front of the car, Haleigh let the self-hate wash over her as she spoke her thoughts aloud.

"You're too good for me, Cooper Ridgeway."

Chapter 11

By the time Cooper reached the driver's seat, Haleigh was snoring. First, she took his head off over the Ruby committee, and then she slammed back enough alcohol to get herself toasted in a matter of minutes. Since he was pretty sure the theater wasn't the real source of her sudden mood change, Cooper laid the blame at Meredith Mitchner's feet.

If he hadn't overheard all those conversations between Haleigh and his sister, Cooper would be as clueless as the rest of the town about the older woman's true nature. She'd been genial enough at school gatherings. Conversed with his mother about whatever mothers talked about when their kids were friends. But, based on his teenage eavesdropping, she'd been a completely different person at home.

Snippets of Haleigh's complaints came back to him. Phrases like *I can't do anything right* and *the woman hates everything about me* made him cringe. True or not, no kid should ever be made to feel the way Haleigh had. Unfortunately, Cooper knew the feeling all too well, as his father, too, had a knack for throwing verbal punches in his son's direction. The constant reminders of every way in which Cooper had disappointed Malcolm Ridgeway were impossible to forget.

At least Cooper understood the source of his father's hostility. A failed academic, the elder Ridgeway had expected his son to accomplish everything he'd been unable to do. As if he could achieve success through one degree of separation. The fact that Cooper wasn't going to be the book-smart type had been apparent early on, but that hadn't stopped his father's attempts to force-feed facts, figures, and philosophy to his child.

When Cooper hadn't coughed them back up in the right order, or repeated them with enough eloquence to meet his father's expectations, things got ugly. Heavy books flew across the room. Beloved toys were ripped away, and long hours were spent in his room to "think about what he'd done."

Until age thirteen, he'd believed himself the dumbest person on the planet, because no matter how long Cooper stared at his bedroom walls, he never could figure out why he was being punished. Abby didn't have any answers either. Their father hadn't been as hard on Cooper's twin, but then he'd barely acknowledged her presence. An entirely different cross that no child should have to bear.

"I give you everything," Haleigh mumbled from the passenger seat. Her eyes were still closed and her lips pushed forward in a pout. "Why can't you ever be happy?"

Afraid the waterworks might start next, Cooper tapped the side of her leg. "Wake up, Hal. We're almost home."

"I don't want to go home," she argued as her head flopped toward the door. "Home sucks."

Cooper wasn't sure if that was her liquor-soaked brain wanting more alcohol, or if by *home* she thought he meant her mother's house.

"Come on, hon," he said as he parked next to Abby's red Camry. "We're here now. At Abby's house."

She'd have to wake up enough to at least down some water before bed. Otherwise, she was going to feel like hell in the morning. After undoing his own seat belt, Cooper freed Haleigh, who fell against his arm and nestled into his shoulder. He'd heard somewhere that alcohol always told the truth. If that was the case, his drunk little friend liked him more than she let on while sober.

"Lean this way," he said, lowering her down to the console between the seats. "I'll be right over to get you." After a quick trip around the car, he gave Haleigh a gentle shake. "Time to get on your feet, darling." He could carry her, but Cooper preferred to minimize her embarrassment in front of Abby and Jessi. At barely ten in the evening, chances were good that both would be awake.

When he tapped her cheeks, Haleigh finally stirred. "Stop that," she ordered, swatting his hands away. "I'm good. Just give me a second."

Her words were clearer. That was a good sign.

Brown eyes blinked open as she slapped her lips together. "My mouth is dry."

"We'll get you water inside."

"Let me try standing up." Moving slowly and with a tight grip on his sleeve, she set both feet on the driveway. "No spinning so far," she reported. "But my head is still buzzing."

Cooper chuckled. "That's what rum will do to you."

"I think the bartender skimped on the Coke part."

"If Denny made them, that's probably true."

Haleigh pinned him with a one-eyed glare. "Do you know *everybody*?"

"I've lived here all my life," he said with a shrug. "It's a small town."

"Yes, it is. Tell me I didn't do anything that's going to race through the gossip mills tomorrow."

He hadn't checked for witnesses during their exit, but saw no need to add to her worries. "You didn't dance on the tables or flash your bottom, so I think you're good."

Massaging her temples, she said, "You just described my first two years of college."

With complete honesty, he said, "Wish I could have seen that."

"Trust me," she answered, "no one needed to see that." After a deep breath, she squared her shoulders. "Let's do this."

Once upright, Haleigh listed to the right, but Cooper caught her. "Maybe a little slower," he said with her hands in his. "That buzz isn't going away for a while."

"The sad thing is," she said, gingerly putting one foot in front of the other, "I'd go back for more if I thought I could get myself there."

Letting her set the pace, Cooper asked, "You want to tell me what's so bad that you're trying to drown it in booze?"

She stopped and met his eye. "Not really."

Disappointed, he said, "Fair enough."

Haleigh squeezed his hands. "Cooper, I know you mean well, but I'm not dumping the black hole that is my mental baggage in your lap. However, if you don't take two steps to the side, I am going to toss what little is in my stomach all over your boots."

Cooper heeded the warning just in time. As Haleigh retched into Abby's flower bed, he held her hair out of her face and kept a soothing hand on her back. When she was finished, he handed her the handkerchief from his back pocket.

"How do you always happen to have one of these handy?" she asked, dabbing at her chin.

There were things Cooper didn't feel like sharing tonight either. "Just do. You ready to go inside?"

She nodded. "Yeah, but I feel bad about Abby's flowers."

They stepped onto the porch side by side. "I'll come out and hose it away."

Pushing through the front door, Haleigh sighed. "Of course you will."

Toothpaste was Haleigh's first priority. Cooper stayed silent behind her as they made their way into the house. The TV was on in the living room, but the sound had been muted. In the glow of a pretty young woman twirling in a wedding dress she was probably about to say yes to, Haleigh located Abby passed out in the recliner with a sleeping Emma on her chest.

"Where's Jessi?" Cooper asked, obviously not spotting the sleeping child.

Haleigh held one finger over her lips. "Probably in bed," she whispered back as she pointed toward the infant. "Emma gives new meaning to the phrase *up all night*. If you wake her, we'll all kill you. Slowly. And with malice."

Cooper held his hands up in surrender and kept his piehole shut. This had been the crappiest night she'd had in a while, and having Mr. Perfect witness most of it put a nice coating of humiliation on top of an already thick helping of personal disgust.

Why did she let her mother get to her? Better yet, why did she cling to the hope that anything would ever change in their relationship? That a miracle would happen and the angels would sing and her mother would actually *like* her?

And maybe the drunk fairy would fly through her window tonight and leave Haleigh's dignity beneath her pillow.

"I'll be right back," she said, about to release Cooper from his baby-sitting duties and send him on his way. Until she realized he'd driven her car. Which meant he had no way to get back to his own. Dragging him quietly into the kitchen, she kept her voice low. "How are you getting home?"

He ran a hand through his thick hair, leaving curls standing on end. "I'd planned to have Abby drive me back to the bar, but I guess that's not an option."

"Why didn't you just bring me home in your truck?"

"Because I assumed you have to be at the hospital tomorrow and would need your car."

Hot he may be, but this selfless streak was getting old. Did the man ever put himself first? *Ever?*

"Nice," she said, slapping him on the chest. "Now what? You can't stay here all night." There was no way she could sleep knowing he was right there, under the same roof, available to make all of her lewd dreams come true. "You need to call a cab."

Cooper snorted. "We aren't in Memphis, Hal. There are no cabs in Ardent Springs." He crossed the room to drag a glass out of the cupboard. "You need water."

As he bent to retrieve a bottle from the bottom of the fridge, Haleigh couldn't decide which was more frustrating—his unflinching gallantry or that perfect ass.

"You should call Spencer to come and get you."

"Relax, Hal," he said, filling the glass as if Haleigh was too special to drink from a plastic bottle. "It's not like we've never slept in the same house before. I can behave if you can."

Wearing the sexiest grin she'd ever seen, Cooper slid the glass across the island, and all Haleigh could think about was all the things she'd like to do to him right there in the kitchen.

Instead of rum and Coke, she'd gotten rum and horny.

"I'm not the least bit worried about either of us behaving." Lies. All lies. "But people will talk."

"Uh-huh. Because me sleeping at my sister's house while two other females and a newborn are here would be extremely scandalous." Snagging his own bottle from the fridge, he added, "Besides. My truck isn't even outside, so no one would know I was here anyway."

I know! Haleigh's brain screamed. Closing her eyes, mostly to avoid watching Cooper wrap his lips around the mouth of the bottle, she berated herself to get a grip. The alcohol was wearing off, thank cheezits, and that meant sanity should return any second. Until it did, she'd have to rely on her shoddy self-control to get them through this.

Opening one eye, she found Cooper watching her. "Still here," he said with a wave.

"Still hot," she muttered. At his raised brow, she corrected, "High! Or drunk really. That's what I meant. I'm still drunk. That's why I'm acting like an idiot right now. And why I need to go to bed before I embarrass myself further. Not that much could top the puking incident. Did I thank you for holding my hair back?"

Blessed be, the babbling phase had begun. Haleigh had been sober for so long, she'd forgotten about this part.

"You didn't, but you're welcome," he said. "And there's nothing to be embarrassed about. Everybody needs to let off steam now and then. It's good to let your hair down." He leaned farther across the island until his dimple was close enough to lick. "To do something you wouldn't normally do."

"I can't argue with that," she said, lost in the spell of his voice and his lips and if she leaned just a little closer . . .

"But you don't want to get *too* crazy," Cooper said, backing away and leaving Haleigh in a blinking fog of lust. "Nobody wants to do something they'll regret the next day."

Haleigh had been wrong. Cooper was not a good guy. He was evil. Pure evil. And if she didn't know better, she'd swear that he knew exactly what he was doing to her. A highly sobering thought.

"You're right." Raising her glass in his direction, Haleigh put on her most innocent smile and headed for the hallway. "Thanks for looking out for me, Cooper. Without you around, there's no telling what I might have done tonight."

Fighting the urge to see his response to that loaded statement, Haleigh kept her eyes forward and her feet moving. The buzz had dropped to little more than a hum in her ears, but the rest of her body was still vibrating with the need to hold Cooper to his earlier promise of letting her see him in his underwear.

This *was* a sleepover, after all. And getting him naked would be a lot easier if he was already in his unmentionables.

Haleigh slammed the door on that thought. Literally. And then paid the ultimate price as Emma's wail echoed through the house.

How did anyone sleep with a baby in the house? No wonder new parents were freaking zombies. And this definitely explained Carrie's recent mood swings. At least they'd been able to tag out and hand the pissed off little thing to the next person. Well, everyone but Haleigh, who never bothered to come back out of her room.

Cooper had been tempted more than once to carry Emma in there and leave her on the bed next to Haleigh's ear. Would have served her right. And not just for waking up the baby.

Newborn or no, he likely wouldn't have gotten much sleep anyway. Who knew what she might have done. If he'd played his cards right, she might have done *him*.

Being a good guy sucked.

When he and Haleigh finally did have sex—and they *would* be having sex—neither of them would be drunk. Or have recently hurled into a bed of pansies. Speaking of, he still needed to get the hose for that.

Last time he'd seen the clock, it had read three forty-five when Cooper had passed an exhausted Emma off to an even more exhausted Jessi, who carried with her a bottle and a dream. That her baby would pass out and stay out for at least five hours. Heck, four would have been an improvement.

At the same moment the scent of fresh coffee hit his nose, Cooper heard a door open down the hall. Jessi was in the kitchen, and Abby in the shower, so that left only one person. How nice of Haleigh to join them.

She breezed by the couch without so much as a glance in his direction. As she rounded the corner, he heard her say, "Coffee. Now."

Cooper could have told her that one bottle of water was not going to be enough.

Several obvious sounds followed. A cupboard opened and closed. A mug hit the counter. Coffee filled the mug. All followed by a woman's low moan.

And now all of Cooper was up and ready for the day. He made a quick trip to the facilities, brushed his teeth with his finger, and smoothed his hair as best he could. He'd been meaning to get a haircut for a couple weeks but hadn't gotten around to it. That had to change today.

Ready as he'd ever be, Cooper strolled toward the kitchen, but stopped short when Jessi's voice caught his ear.

"I don't get it," she said. "Why are you and Cooper not a thing?"

Something he'd like to know as well.

"Anyone ever tell you you're a nosy kid?" Haleigh replied.

Just answer the kid's question already.

"Just answer the question," Jessi echoed. "He's hot. He clearly has the hots for you." Even the teenager figured that out? "I've seen you checking out his ass more than once."

"I'm not going to argue that Cooper isn't hot," Haleigh said. "I'd have to be dead not to notice that. And he's sweet and funny and probably the best guy I've ever met."

Jessi's tone turned sarcastic. "Right. Who would want a guy like that?"

"I didn't say I don't want him—"

"Good, you're ready," Abby said from behind him, startling Cooper.

"Were you a ninja in a former life?" he asked. "Warn a guy, would ya?"

Abby propped her hands on her hips. "Maybe if you weren't eaves-dropping, you'd have heard me."

"I wasn't eavesdropping," he defended. "I was trying not to inter-rupt their conversation."

"Then you should have tried not interrupting from the couch." Stepping around him, she said, "All right, girls. We're heading out."

Haleigh lifted a mug that read *Death Before Decaf* in silent salute while Jessi said, "Take me with you. I can have Emma ready in five minutes."

"We've been over this, Jessi. I can't take you and the baby to work."

"But I'm going crazy. I've forgotten what the sky looks like."

Abby filled her travel mug with coffee as she said, "Step outside and look up. It's in the same place it's always been."

Even Cooper thought that was a bit harsh. "See if our mom will sit with Emma this evening, and I'll come take you for a ride."

"Mama has a date," Abby said, then stared at the silent faces gaping back at her. "What?"

"Since when does our mother date?" Cooper asked. "And why haven't I heard about this before now? Who is he? Have you met him?"

Grabbing a breakfast bar from the pantry, Abby said, "Gee, I won-der why she hasn't told you? Could it be that reaction right there?" She grabbed her keys off the hook by the light switch. "See you ladies tonight. Haleigh Rae, find me at work. I'd like to hear the story of why I'm taking my brother home at seven in the morning."

When had his cheerful sister gotten so stern?

"Hey," he said, tracking her into the foyer. "I want to know who Mama's dating."

"Just move it," she tossed over her shoulder. "I'll tell you on the way."

Chapter 12

Jessi stared at Haleigh with wide eyes. "Do you think he heard us?"

"I don't know," she replied, distracted by Abby's parting comment. Haleigh knew that tone. Abby wasn't happy with her. But then Haleigh wasn't all that happy with herself, either. Last night had been bad. Very bad. She'd be lucky if Raquel didn't drive over from Memphis just to smack her upside the head. A beating she well deserved. "He's too upstanding to eavesdrop, so I doubt it."

"Things could get interesting if he heard you say you want him."

Haleigh nearly spilled her coffee. "I never said I wanted Cooper."

"Yes, you did," Jessi corrected. "You said it's not that you don't want him, which means you want him."

"That is not the same thing." Her throbbing temples were hindering her ability to think. Had she said she wanted Cooper?

"It most definitely is, though your version was about to come with a *but* until Cooper screamed like a girl and you shut up." Sliding off her stool, Jessi filled a mug with hot water and popped it into the microwave. "I was starting to think y'all were the most boring people ever. Now I see the drama is just in the early stages."

Drama? Her life may have its moments, but she did not live in some cheesy soap opera.

"Sorry to disappoint you, but there is no drama. Just because I'm attracted to Cooper doesn't mean anything is going to happen. For one, I'd drive him crazy. He's like sunshine and rainbows, and I'm thunderclouds and mud puddles. He's the boy next door, and I'm the emotional train wreck who should have a ring of those orange construction cones set up all around me."

Jessi held silent for several seconds while staring at Haleigh as if she could see through her skull.

"Nope," she said. "I'm not buying it."

Haleigh struggled not to grind her teeth. "Not buying what?"

"You're no train wreck, doc. I was raised by a train wreck, and you don't even qualify as a mild fender bender."

"You've known me for less than a week."

"Did you miss the *raised by* part?" Jessi asked. The microwave dinged and the girl continued her diatribe as she made her tea. "Let's start with the obvious—you're a doctor. Employed, smart, and dedicated, because you have to have dedication to endure, like, eighteen years of college to be a doctor."

"Eight," Haleigh corrected.

"Same thing. Next, you don't dress like a train wreck."

"There's a train wreck dress code?" Haleigh drawled. "Enlighten me."

With a shake of her head, Jessi said, "Sarcasm doesn't bother me. Now we move on to your lack of a social life. Train wrecks are notorious for their need for attention. After Calvin, Mama never went forty-eight hours without bringing a man home. Male attention is like oxygen in her world." Jessi set the tea bag in the sink and proceeded to grab the milk from the fridge. "You, on the other hand, don't seem interested in men at all." With a pointed look, she added, "Except for Cooper."

"I've known him my whole life."

"Then you know his history. You know, that's the trouble with dating a guy you just met. He's cute, he says the right things, and the next thing you know you're searching for your panties in the backseat of his Mustang." More to herself than to Haleigh, Jessi mumbled, "Damn, that was a nice car. Anyway, that's when you find some other girl's panties under the passenger seat and realize that new guy is a two-timing jerk who didn't deserve you, but by then the damage is done."

Sidetracked from the subject, Haleigh said, "You got pregnant in the backseat of a Mustang?"

"Hey," Jessi barked. "Don't judge. Train wreck mother. Not a great role model, okay?"

"Right. Sorry. I just . . ." Haleigh tapped the side of her coffee cup. "Is the backseat of a Mustang really big enough for that?"

It was Jessi's turn to look surprised. "Are you saying you've never done it in a car?"

Haleigh resisted the urge to defend herself by sharing a few of the less conventional places she'd had sex during college.

"As revelatory as this conversation has been, the point is that Cooper and I are a no-go. Period. Besides the fact that he deserves a woman the complete opposite of me, there's also the issue of bringing him home to my mother. She's still mourning my broken engagement to a plastic surgeon. I can only imagine her reaction upon hearing I'm going to spend my future with a mechanic."

"Wow," Jessi said. "I did not see that coming."

"What?" Haleigh asked.

"I just didn't figure you for one of those bitchy snobs."

"What did you call me?"

"Don't get snippy with me, doc. You just said a mechanic isn't good enough for you. That's seriously crappy. Cooper didn't have to take me to the hospital that night he found me. But he did. *And* he stayed. Then he made sure I had someplace to go. If that isn't good enough for you, then I'm sorry, but that makes you a bitch." Tea in hand, Jessi headed out of the kitchen. "I need a shower."

"Wait." Haleigh chased her into the living room. "I never said he isn't good enough for *me*. I said my mother wouldn't approve."

Jessi spun, her eyes flashing. "Who cares? Aren't you like forty? I mean, you're a freaking adult. You don't need your mommy's approval if he's the right guy." Painting Haleigh with a look of disgust, she said, "Grow up, for cripes' sake. And if you don't have the guts to go after Cooper, don't use your mother as an excuse."

"I—" Haleigh started, but Jessi stormed off.

The question echoed in Haleigh's brain. *Who cares?* Haleigh cared. She wanted her mother's approval. Jessi didn't understand the dynamic Haleigh grew up with, or the guilt she carried for being the thorn in her mother's side. The one that her father had twisted and buried deeper all those years.

"I don't have to explain my life to anyone," she said, charging down the hall to her own room. At least this time she remembered not to slam the door.

"I don't understand why you kept me in the dark about this," Cooper said.

"I didn't keep you in the dark," his mother hedged. "I just didn't tell you yet."

"That's the same thing." He cut into the chicken-fried steak she'd brought him for lunch. "How can I make sure you're okay if I don't know that you're hopping all over town with some guy I don't even know?"

Linda Ridgeway rolled her eyes. "Oh, please. Bruce is on the Ruby committee with you, and I know for a fact that he's volunteered to help with your car show fundraiser thing, so it isn't as if he's a total stranger to you."

Bruce Clemens owned the local bookstore, called Bound to Please, and was a nice enough guy. But that didn't mean Cooper wanted his mother dating him. Or anyone else for that matter.

"So he's been looking me in the eye and conveniently not saying a word about having the hots for my mother."

"Cooper Daniel, I will not have you implying that Bruce has done anything wrong. We are single, consenting adults, and do not need your permission to spend a little time together."

Properly chastised, Cooper tried to see the situation from his mother's point of view. She *was* only fifty-three years old, and in great health, thank goodness. And he had to admit that there was no reason for her to spend her remaining years living like a nun.

"I'm not suggesting you need anyone's permission, and I do want you to be happy," he conceded. "I guess I just need to get used to the idea of you, you know, dating."

His mother's carefree laughter returned. "You make it sound like I've taken up pole dancing. Goodness, Cooper, I'm having a nice time with a man who thinks I'm pretty."

"You're beautiful," Cooper declared. "You don't need some bookstore owner to tell you that."

"Actually, I do." Laying her hand along his stubble-covered jaw, she said, "But it's nice to hear it from you as well." After a wistful sigh, she pulled her hand away to prop it beneath her chin. "Enough about me. Tell me what's going on between you and Haleigh Rae."

Cooper hadn't seen that one coming. "I don't know what you're talking about," he said before shoving a forkful of food in his mouth.

"Oh no," Mama said, wiggling a finger in front of his nose. "If we can talk about my love life, we can talk about yours. Abby said you spent the night at her house last night."

"On the couch," he clarified around the steak.

Throwing a folded paper towel his way, she said, "You know better than to talk with your mouth full."

Chewing the rest of the meat, he swallowed and said, "Haleigh had too much to drink at Brubaker's, so I left my truck at the bar and drove her home. Then I slept on the couch. End of story."

If he did make a move in Haleigh's direction, the odds were still in favor of her telling him to go to hell. For the sake of his pride, he'd prefer as few people as possible know of his potential humiliation. Add in his mother's unwavering determination to see her son married, mostly for the sake of getting herself some grandkids to spoil, and the slightest whiff of him and Haleigh getting together would have her doing who-knew-what to see them tripping down the aisle as soon as possible.

"You don't really expect me to believe that. You've been in love with the girl since you hit puberty. Maybe before."

Sweet corn spewed across his desk. "How do you know that?"

She shook her head as she gathered the corn in another paper towel. "I'm your mother, Cooper. I know everything."

He didn't like the sound of that.

"Now, what are you going to do about Haleigh Rae?"

"I'm not going to do anything about Haleigh Rae. And you're not going to do anything, either," he ordered. "No meddling. Promise me."

"You aren't getting any younger, you know."

They'd been over this more times than he could count. "For the last time, when I marry, I'm only doing it once. That's it. And that means no wedding until I find a girl that I can't live without. So far, that hasn't happened, but you'll be the first to know if it does."

Leaning forward as if sharing a great secret, she said, "Cooper, you've loved that girl forever. You have to at least give it a try."

He copied her movements. "Like I said, I'll let you know if the right girl comes around."

As the implication sank in, Linda Ridgeway sat back with a wide grin splitting her face. Nodding her approval, she said, "That's my boy."

Haleigh's shift didn't start until noon, which gave her plenty of time to shower and make a call before arriving at the hospital an hour early to track down Abby. As expected, Raquel had been disappointed but supportive, apologizing for being out of reach while dinging Haleigh for walking into the bar in the first place. An addict knew better than to tempt fate, especially when her defenses were down.

She took the scolding without argument or offense. Every word her sponsor said had been the truth. They'd agreed that avoiding future encounters with her mother would be the best way to go, but since Haleigh wasn't prepared to cut her mother out of her life, she'd agreed to search for a local counselor to get herself back on track.

Feeling like a failure was nothing new, but stung nonetheless. What mattered now was getting back on the wagon and staying there.

As she made the drive to the hospital, Haleigh contemplated the impending conversation with Abby, which allowed her *not* to think about Jessi's lecture. Though she had sunk to the childish level of leaving a sticky note on the fridge informing the little know-it-all that Haleigh was only thirty-one, thank you very much.

What did the girl know anyway? Clearly, her mother had set the bar pretty low when it came to standards for her daughter. With a parent like the one Jessi described, why would any child care about winning her approval? The careless woman didn't even know where her daughter was right now. The daughter who was supposedly still pregnant.

"I have fifteen minutes," Abby said, meeting Haleigh near the elevators outside neurology. "We can talk in the lounge up here."

Her tone was all business. Not a good sign.

"Whatever you want," Haleigh said, keeping up with her friend's brisk pace.

Thankfully, the lounge was empty since Abby didn't pull any punches. The moment they stepped through the door, she said, "I thought you gave up drinking."

"I did," Haleigh defended. "It was one slip."

"If Cooper had to bring you home, it was more than a slip," Abby said, slamming her hands into the pockets of her scrubs. "What's going on between the two of you?"

"Hold on a minute." Haleigh got enough of this crap from her mother. She didn't need it from her best friend, too. "I had a rough night and threw back a couple drinks. Unfortunately, I did it on an empty stomach and a couple was all it took to go too far. I didn't ask Cooper to bring me home. In fact, I didn't have a choice in the matter since he threatened to throw me over his shoulder and carry me out of the bar."

Tapping her foot, Abby said, "I heard you in the kitchen last night. You were flirting."

"I was drunk." This was ridiculous. Haleigh had screwed up. There was no denying that. But she hadn't committed any sins with Cooper. "I'm going to ignore this interrogation because I know you're still not in a good place. And having Emma around isn't helping. To sum up, I fell off the wagon. I'm seeking counseling to make sure it doesn't happen again. And I'm not flirting with your brother. End of discussion."

Before Haleigh reached the door, Abby said, "I don't want to see him hurt." When her friend turned around, she added, "I don't want to see either of you hurt, but Cooper isn't like you. He wears his heart on his sleeve. Easier for someone to break."

Fighting to hide her feelings, Haleigh shook her head. "I don't plan on hurting him, Abby."

"I know," her oldest friend said. "But that doesn't mean that you won't."

Which was the exact reason why Haleigh wouldn't cross that line.

"No one knows my ability to leave chaos in my wake better than I do," Haleigh said. "You have my word, Abby. I won't hurt him."

Again she turned to leave, but Abby stopped her. "Are you okay? What happened last night to set you off?"

Crossing her arms, Haleigh said, "My mother suggested that for once in my life I should put her first."

Abby's shoulders fell. "Wow."

"Yeah. Wow."

Abby Ridgeway had been Haleigh's confidante since they were nine years old. She knew every ugly and twisted part of her past. Without her friend as witness, Haleigh might wonder if her childhood had really been so bad, or if the painful memories were more nightmare than reality.

That *wow* confirmed the truth.

With a philosophic smile, Haleigh said, "Nothing I shouldn't be used to, right? I'm sorry I upset you. It won't happen again."

"I love your guts, Haleigh Rae," Abby said with an apologetic tone.

When the girls were eleven, Haleigh had come to a life-changing conclusion that she had to share with her best friend immediately. *My mother hates my guts,* Haleigh had declared, to which Abby had responded, *I love your guts.* They'd been using the phrase ever since.

The words made Haleigh smile despite the ache in her chest. "I love your guts, too, Abby Lou."

And maybe someday she'd love her own as well.

Chapter 13

Cooper was getting a complex about females puking in his presence. No sooner had he arrived at Abby's house Monday morning to drive Jessi and the munchkin to the pediatrician's office, than Emma upchucked down the front of her little pink outfit.

"Come on, Emma," Jessi pleaded. "We're already late as it is."

"I'll get you there on time," Cooper said. "Get her changed and meet me at the car."

Due to Cooper's truck being circa 1975, strapping a baby into the middle of his bench seat wasn't an option. Fortunately for Jessi, Abby had the day off and had offered up her Camry.

As Jessi rushed off, Cooper headed for the door and ran into Abby exiting the laundry room with a basket full of clothes.

"If those are yours, I think they shrunk," he said, knowing full well that the tiny items belonged to Emma.

Abby wasn't amused. "Forgive me if I'm not in the mood for laundry humor."

"You haven't been in the mood for any kind of humor lately," he observed. He understood that she was grieving, but that didn't stop Cooper from missing the twin he'd known his whole life. "Why don't you come with us? I'll buy lunch for everyone."

She led him to the living room, where she dropped onto the couch and settled the basket between her feet. "Don't you have a business to run?"

"Frankie and Ian are working the garage, and Kelly can handle the counter without me for a few hours." Abby knew that Cooper had enough employees to keep the garage running without his constant supervision. Which meant she was being a snot for no reason. "When was the last time you did something other than work or volunteer at one of those veterans' charities?"

Snapping a baby blanket in the air, she said, "Those charities are important. Those men and women sacrificed everything for the rest of us, and they deserve our help. Forgive me for wanting to give back."

"Abby," he said, and waited for her to meet his eye. "No matter how much money you raise, you can't bring Kyle back. And you know he'd hate to see you cut yourself off like this."

"What do you know about it, Cooper? You've never committed to anything other than a metal box on four wheels." Green eyes that matched his own snapped fire. "How about, when you lose the love of your life, then you can tell me how to live mine."

Shortly after Kyle had died, while Abby had been walking around in a daze acting as if her husband might stroll through the door at any minute, their mother had made Cooper read about the five stages of grief. Those early months had been a textbook case of denial, but Abby had clearly drifted into the next stage—anger.

His sister had no more control over her emotions right now than she did the weather, but knowing the source of the storm didn't make it any easier to bear.

"You're right," he said, backing away. "What do I know?"

When he reached the front hall, Abby called after him. "Cooper, come back here."

Reluctant to take more abuse, he ignored the plea and kept walking. "Please," she said as she caught up to him. "I shouldn't have said that. I'm sorry."

Cooper shook his head as he turned. "No, you shouldn't have. But you're right, I don't know a damn thing about what you're going through."

"Maybe not," she agreed, "but you're right about Kyle. He'd hate to see me hiding away like this. I just need more time, okay?"

"Okay." Cooper hugged his sister tight before dropping a kiss on the top of her head. "I'm here for you, sis. Whether you want to talk or yell or punch something, I'm here."

She sniffed as she pulled away. "I appreciate that."

As he tugged on his sister's ponytail, Jessi stepped into the foyer and hesitated. "I'm sorry. Am I interrupting a family moment?"

Abby laughed. "We were just getting something straight," she said. "You guys better go or you're going to be late."

"I changed her as fast as I could." Jessi handed the baby-filled car seat over to Cooper. "She wouldn't stop squirming long enough to get her legs in the holes."

"Like I said, I'll get you there on time."

Cooper and Jessi rushed out the door as Abby yelled, "No speeding, little brother."

Jessi snorted. "Did she just call you *little brother?*"

"She beat me by a minute," he explained while locking Emma into the backseat. "And she's never let me forget it."

"It must be cool to have a twin," she said wistfully as she buckled herself in.

"It has its moments," he answered. "Don't you have any siblings?"

Shaking her head, she said, "Nah. Mama got herself fixed when I was a kid. Said I crimped her style enough."

Just when Cooper thought he knew how having a crappy parent felt, Jessi went and proved him wrong. Aware that the kid would rather stick another hole in her face than accept his sympathy, he said, "If that's the example you had to follow, I'd say you turned out pretty good, short stuff."

Looking both embarrassed and pleased, Jessi said, "Thanks, dude. Do you think my dad will feel the same way?"

Cooper hadn't seen that question coming. One week into their search and they'd yet to catch a lead. Caleb had asked Hattie Silvester, who owned the newspaper and had grown up in Ardent Springs, but the initials hadn't rung a bell with her. Spencer had consulted Lorelei's grandmother as well as Buford Stallings and Lorelei's father, Mike Lowry, both of whom could be around the age Jessi's father might be today.

But again, no one remembered anyone going by J.T. It was looking more and more like Jessi's mom had sent her on a wild-goose chase for a man who didn't exist.

"Are you sure you want to keep looking?" Cooper asked. "The guy bailed on you and your mom. That doesn't sound like a good guy to me."

Keeping her head up, Jessi stared out the windshield as she said, "I need to do this, Cooper. I really appreciate y'all taking me in, but I've gotta see this through. This might be my only shot to have a real family."

Feeling like a protective big brother, he said, "I know we called this stay at Abby's temporary, but you know nobody is kicking you out, right?"

"I still feel bad for crashing like this. I tried to get Abby to leave that laundry alone. She shouldn't have to fold Emma's clothes on her day off." Leaning an elbow on the door ledge, she added, "And my funds are running out. I need to get a job somewhere."

Jessi had been carrying more money than any of them had expected when she'd come to town. It turned out she'd been saving through her entire pregnancy. His mother had organized a diaper collection among her friends, which left Jessi's funds to cover all of Emma's formula so far. With the clothing and blanket donations from Carrie, plus the car seat Cooper bought, the baby was well taken care of.

For now.

"Aren't new moms supposed to wait like six weeks before doing anything?"

"Broke new moms don't have that luxury," she said. "And maybe if I get a job I'll come across someone who knows this J.T. person."

He had to admire her staunch determination. "I'm asking everyone I can think of," he said, assuring her that they were taking the search seriously. "If he's around, we'll find him."

She nodded. "He's here. I can feel it."

Growing certain that the opposite was true, Cooper held his tongue. If they didn't get lucky in the next week, their only alternative would be to go public with the search. Something he was reluctant to do. Regardless of how things had gone down, learning a man had a long-lost daughter could have a less than positive effect on a family.

That meant they needed to exhaust all other avenues before outing the guy publicly. For all their sakes, Cooper hoped something would turn up soon.

Between late Saturday afternoon and lunchtime on Monday, Haleigh had delivered seventeen babies. A record for her career, and a feat she never wanted to achieve again. Whatever had leaked into the Ardent Springs water supply nine months before, Haleigh was just glad that she hadn't been around to drink it.

The weekend baby boom had kept her so busy, she hadn't seen Abby since their eye-opening chat two days before. Losing Kyle had changed her friend. Though less outgoing than her twin, Abby had been just as sweet and generous as her brother. Always ready with a positive word and a ready smile. Abigail Ridgeway had been the saving grace that kept Haleigh from succumbing to the permeating darkness at home. A source of acceptance without limit or condition.

For Abby to imply that Haleigh was little more than a wrecking ball destined to destroy anyone who stepped too close hit like a left hook. If the only person who had ever believed in her saw nothing left to redeem, who was Haleigh to argue?

The only person who had anything nice to say about Haleigh as a person was Cooper. Poor, blind Cooper. Even if Abby hadn't warned her off, she'd have kept a distance between them. If they got too close, he'd see what Haleigh really was. Delusion or not, Cooper's misplaced faith might be the only weapon to keep her demons at bay. If just one person believed she was worth saving, then maybe she was.

"That's four twenty-five," said the young man behind the register.

Haleigh had taken advantage of the respite to grab a coffee and a muffin from the cafeteria. She handed over a five, and then pocketed the change.

"I was hoping I'd find you here," said a gentle voice from her right.

The heat of humiliation danced up Haleigh's neck. She'd hoped to avoid the number one witness to her Brubaker's performance.

"Hey, Carrie. How are you?" To the drooling baby on the woman's hip, Haleigh said, "You're getting cuter every day, little one."

"She is, isn't she?" Carrie beamed. "I know you're busy, but do you have two minutes you can spare? I'd like to talk to you about something."

Certain this would be another conversation about Cooper, Haleigh said, "I'm not sure . . ."

"Please. It's about something you said Friday night."

"Whatever it was, I'm sorry. I wasn't myself that night." A sorry excuse, but nothing better came to mind.

"There's nothing to apologize for," Carrie assured her. "We all have our off days. But you said something about there being more important needs in this area than a restored movie theater."

She didn't recall making that statement to anyone other than Cooper, but she wasn't about to contradict the woman. "I might have said that."

"You did, and I agree with you."

Someone agreed with her? Maybe she did want to have this conversation. Glancing down at the food in her hands, she said, "Let's find a seat. That little one has to be getting heavy, and I'd really like to eat this."

Carrie smiled. "We can do that."

The pair found an empty table in the corner. Haleigh set down her coffee and muffin, and then retrieved a high chair from beside the drinks station. When she returned, she realized that Molly might not be big enough for a high chair.

"Can she sit in this?"

"Sure," Carrie answered, whipping a piglet-covered contraption from her diaper bag. "I just need you to hold her while I put this in the chair first."

Before Haleigh could argue, she found a wide-eyed four-month-old blinking up at her. Instead of letting out a wail of protest, the baby nestled into her shoulder as if they were old friends.

"I think she likes me."

Carrie glanced up. "She should. You *are* the first person to ever hold her, after all."

A humbling thought. And true hundreds of times over, but Haleigh had never considered her job in that context. Feeling more at ease, Haleigh settled into her chair cuddling Molly close. "This is kind of nice."

Dark brows drew together. "Dr. Mitchner, you act like holding a baby is a new experience."

"Please, call me Haleigh," she said. "And in this context, it *is* a new experience."

Sliding the piglet cover over the back of the high chair, Carrie said, "That's silly. You deal with babies all day."

A common misconception. "I deal with mothers all day. I only hold babies for a matter of seconds before I pass them off to someone way more qualified to deal with them. And they're usually screaming at me, not all quiet and loving like this sweet girl."

"Huh," Carrie said. "I guess that makes sense. Now I almost feel bad about putting her in the high chair."

Haleigh picked up the muffin with her free hand. "I can eat around her. Tell me again what we agree on."

"That needs are being ignored in this area, but I'm not sure you'll agree with me on what we should do about it."

That sounded like the beginning of a dangerous proposition. "I'm listening," Haleigh mumbled around a blueberry, before brushing crumbs from Molly's back.

With a deep breath, Carrie said, "I'm not sure how much you know about my life before Molly's dad died, but to make a long story short, I endured an abusive situation because I had no place else to go. No family. No friends—Patch made sure of that—and no shelters. The last is the need I'd like to address."

"You want to start a shelter?"

"I wish," she snorted. "I'm not qualified to start something so ambitious. But I would like to help someone else start one. Someone more qualified to get the project off the ground. Like maybe a person with a medical background like yours."

"You've got the wrong someone in mind," Haleigh said. "That kind of endeavor would require a real leader. That's not me."

"You were class president, editor of the school newspaper, chair of the yearbook committee, and head of the science club your senior year of high school. *And* you led the debate team to a regional championship," Carrie reminded her.

"How do you know all that?"

"I was only two years behind you in school."

"Oh, right." Molly pulled her knees up against Haleigh's stomach and tickled her neck with an adorable and very contented sigh. Haleigh's ovaries actually attempted to leap out of her body. "Does she always do that?" she asked.

Carrie smiled. "Not with everyone. Come on, Haleigh. Will you at least think about it?"

"I wouldn't know where to start on something like that. I mean, where would we even put it?"

To Haleigh's surprise, Carrie whipped a manila folder from her diaper bag. "I've done some research on that. The old band camp out on Highway 76 is up for sale, and it's the perfect location, with several dorm-like rooms plus office space."

Haleigh ignored the folder dangling inches in front of her nose. "What the heck kind of magical bag is that?" she asked. "I'm afraid you're going to pull out a tuba next. Or maybe a hula hoop."

The folder dropped to the table. "Do you know what it's like to be punched?" Carrie asked. "Or slammed against a wall?"

Jaw tight, Haleigh said, "You're not fighting fair, Carrie."

"This is too important to fight fair. There are women suffering right now because they have no alternative. We can change that."

She'd never suffered physical abuse, but Haleigh did know how it felt to be a scared young girl without a lot of options. And something like this might have been an option for Jessi when she'd had nowhere else to go. If the thickness of the folder was any indication, Carrie had already done a lot of the preliminary research.

Still, where would she find the time for something like this? Working sixty to seventy hours a week at the hospital while appeasing her mother with regular dinners in her downtime didn't leave room for a new project.

As Haleigh opened her mouth to refuse Carrie's request, their conversation was interrupted.

Chapter 14

"Lookee here," Cooper said, "three of my favorite ladies in one place."

At the sound of his voice, Molly lifted her head fast enough to buck Haleigh's chin, then promptly lifted her arms to be picked up. He took her without hesitation, immediately shooting raspberries into her belly. The little girl laughed with glee.

The man was a natural. By the time he tucked the tiny thing against his chest, his shirt was spotted with drool and Haleigh's ovaries were doing a Kermit flail. Even the echo of Abby's warning did nothing to calm the WANT voice screaming through her head.

You promised, she reminded herself, even while her ovaries bartered with her brain. Just one night. Or maybe a weekend. Okay, a solid week and she'd have her fill.

Which might have been the biggest lie she'd told herself in months.

～

Haleigh looked everywhere *but* at Cooper. Even so, he didn't have to see her eyes to feel the tension coming off her body.

"What are y'all up to today?"

"Nothing," Haleigh said, but Carrie spoke over her.

"I'm trying to convince Haleigh to help me start a women's shelter in the area."

The doc didn't look happy about Carrie sharing that detail. In fact, she looked as if she were bracing for a blow. He didn't see why, since this sounded like what she'd been talking about Friday night when he brought up the theater project.

"That's a great idea," he said, enjoying Haleigh's shocked expression. At least now she was looking at him.

Eyes narrowed, she said, "What did you say?"

"I said it's a great idea. You should do it." Molly grabbed his lips and Cooper wrestled her hand away. "Friday night you said more important needs than a theater were being ignored. If you believe that, then do something about it."

"I . . ." she sputtered. "That's not what I meant."

"So girls like Jessi aren't stuck with no place to go?"

"Yes, that's a problem."

"Okay then. Now you have a chance to change it."

The idea seemed simple enough. Haleigh had the intelligence, the determination, and the experience to make a difference. Not that delivering babies wasn't making a difference, but this option would have more far-reaching effects.

"See," Carrie said. "Even Cooper agrees."

"Cooper was a saint in a former life. Of course he agrees."

"That's me," he said, rocking on his heels. "The patron saint of motor oil." Molly chimed in with some incoherent gibberish, and Cooper nodded in agreement. "Even Molly thinks you should do it."

Haleigh squirmed in her seat as if something more than the shelter idea was making her uncomfortable.

"Fine," she snapped. "You two can stop ganging up on me. I'll think about it, but I'm not committing to anything." Snatching a folder off the table, she added, "If I decide not to do it, I promise to at least recommend someone who would be a better choice."

"There is no better choice," Carrie said stubbornly. "You're the perfect person to make this happen."

"What makes you so sure?"

"What makes you so sure you aren't?" Cooper asked.

She met his challenge with a level glare. "Lack of time, for one thing. Then there's lack of connections and experience."

"The only thing you're lacking is faith in yourself, and we have more than enough to make up for that."

History had proven that once Haleigh set her mind to something, nothing stood in her way. Whether scoring perfect grades or earning her MD, she'd achieved every goal she'd set for herself.

"Like I said, I'll think about it."

"Good." Carrie bounced out of her seat. "Now we have to get moving." She whipped some pink contraption off the high chair near Cooper's hip and stuffed it into the diaper bag. "Little one's good mood is about to go out the window. Today is her four-month shots."

"I should go, too," Haleigh said, wrapping up the remnants of a half-eaten muffin.

"I'd like to talk to you if you have a minute," Cooper said. His run-in with Abby had left him worried, and the only other person who knew her as well as he did was Haleigh.

She tossed the garbage in the can behind her seat. "I need to do my rounds."

"It's about Abby," he explained. "I'm worried about her."

With a glance to her watch, she said, "We'll have to make it fast."

"Let us get out of your way," Carrie said, taking Molly. "My number is in the file. Give me a call when you make your decision or if you have any questions. See you later, Cooper."

As mom and baby disappeared out of view, Cooper took the seat that Carrie had occupied. "How does Abby seem to you?" he asked.

Haleigh lifted one shoulder. "Distant. Irritable. Sad."

"So, not like Abby at all."

"Cooper, she lost her husband. We can't expect her to be back to normal on our schedule."

"I know," he said. But he hated seeing her hide away, as if her life had ended along with Kyle's. "This morning, she nearly ripped my head off for making a joke about the laundry."

"Yeah," Haleigh agreed. "Her fuse has gotten way shorter lately."

At least he wasn't the only person to see it. "I get that this is grief, and she needs to go through it her own way, but there has to be something we can do to help."

One side of her mouth curled up. "That white horse of yours isn't going to work in this situation."

"So we don't even try?" He couldn't stand to sit back and do nothing. "Are you working this Saturday?"

"Until six, yeah. Why?"

"I'm having a cookout, and I want you to convince Abby to come. I already know she has the night off. We normally start around five, but I can wait a little longer to put the food on the grill."

Haleigh ran a hand through her loose curls. "After a twelve-hour shift, you want me to drag Abby out for some hot dogs?"

"You've never been to one of my cookouts," he said, highly offended. Hot dogs. Please. "Try chicken, ribs, and a smoked brisket. Plus the sides that Caleb will bring. And, of course, Lorelei is in charge of desserts."

"That does sound good." Haleigh tapped the side of her coffee cup. "But did you miss the twelve-hour shift part? And getting Abby to come is a long shot at best."

"Just get her out for one hour. Lie to her if you have to."

"Ha!" she laughed. "Now I know I'm hearing things. Did the unflinchingly honest Cooper Ridgeway just tell me to lie?"

What *was* her hang-up with this Saint Cooper crap? She made him sound like a self-righteous asshole.

"One of these days, I'm going to show you how *un*-saintly I am. Just because I didn't take advantage of you Friday night doesn't mean I didn't think about it."

He'd sure as hell thought about it. And he'd been thinking about it ever since. Yes, he wanted to get Abby out of the house, but he also wanted Haleigh at the cookout. He'd planned to ask her anyway, but the plan had changed after his encounter with his sister.

"Nothing would have happened Friday night," she stated. "No matter how drunk I was."

"That's not what the alcohol was saying." Cooper was upstanding, but he wasn't stupid. If he hadn't backed off after buckling her in, he'd have tasted the rum on her lips and not cared about right or wrong. And she wouldn't have stopped him.

Then again, maybe he *was* stupid.

"Alcohol lies," she argued.

"You and I both know that isn't true."

Taking a different tack, she said, "It's just a physical attraction. It doesn't mean anything."

Cooper leaned back in his chair. "It means something to me."

"And that's where we differ." Haleigh tucked Carrie's folder under her arm as she rose from her chair. "I'll see what I can do about Abby, but I doubt she'll agree to come."

"Haleigh, hold up," he said, not wanting her to walk away mad.

"Forget it, Cooper." She gave him a pleading look. "Do us both a favor and forget it."

In the end, Haleigh hadn't needed to lie. She simply informed Abby that Cooper had invited them all to a cookout at his house on Saturday and she was going with or without his sister. The fact that her best friend didn't trust her, or that Abby even felt the need to protect Cooper from her, should have been highly insulting. But the truth was, Haleigh didn't trust herself either.

Cooper had been right about the night she'd gotten drunk at Brubaker's. She'd wanted to kiss him in that car. Hell, she'd wanted to do a lot more than kiss. When sober, common sense prevailed and Haleigh had no trouble acting like a sensible woman. When not sober, she tended to be a certified hussy.

Now that she'd had time to dwell on it, the night at Brubaker's had been a long time coming. It was a wonder she hadn't nose-dived off the wagon sooner considering she'd been dining with her mother on a regular basis for the last six months. Meredith Mitchner could drive anyone to drink. She'd certainly pushed Haleigh onto the path all those years ago.

Not that Haleigh blamed her mother for her addiction. She'd learned a long time ago that diving into a bottle had been her choice. Her unhealthy way of dealing with an unhealthy situation. During the week, she'd found a counselor who specialized in addiction, but the earliest appointment Haleigh could get was still a month away.

"Are you sure they won't mind my coming?" Jessi asked.

"For the last time," Abby said, "no one will mind. They're going to be so excited to see Emma's chubby little cheeks that you'll probably have babysitters lined up around the grill before the food is served."

"It'll help if you don't tell them how little she sleeps," Haleigh mumbled, and received a poke from her best friend. "Ow," she whined. "Unnecessary."

"She'll eventually sleep more, right?" Jessi said.

"And cry less?" Haleigh asked.

Abby twisted to look at both of them from the passenger seat. "Why are y'all asking me? I've never had a baby, remember?"

They needed to change the subject quick.

"Does Cooper have these cookouts often?" Haleigh inquired.

Her passenger nodded. "From the minute it's warm enough until we're all bundled up and holding our hands to the fire to stave off frostbite."

Haleigh suspected she knew the answer to the next question, but asked anyway. "How long has it been since you went to one?"

With her eyes locked on the passing scenery, Abby said, "I haven't felt like it for a while."

A while meaning since Kyle died, no doubt.

"What is there to do besides sit around eating and gossiping?" Jessi's voice implied she found neither of these options entertaining. "I'm not even going to know anyone."

Could these two get any more annoying? Good reason or not, Abby's woe-is-me rut was getting old. And Miss Too-Cool-For-A-Cookout had jumped at the chance to come when Haleigh had first mentioned it. Now, as if to protect her teenage coolness, she deployed the eye-rolling attitude.

"Look," Haleigh said. "I just worked twelve hours after pulling three sixteen-hour shifts in the last three days. If anyone has reason to be unpleasant at this soiree, it's me. But I'm not going to do that. And neither are the two of you." Her index finger bounced from one passenger to the other. "It's a beautiful night, and we are going to be social. We're going to eat good food, enjoy the stars, and have a freaking good time." Catching Jessi's wide-eyed stare in the rearview mirror, she added, "Everybody got that?"

"Good time," Jessi repeated. "Yes, ma'am."

Silence loomed from beside her.

"Abigail?"

"I will be a veritable ball of glee."

Sarcasm was a side-step away from jovial. In some countries.

"I'll take it," Haleigh said, contemplating how quickly they could leave without appearing rude.

Chapter 15

"You're killing me, dude," said Ian O'Malley while rubbing his inexplicably flat abs. "I haven't eaten since lunch. What are we waiting for?"

Young Mr. O'Malley, Cooper's cousin on his mother's side, swallowed more calories in a day than could be found in one of Lorelei's cookie displays, yet he remained skinny as a rail. The family had long ago determined that Ian had the metabolism of a hummingbird. Ironic, since he moved at the speed of a drunk slug.

"Not everyone is here yet," Cooper explained, not for the first time. "The grill is hot and once the meat hits the fire, it won't take long."

"Let me cut the brisket," Ian begged. "That's been done for hours. If I don't get something soon, I'm gonna start gnawing on my boots."

"If you don't shut up, you're going to be *sitting* on my boot."

"Aw, jeez," the younger man grumbled.

"Time to set up the buffet line," Lorelei said as she and Caleb positioned bowls and casserole dishes on the table to Cooper's right.

"Everyone isn't here yet," he reminded them. Abby had let him know two days before that all four females in the house would be joining them. And they would get their food hot and fresh off the grill like everyone else.

"Relax, big boy," Caleb said. "Carrie says Haleigh's car just pulled up."

Unexpected nerves sent his stomach buzzing like a hive knocked from a tree. Haleigh had been to his house before, but she hadn't seen his pride and joy. Like any man, Cooper felt the inside of the house served no other purpose than to hold his stuff and keep him from getting wet in the rain.

But the backyard. That was where a man *lived*.

"I hope we aren't too late," Haleigh said as she handed Cooper a bucket of fried chicken. "The drive-thru was slow. My mother would be scandalized if I showed up at a social gathering empty-handed."

Cooper couldn't respond. Haleigh never failed to look pretty, but with the color high on her cheeks, a layer of gloss on her lips, and hair shining like spun gold in the light of the tiki torches, she took his breath away. Signs of exhaustion around her eyes were the only hint of imperfection in an otherwise flawless face.

Pulling himself together, he said, "You can never have too much food when Ian is around."

"Ian?" she asked.

"You remember the little kid who went around stealing everyone's bread during Thanksgiving dinner?"

"Sticky Fingers O'Malley?"

Cooper chuckled at the old nickname. "We all thought he'd grow up to be a thief, but it turned out he just likes food. A lot."

Abby walked by with a wave, but said nothing. Jessi approached holding Emma on her shoulder. "Where can I change her?" she asked.

"I'll show you," Carrie answered before Cooper could open his mouth. "The bed in the back bedroom works great."

As the two mothers disappeared into the house, Haleigh said, "Carrie knows a lot about your bedrooms."

Refusing to take the bait, he said, "Is there a question in there somewhere?"

She shook her head. "You two just seem like a sensible pairing. Spencer and Lorelei. Caleb and Snow. You and Carrie."

Leaning close as if sharing a secret, Cooper said, "If you're trying to suss out the truth of my availability, I promise that I am one hundred percent single."

"You're so full of yourself," she said with a grin. "It's a wonder all those baseball caps you wear actually fit on your big head."

He raised a brow. "You really want to give me an opening like that?"

"Please." Her efforts to appear unamused failed miserably.

Loading the grill with marinated ribs, he said, "You're in a good mood tonight."

With a teasing smirk, she said, "Is there a question in there somewhere?"

"A smart-ass remark. Definitely the sign of a good mood."

Haleigh sighed. "I didn't want to come any more than Abby did, but that's the reason I'm here. If we're both antisocial at the same time, there's no hope for either of us. She's dragged me from the abyss on more than one occasion. It's about time that I returned the favor."

Cooper took the opportunity to point out what Haleigh would never see on her own. "That's the kind of thing that a good person would do."

"More like a guilty person," she snorted. "I'm running out of IOUs to hand out."

If they kept going in this direction, he and Haleigh would end up in another standoff. Cooper brought them back to the subject of Abby.

"Do you think having Jessi and the baby around is making her worse?"

Snatching a peanut-butter-filled celery stalk from the table, Haleigh looked to be contemplating her answer. "She was already moody before Jessi moved in. And the only time I see her smile anymore is when she's holding Emma and doesn't think anyone is watching."

"I talked to Miss Hattie about this J.T. person." Cooper flipped the chicken breasts. "She'd never heard of anyone in town going by that name, and she's lived here her whole life."

"It's obvious that Jessi's mother made up this J.T. person," Haleigh sighed. "But how are we going to tell her that? And if she does finally give up this pointless hunt, where will she go?"

He felt as if they were devising a way to tell a child that Santa Claus was a fraud. "What's the harm in letting her think we're still looking for him?"

"Again with the lying," she said. "But in this case, a tiny fib might not be a bad idea. Still, are you going to tell Abby that this temporary arrangement might not be so temporary? She's been the person most put out by all this."

Cooper spotted Abby talking to Lorelei and Snow. She was almost smiling. Getting her out was definitely the right thing to do.

"I'll tell her. Which reminds me, how did you get her to come?"

"Funny story," Haleigh said, but she didn't sound amused. "No lie required. I simply told her about the invitation and said I was coming whether she did or not."

That didn't explain why Abby agreed to come. "You lost me," he said.

Pointing toward Abby with her celery stick, she said, "She doesn't trust my intentions toward you."

Liking the sound of that, Cooper said, "You have intentions toward me? I think we should explore this further."

Haleigh rolled her eyes. "She *thinks* I'm going to break your heart. Which is ridiculous because you're Cooper and I'm a walking disaster and no one knows either of those facts better than I do."

He definitely didn't like the sound of that. "Skipping the *I'm Cooper* bit, because I have a feeling that's the sainthood bull crap again, let's clear up the second part. You are not a walking disaster."

"Come on, Coop," Ian cut in. "I'm shriveling down to nothing over here, and the smell coming off that grill says the food is done." Sparing Haleigh a glance, his cousin did a double take. "Hello, gorgeous."

"Hey yourself, O'Malley. The last time I saw you, your head had yet to grow into your ears." Haleigh grinned. "It's nice to see some things never change."

"Dude," he mumbled out the side of his mouth as if Haleigh couldn't hear him. "How does she know my name?"

Cooper transferred a rack of ribs onto a platter, then waved his tongs toward his cousin. "Big ears and very little between them," he said. "Ian, this is Haleigh Rae Mitchner. She's Abby's best friend who used to spend holidays with us. Which means she knows not to let you too close to her plate."

"Aw, I don't steal rolls anymore."

"A true sign of maturity," Haleigh said with a wink.

"That smells awesome," Jessi said as she joined them, hands empty and looking like the cat who'd just spotted a canary. "Hi," she greeted Ian. "I don't think we've met."

Of course they hadn't met. She'd been in town less than two weeks, and spent most of that time shut in with a newborn.

"I'm Ian," the bean stalk said with a familiar look of awe on his face. "Ian O'Malley. Cooper here's my cousin."

"I like the name Ian."

"Jessi is pretty, too."

Well, hell. "I thought you were hungry," Cooper said to Ian. "Get yourself a plate."

"I can wait," he answered, eyes locked on Jessi's brown ones. "Did you get a drink yet?" he asked her.

"Not yet. You want to show me where they are?"

"Yes, ma'am."

As the pair walked off, Cooper yelled, "Nonalcoholic," but the kids had already tuned him out.

"That girl moves fast," Haleigh said.

Cooper loaded the platter with the rest of the ribs. "Too fast. She'll eat that boy up and he won't know what hit him."

Haleigh watched the young couple with a tilt of her head. "I don't know. Maybe a boy like Ian would be good for her."

"You mean spending time with a guy who doesn't knock girls up and then take off?"

"Yeah," Haleigh agreed. "Why not?"

"Why not, indeed," he said, recognizing an opening when it came his way. "Which leads to the conclusion that spending time with a nice guy who doesn't treat a woman like crap would be good for *you*."

With narrowed eyes, Haleigh held Cooper's gaze as she yelled, "Food is up! Everybody come eat."

The food was excellent. And the company wasn't so bad either. As often happened at these sorts of gatherings, the women split off on their own, while the men lingered around the grill, patting each other on the back and talking about sports or things that go boom. At least that's what Haleigh assumed men talked about.

Most men, she corrected. Marcus preferred subjects such as net worth and Italian leather shoes.

"How do you like being home?" Lorelei asked Haleigh. "I can't imagine leaving Memphis for Ardent Springs."

"You left LA," Haleigh pointed out.

"Touché. But I never intended to stay here."

Venturing into territory that likely wasn't any of her business, Haleigh asked, "Then why did you?"

"For *lurve*," Snow answered for her friend.

Without argument, Lorelei said, "Damn right. Nothing else would have done it."

"I've never lived anywhere else," Abby said, "but I don't think Ardent Springs is so bad."

"Neither does Lorelei," Carrie chimed in. "Regardless of what she says."

"Hey." Lorelei pointed at Carrie. "I have a rep to protect."

A collective spurt of laughter erupted at that statement, though Haleigh couldn't help but notice Abby's lack of mirth.

"Speaking of love," Snow said, "your new mother seems to be smitten over there."

Ian and Jessi had been the one exception to the gender break out. They'd been talking since dinner, and Haleigh had to give the young man credit for not running scared the moment he met Emma. Especially since her choice of greeting had been to hurl down the front of his shirt. He was currently pushing them both on Cooper's rope swing.

"From what I've heard, her taste in guys has left much to be desired," Haleigh said. "Please tell me Ian doesn't fancy himself a playboy?"

"Hardly," Abby snorted. "He rarely musters up the courage to talk to a girl. I'm surprised he made it this far."

"Jessi made the first move, and I don't think she gave him a choice but to talk to her."

"I like a girl with chutzpah," Lorelei said.

"Chutzpah is what landed her in the maternity ward," Haleigh pointed out. "If she manages to grow a little common sense to go with it, her future will be a lot simpler."

"She's already a single mom," Abby said. "How simple could it be?"

"I'm a single mom, and my life isn't so bad," Carrie interjected. "You make it sound like a handicap."

Abby doubled-down. "Her life is going to be harder now than it would have been if she'd not had a baby. That's just a fact."

"You don't know that," Carrie argued. "There are worse things in life than having a baby on your own. She could have ended up with a guy who used her for a punching bag. Trust me, that's a crappier life than raising a little one by yourself."

"Who wants another drink?" Haleigh asked. "I'm buying." Why Abby had turned anti-single-mom was a mystery, but this was no time for a cat fight.

"I need to check on Molly," Carrie said. The little girl had fallen asleep less than an hour before and had been put down in a playpen in the kitchen.

As the offended mother strode into the house, Abby said, "I need a break," and took off around the side of Cooper's house, presumably toward the front porch. Or maybe to the car. Haleigh wouldn't be surprised if she sat in the Fusion for the rest of the evening. At least she hadn't demanded that they leave. Yet. Shocking as it sounded, Haleigh was actually having a good time.

She hadn't hung out with a group of women in a long time, and the lazy feeling of having nowhere to be and nothing that she *should* be doing felt refreshingly liberating. Technically, she should have been sleeping, but as someone famous once said, she could sleep when she was dead.

Or retired. Either way, Haleigh wasn't ready for the cookout to end. Lorelei broke the silence. "That wasn't awkward at all."

"Not a bit," Haleigh agreed. She could have apologized for her friend, but Abby's behavior belonged to Abby alone. If anyone gave an apology, it would have to be her.

"Oh, hey," Lorelei said. "Has Cooper introduced you to his ladies?"

"Um . . ." Haleigh mumbled. "His *what*?"

"Cooper!" she hollered across the expansive back yard. "You need to show Haleigh where you keep your girls."

As if this wasn't the most bizarre request ever, Cooper saluted with his beer bottle, excused himself from the men, and headed their way.

"Okay," Haleigh said, dragging the word out. "This should be interesting."

"It's quite posh, actually," Snow assured her as Cooper took Haleigh's hand.

"Come on," he said. "Let's take a walk."

Too stunned and confused to argue, Haleigh allowed Cooper to lead her into a copse of trees. The daunting thought occurred that this was exactly how teenage girls ended up murdered in all those horror movies. Lured by the cute guy to find a secluded spot where they could get frisky, and then *bam*, out jumped the serial killer.

"Whoever these girls are, they're alive, right?"

"From saint to murderer," he said, navigating them along a stone pathway. "You really need to make up your mind about me."

"Just keep walking, smart-ass," she murmured. "And don't get any funny ideas."

Heaven knew she was having enough for the both of them.

Chapter 16

"I'm not sure if they're outside or not, but they make an appearance when I turn on the light." Cooper flipped two switches on the side of the shed and waited.

"You have to be kidding me," Haleigh said. "Is that a chicken coop?"

"Yes, ma'am."

"Are there chickens in it?"

"Nope," he teased. "Rhinos."

That earned him a smack on the arm. "Don't be a jerk. I can't believe you have chickens." When she noticed the sign over the door, she said, "Coop's Coop? Really?"

He gave a half shrug. "That's what it is."

As Haleigh inspected his latest project, Cooper took the opportunity to study her. In the moonlight, her hair glowed like braided reeds of wheat, while her lashes created tiny shadows on her cheeks. The face almost always etched with skepticism softened to resemble the girl who'd teased him over his cereal bowl and helped him pass geometry.

When they were kids, Haleigh had been fearless. The first to jump in the pool or flip on the trampoline. In their teen years, she'd pulled back. Preferred studying over skateboards. The library over loud parties on the river bank. Cooper couldn't help but believe the gutsy young girl remained buried in there somewhere. Based on the look that crossed her face as the girls popped out of the coop, his suspicions were confirmed.

"Oh my gosh," she said. "There they are. I haven't seen chickens up close like this since elementary school when they took us out to Silvestri's farm and called it a field trip."

"I loved those trips," Cooper said, remembering how Haleigh had shrieked as they chased the pigs. "You would have caught that piglet if the other one hadn't tripped you up."

Haleigh grinned. "I had the taste of mud in my mouth for a week." Wrapping her fingers around the chicken wire, she said, "I can't remember the last time I thought about those trips. Feels like a lifetime ago."

"A couple decades," he said. "Not so long."

"Leave it to you to put a positive spin on us getting twenty years older." Moving toward the entrance to the run, she said, "Can we go in?"

"Sure," he said. "I don't normally feed them this late, but you can throw down some scratch. First, I need to tell you a little about them, so you're prepared."

She stared at him as if he'd offered to explain why water is wet. "They're chickens, Cooper. What else is there to know?"

"The pecking order is very important," he pointed out.

"Is that supposed to be a pun?" she asked.

Cooper had half a notion to send her in uninformed and let her find out for herself. "Do you want to get closer or not?"

Haleigh sobered, but struggled to keep the smile from her face. "Yes. Of course. Teach me, old wise chicken-tamer."

"You'll thank me for this." Pointing through the chicken wire, he said, "You see that darker one there? That's Mabel. She rules the roost."

A snort escaped through her smirk. "You're doing that on purpose."

Ignoring her, he continued. "The other two with lighter feathers around their necks are Trixie and Dixie. They try to ruffle Mabel's feathers now and then, but she rules with an iron beak, so they pretty much stay in line."

"You really need to get out more," Haleigh drawled. "You've been cooped up way too much." She found her own joke hysterical, but Cooper kept a straight face. Barely. "So you're the only one who gets to play with puns?" she asked. "Fine. Where's this scratch stuff?"

"I'll get you a bucket." After retrieving the treat from behind the coop, he said, "Toss it on the ground in front of you and they'll come get it."

"I've got this," she said, a look of determination on her moonlit face. In a moment of sanity, she said, "You're coming in with me, right? In case they attack me."

"What am I supposed to do if they attack you?" he asked. He knew exactly what to do, but Haleigh didn't need to know that.

"They're your cockamamie birds, Cooper. I don't know. Yell and wave your arms."

"They're chickens, Haleigh, not grizzly bears."

"Whatever." As if sneaking up on a sleeping tiger, she tiptoed to the latched door. "Here we go."

Cooper let Haleigh enter before sliding in behind her. The girls were used to him coming in during the day, but a night visit was unusual. He wasn't sure how they'd react. "No sudden moves. Start scattering."

"Wouldn't scattering be a sudden move?" she asked, backing up against him as the chickens approached. "They don't look happy to see me."

"They always look like that." Though they didn't usually crowd him into a corner. "Toss the scratch already."

"I'm tossing," she said, throwing handfuls of corn and oats on the ground. "They're getting closer."

"You dropped the scratch at your feet," he reminded her. "I told you they'd come and get it."

Dropping the bucket to the ground, she said, "I don't want to do this anymore."

As he reached for the bucket, Mabel pecked his hand hard enough to draw blood. "Dammit," Cooper hollered. "Get over to the door."

The minute Haleigh stepped right, Mabel came off the ground like a raging demon bird. Cooper used his arm to protect Haleigh's face, careful not to swing at the hen, and prodded the panicking woman along until he could reach the latch. Trixie and Dixie raised a racket, as if cheering Mabel on, while Haleigh's screeching nearly drowned them out.

The old bird landed another bruising peck on Cooper's thigh before he swung Haleigh out and latched the door behind them. They stood face-to-face with Haleigh's back against the run, both struggling for breath, until an unexpected cackle split the night air. For a second, Cooper feared Mabel had gotten out during their escape, only to realize that the sound wasn't coming from the chickens at all.

It was coming from Haleigh.

Peals of laughter echoed through the trees as breathing turned to wheezing. When her forehead hit Cooper's chest, the scent of strawberries filled his senses, and he grasped the chicken wire as she pushed against him.

Being attacked by his chickens didn't strike Cooper as all that funny, but her snickering, punctuated by the occasional snort, proved contagious. Before he knew it, Cooper was chuckling right along with her.

"You're insane, you know that?" he said. "She could have taken your eye out."

Haleigh's hands flapped in the air. "We just got attacked by a freaking chicken," she said, before succumbing to the hilarity once more.

With dancing eyes, she added in a loud whisper, "I thought I was going to pee myself."

"That's attractive," he replied, enjoying the more carefree doctor smiling up at him. "Mabel probably would have taken that as a challenge."

She squealed at the comment. "I can see the headline now," she sputtered. "Woman's death suspected to be *fowl* play."

Cooper groaned. "I can't believe you went there."

"Oh, come on," she said, tugging on the front of his shirt. "That's funny and you know it."

Sliding the hair off her face, he said, "I like when you laugh. You should do it more often."

Her shoulders fell with a deep sigh. "I do feel better. Maybe laughter really is the best medicine."

"It isn't a cure-all, but it's a start." Cooper straightened to bring his body closer to hers. "I'm really glad you came tonight."

"I am too. But I don't think—"

"Shhh . . ." he said, dropping a finger over her glossy lips. "For once in your life, Haleigh Rae, don't think. Just feel."

When he leaned down, she brushed her nose against his. "Feeling isn't my forte."

As their breaths mingled, the tang of barbeque sauce mixed with hops and sweet tea. "Just follow my lead, darling."

The moment their lips met, Cooper felt as if he'd come home. He tugged at her bottom lip as she pressed against him, her hands sliding up his chest before shoving into his hair. Gripping her hips, he trailed gentle kisses down the column of her neck.

"How does that feel?" he asked, giving her earlobe a quick bite.

Haleigh nodded her head. "Good. Yeah." On the verge of panting, she mumbled, "Real good."

"Then let's make it even better." Cooper shifted Haleigh to the right until she stood flat against the shed. She protested at the break in contact, tugging hard on the collar of his flannel. To the unspoken plea, he said, "You've got it, doc," before covering her mouth with his. She took everything he offered, and gave double in return. Hot, wet, and demanding, Haleigh turned kissing into a combat sport, tasting, scratching, and grinding her way to total domination. But Cooper wasn't ready to admit defeat just yet.

Dipping his hands under her bottom, he jerked Haleigh's feet off the ground as he lifted her high enough to meet him nose to nose. Her eyes were molten whiskey in the glow of the floodlight, her lips red and inviting as she traced a thumb over his lower lip.

As if surprised by the revelation, she whispered, "This feels right."

He nodded as her legs tightened around his hips. "It's about time you saw the light," he said, leaning in to taste her again.

Cooper Ridgeway was one hell of a kisser. And damn sturdy, too. Haleigh had never been swept off her feet, literally, and enjoyed the experience immensely. Of course, the man doing the sweeping had something to do with that.

He tasted like a head rush and felt like a Mack truck. She could hold on to his broad shoulders all night, and considered doing just that. To think, she could have been taking this ride long before now.

As if trying to drive her crazy, Cooper kept slowing the tempo. Sliding from full throttle to idle with annoying control, and drawing her body tighter by the second. Desperate for skin, she tugged hard on the ends of his shirt and heard the satisfying ping of buttons popping. With the shirt open, she explored the hard body beneath the material, dragging a gratifying groan from Cooper's lips. The sound emanated from deep in his chest, sending dizzying vibrations through her fingertips.

"You're perfect," she said, tasting the salt at the base of his throat.

With a tattered breath, he said, "That's my line."

She dismissed the inference, as Cooper's perfection echoed inside and out. Haleigh moved through life in a pretty shell, but the ugliness was always there, close to the surface and clawing to get out.

In Cooper's arms, she didn't feel worthless or inadequate or disappointing, which made this exchange all the more dangerous. Haleigh could easily see herself replacing one demon-suppressant for another. Only drowning in Cooper would be way better than losing herself at the bottom of a bottle had ever been.

While that thought circled through her mind, Cooper's powerful hands drifted up her rib cage, setting tiny fires along her nerve endings. Haleigh clung to him, wanting more but not willing to sacrifice his heat to find a better location to carry on.

When his thumbs found her nipples through thin satin, her body kicked into another gear as she sucked on his tongue, desperate for more.

"What's going on back here?" a female voice spoke from the trees, followed by at least two gasps and an "Aw, shit." The expletive came from a man who proceeded to take charge, saying, "Everybody back to the party."

Cooper slammed his hands on the side of the building, presumably shielding Haleigh from the onlookers. As if he could protect her from the fallout of this colossal mistake.

This is not a mistake! screamed a voice in Haleigh's head. One she didn't recognize but wanted to believe.

With his forehead pressed to hers, Cooper said, "I need less nosy friends."

The joke broke the tension, and she couldn't help but laugh. "That first voice was Abby's, wasn't it?"

"Yep." Cooper lifted her to the ground as if setting down a priceless piece of crystal. "Afraid so. They must have heard the screaming with the chickens." Attempting to button his shirt, he looked down in confusion. "When did you do this?"

"Somewhere around the time you slid your tongue in my ear." Haleigh righted her clothes. "This should make for a fun ride home."

"Hey," he said, lifting her face with a finger beneath her chin. "We haven't done anything wrong."

She managed a halfhearted smile. "For once, I agree with you."

Dark brows shot up. "Seriously?"

Cupping his face with both hands, Haleigh rose up to her toes to drop a quick kiss on his lips and said, "Seriously." And then she gave a gentle tap with her left hand. "But that doesn't mean this is going to happen again." Knowing the jury was still out, she added, "Maybe."

"Oh, this will happen again," he said, confidence brimming. "That was too good not to repeat."

"Repeating behaviors that make me feel good has led me into more trouble than I can tell you," she said. "We're still the same mismatched people we were before . . ." Haleigh waved a hand in the air. "Before whatever that was."

"That," Cooper said, pulling her into his arms, "was chemistry. And it's been brewing for a long time."

"You're confusing chemistry with coffee," she corrected, settling against his body. "And we aren't the only variables in this equation. I made Abby a promise that I wouldn't hurt you."

His arms tightened. "Then don't."

As if anything in Haleigh's life was that easy.

Going for total honesty, she said, "If we follow the road less taken here, I can't make any guarantees."

Cooper acknowledged the confession with a nod. "Fair enough. But while we're putting our cards on the table, you need to know this. I want you. And I'm willing to step out on whatever crazy limb it takes to make you see that. Your good side and your bad. Whatever fatal flaw you think makes you less deserving than the rest of us. That's what I'm in for. So don't think I'm going to be easy to spook, because I'm not."

The speech took Haleigh by surprise. And touched a nerve. Her whole life had been a fight for acceptance and always coming up short. With Cooper, she didn't have to fight for anything.

Uncomfortable with the abrupt leap from hormone rush to something serious, she attempted to defuse the bomb he'd just dropped in her lap. "That's a big jump from one make-out session."

"We both know this thing between us didn't start with a chicken attack."

Haleigh couldn't resist the giggle. "If this works and we have kids someday, I'm totally telling them it started with a chicken attack."

Taking her hand, he led the way back to the stone path. "And I'm telling them that you ripped all the buttons off my shirt."

"Don't you dare," she ordered, poking him in the ribs. They walked the rest of the way in silence. At the entrance to the clearing, Haleigh tugged on Cooper's hand until he stopped and turned her way. "You know this is all just kidding around, right?"

By the look on his face, he didn't know any such thing. "If it makes you feel better, you can believe that. For now. But I meant every word I said back there."

A knot of apprehension tightened in Haleigh's chest. Cooper had essentially just handed over his heart on a silver platter. If there was ever a day she wanted *not* to screw something up, this was it.

"Duly noted," she said, trying to keep things light. Peeking through the branches, she braced herself. "Time to pay the piper, I guess."

"No one will say a word," Cooper assured her, dropping a hand to the small of her back. "And I'll handle it if they do."

As they stepped into the yard, Haleigh's eyes were locked on Cooper's face. The white knight was in full armor and ready to fight for her honor. Maybe having a hero by your side wasn't such a bad thing after all.

Chapter 17

To say that the drive home was tense was like saying a bonfire is kind of hot.

The moment that Cooper and Haleigh stepped out of the trees, the partygoers had fallen into a collective silence. Except for Jessi and Ian, who were still wrapped up in whatever fascinating conversation they'd been conducting for the last two hours. Though reluctant to leave her alone, Cooper had eventually agreed that there was no reason for Haleigh to accompany him into the house for a new shirt.

As if that wouldn't make the situation worse *at all*.

Within minutes, Abby had relayed her desire to leave. No one spoke on the way home, which afforded Haleigh much-needed time to think.

One week ago, she'd been sure that *nothing* would ever happen between her and Cooper. Even one day ago, Haleigh's intentions had been in the right place. As her best friend's brother and an incredibly upstanding guy with everything going for him, Cooper Ridgeway was without a doubt off-limits. *Verboten.* Absolutely no touchy.

And then she'd touched. And kissed. And felt not only beautiful and desired, but accepted and worthwhile. There were no ulterior motives with Cooper. No judgment and no impossible standards to meet. Bottom line? He liked her. He didn't want to use her or show her off. He just liked her, and that was a rarity in her world.

Did she deserve Cooper? Of course not. But Haleigh would give anything to feel like that again. Besides, who was to say that Cooper wasn't right about her? Maybe she wasn't irredeemable in the grand scheme of things. Haleigh had never sold drugs to kids. Never robbed a liquor store. Heck, she'd never so much as tapped a dog with her bumper. There had been that one raccoon on a late-night drive from Memphis a few years ago, but Haleigh was pretty sure the critter had survived.

The point was, maybe she didn't deserve him *right now*, but she could. Eventually. After all, if anyone could make her a better person, it was Cooper.

"I'm going to bed," Abby said the minute they walked into the house.

"What crawled up her butt?" Jessi asked as she lowered the car seat onto the couch to unbuckle Emma. "And what was up on the way home? I'm surprised the windshield didn't freeze over."

Haleigh debated whether or not to spill the dirty details. Since Jessi was likely to hear them eventually, better to take the opportunity to at least let her hear Haleigh's version first.

"When Cooper took me back to see his chickens—"

"Wait," Jessi stopped her. "Tell me that's a euphemism."

"You want to hear this or not?" Haleigh asked, her patience at an end.

"Fine," the teenager said, not bothering to hide the eye roll. "Go on."

Dropping into a chair, Haleigh pinched the bridge of her nose as she continued. "We went into the run to give the chickens some kind of treat, and they weren't very happy about the intrusion. One in particular scared the crap out of me, and I ended up screaming like an idiot."

"I didn't hear any screaming."

"You didn't hear anything beyond the sound of Ian's voice from the moment you wiggled your tail in his face."

"Excuse me," Jessi said. "Whatever put your panties in a twist had nothing to do with me."

Haleigh sighed. "You're right. That was uncalled for."

"Thank you. Now where does Abby come into the chicken story?"

"Unfortunately, she comes into it at the moment that Cooper and I were getting hot and heavy at the side of the coop. The partygoers came to see what the commotion was, and instead of finding our lifeless, chicken-pecked bodies, they stumbled upon something out of a barnyard porno movie."

Jessi sat down next to the car seat with a sleeping Emma on her shoulder. "First of all, don't ever use the words *barnyard* and *porno* in the same sentence again. Second, why would Abby be ticked about her brother and her best friend getting together? That's, like, the perfect scenario. Who better to get as a new sister than your best friend?"

The child made an excellent point. Abby's attitude didn't say much for their friendship. Not that Haleigh expected her to break into a happy dance, but would it hurt to give her oldest friend the benefit of the doubt?

Considering Haleigh's history, maybe so.

"One of the perks of being best friends since elementary school is that you know everything about each other. In our case, that's also a pitfall. I may look like I have my crap together, but Abby knows better."

Jessi snorted. "You think that's how you look?"

Really? The single mother was passing judgment?

"I could be sleeping right now," Haleigh pointed out.

"Come on," Jessi chimed. "You're a doctor, but you rent a bedroom from a friend. You work more than anyone I've ever met, you don't date, and I'd bet my Doc Martens that you haven't gotten laid in, like, forever."

"It's only been seven months," Haleigh defended. "And I rent that bedroom back there because between student loans, credit cards, and a car payment, plus my mother's mortgage and utilities, I don't have enough left over to get my own place." She hadn't meant to share so much. "Dammit, I don't need this."

The minute Haleigh popped out of her seat, Jessi said, "Doc, wait. I'm being a jerk." Haleigh stood where she was with her arms crossed. She could not take one more hit tonight. "Dude, I'm sorry. I didn't know all that."

"That's because none of it was your business."

"I know. Look, if anyone knows what it's like to get dumped on from every direction, it's me. I really am sorry."

The words sounded sincere. "It's fine. I guess it's good to know that I'm not fooling anyone."

"That's a heavy load you're carrying."

Haleigh snorted. "You don't know the half of it." As the weight of Abby's disapproval settled around her, the urge for a drink hit so hard she could feel the burn in her lungs. "I'm getting some coffee," she said, heading for the kitchen.

"Let me put Emma down and I'll sit with you."

"I appreciate that, but you don't have to stay up on my account."

"I want to," Jessi said, and with a half shrug, added, "I've never had a lot of female friends. Do you mind if I stay up for a while?"

"No," Haleigh said, wishing more than ever that she possessed the magic wand that would change this girl's life. "I don't mind at all. If you promise not to tell, I'll show you where to find the secret cookie stash."

"There's a secret cookie stash?" Jessi asked in awe, looking more like a little girl than a new mother.

"Put the baby to bed," Haleigh said. "I'll have the milk poured before you get back."

The too-cool teen reared her pop-punk head. "Milk and cookies are for kids," she said, as if saving her street cred required pointing this out. When Haleigh simply stared with a raised brow, Jessi caved. "Okay. I'll be right back."

⤫

"We need to talk," Abby said, as she stormed into his office without knocking.

Cooper was in the middle of a tire order, and, so as not to lose his place, he pressed a finger over the current line before looking up. "Sure, Abbs. No need to knock. Come on in."

"Was Saturday night the first time that happened?" she asked, ignoring his sarcasm.

Annoyed by her tone, he said, "Nope. I have cookouts all the time."

"This isn't funny."

"Do you see me laughing?"

Slamming her hands on the edge of his desk, his sister said, "You need to stay away from Haleigh Rae."

"Why is that?" Cooper asked. Having no intention of following his twin's dictates didn't mean he wasn't curious enough to hear her reasons.

Abby dropped into the metal chair behind her. "Just trust me on this."

"Try again," he said, underlining his spot on the order list before dropping the pencil and leaning back. "You don't get to make a demand like that and not back it up."

Tapping her purse strap on the arm of the chair, Abby fidgeted. "You don't know her."

Pointing out the obvious, Cooper said, "I've known Haleigh Rae as long as you have, remember? It's not as if we're strangers."

"I mean," she gritted through a clenched jaw, "you don't know her like *I* know her. She's made some serious mistakes."

"Who hasn't?"

"*Big* mistakes," Abby announced. "She isn't the kind of person you should be with."

Since Cooper was fairly certain that Haleigh never told Abby what happened the summer after graduation, he couldn't help but wonder what other mistakes his sister was talking about. And why she'd betray Haleigh's confidence to keep him away from her.

Crossing his arms, Cooper stared his sister down, waiting for her to elaborate. When she held silent, he said, "Haleigh Rae has repeatedly told me that she isn't a good person. That she's a mess and that I should steer clear."

Green eyes like his own went wide before Abby covered her surprise. "Good. I'm glad. But if that's true, why did I catch the two of you ripping each other's clothes off the other night?"

"Because I don't care what she says." Cooper leaned forward. "Regardless of what Haleigh's mother thinks, or what you seem to think, Haleigh is *not* a bad person. And nothing you say will change that. If she's made mistakes and she wants me to know about them, then she'll tell me. Whatever they are, I'm not going to condemn her for them."

Abby's jaw ticked. "She's been engaged."

Returning attention to the documents on his desk, he said, "So long as she isn't engaged right now, I don't see how that's a problem."

"Three times," Abby said, emphasizing each word. When Cooper met her eye, one dark brow rose. "She goes through men like most women go through shoes."

Curious, but still in Haleigh's corner, he said, "I'm pretty sure women go through more than three pairs of shoes in a week let alone in a decade. Now, like I said, so long as she isn't engaged or married to anyone right now, we don't have a problem." Assuming this statement would end the argument, he retrieved his pencil. "If there's nothing else . . ."

Abby ignored his dismissal, but didn't speak again for nearly a minute. Determined to wait her out, Cooper went on compiling the order, unaware how much he'd underestimated his sister's willingness to betray her best friend's secrets.

"There's one more thing," she said, her voice flat. "Haleigh Rae is an alcoholic." When Cooper's head shot up, she added, "Just like Daddy."

Setting the pencil down slowly, Cooper let the words sink in. Though the first part may have been a fact, the second was an outright lie.

"Unless Haleigh Rae is a mean drunk with a solid left hook, she isn't anything like Daddy. Why would you say something like that?"

"Is that what you want?" Abby asked, jolting out of the chair. "You want to be with someone who puts alcohol over the people they love?"

"I'll say it again. *Haleigh isn't Daddy.*" Cooper charged around the desk. "I don't know what's wrong with you, Abby. In fact, I'm not even sure who you are right now. Haleigh Rae has been your best friend for more than twenty years, and she deserves a hell of a lot better than for you to come barging in here trying to make her sound like a plague on humanity." She opened her mouth, but Cooper had heard enough. "You've said what you came to say, and now you can leave," he spat, pointing to the exit.

Eyes glaring, Abby followed the order, but Cooper stopped her at the door with a warning.

"If I hear one peep that you've repeated this crap to anyone else, you and I are done."

Abby reeled. "That's a horrible thing to say. I would never tell anyone else. I'm only telling you to protect you."

"Protect me from what?" he asked. "She's your oldest friend, Abby. She grew up in our house because she was treated like crap at her own."

Ripping off his hat, he shoved a hand through his hair. "Look," he said, reining in his temper. "So she isn't perfect. So what? Nobody is."

"This is different, Cooper. You remember what it was like. She called that night at Brubaker's a *slip*. How many slips did Daddy have?"

Crossing to his sister, Cooper tried to make her see reality. "Abby girl, it isn't the same. You know better than anyone that Haleigh Rae is *nothing* like him. Daddy was a failure who couldn't live with his own shortcomings. The bitterness made him mean, and the liquor made him meaner. Don't let what he was ruin things between you and Haleigh. Not after all these years."

Staring at the pocket of his T-shirt, she mumbled, "Do what you want, but when you get hurt, don't say I didn't warn you."

Without another word, his sister walked away, leaving a confused and disappointed Cooper behind her. Being angry with the world was one thing. Attempting to destroy her best friend's reputation, even if only to her brother, was another. Something else was going on.

Haleigh hadn't been drunk enough the night after Brubaker's to conjure flashbacks of their father's whiskey-fueled tirades. Unless she was drinking in her room every night, which Cooper doubted based solely on the number of hours she worked, Abby's attitude made no sense. If anything, she should have been even more on Haleigh's side.

Not long ago, their mother had suggested that Abby get some counseling, but she'd claimed to be fine. Based on what had just happened, Cooper intended to make the suggestion himself.

Chapter 18

So this was Cooper's garage.

For some odd reason, Haleigh hadn't expected it to be so . . . nice. The sign over the door read COOPER'S TOTAL AUTO CARE in big, bold letters, while a red neon sign in the window flashed the word OPEN. There were four gas pumps in front of the building, with the typical large canopy. Cars of varying shapes, sizes, and conditions filled nearly all open spaces down each side of the property, presumably waiting for attention. By the looks of things, Cooper would not run out of work anytime soon.

Though they'd exchanged a few flirtatious texts, she hadn't seen him since the cookout, and took the opportunity of a morning off to pay a surprise visit. In truth, the visit was as much a surprise to Haleigh as it would be to Cooper, and her purpose for coming was twofold.

After spending every free minute of the last few days reviewing Carrie's research, Haleigh really wanted to take on the shelter project. It wouldn't be easy, and finding a suitable facility would be the first hurdle. Or rather, the second after procuring the funding. She'd already put in a call to a friend back in Memphis who knew everything about writing grant proposals and would hopefully be willing to offer advice, if not direct assistance.

But Carrie had been right that the old band camp property offered the best option in the area short of building from scratch. There was no way they could construct an entirely new facility that would provide even half of the housing space available at the camp. Not without a major benefactor. With so much of the town focused on raising money for the theater, their best route was to apply for as many grants as possible and use the funds awarded to buy the existing property.

Of course, the grant applications would require a full proposal, including the property they intended to use and the cost involved in obtaining it. According to Carrie, the asking price on the camp was significantly higher than the value, considering the distance from town and the condition of the place. No one had used it in at least five years. Nothing could sit empty for five years and be move-in ready.

Therefore, they needed a personal connection. An in with the owners. That's where Cooper came into the picture. He knew everyone, so surely he'd know the proprietor of JW Property Management.

The second reason was, well, she just wanted to see him. Abby hadn't spoken to her since Saturday night, and as stupid as it sounded, Haleigh needed a friend. Not that Jessi hadn't been a cheerleader during this intense period of awkward silence, but she wasn't Cooper.

With sweaty palms, Haleigh climbed from her car and forced her feet to move. Propelled by sheer will and a hefty dollop of lust, she reached the entrance to the garage, which was two bays wide with both doors completely open, and realized she had no idea where to go. Wasn't there a rule about civilians walking into garages? As in, they shouldn't?

"Can I help you?" a voice behind her said.

Haleigh nearly jumped out of her knickers as she spun on her toes to face a bearded giant wearing glasses with the thickest lenses she'd ever seen. They made his blue eyes look like dinner plates and must have weighed a solid pound each.

"Um . . . I'm looking for Cooper. The guy in charge?"

Well of course the blind lumberjack would know that Cooper was the guy in charge. What a stupid thing to say.

Looking her up and down, the man in filthy overalls leaned slightly right and bellowed his boss's name. Haleigh resisted the urge to cover her ears. What he lacked in eyesight the man more than made up for in volume.

"What?" Cooper yelled from the bowels of the garage. She tried to locate the sound, but Haleigh couldn't see anything other than a Buick with a raised hood.

"There's someone here to see you!" yelled the least helpful man ever.

"Ask 'em what they want," echoed back.

"Oh, for crying out loud." Haleigh marched into the garage, ignoring the protests behind her, and found whom she believed to be Cooper tucked into the guts of the Buick from the waist up. "Is this how you greet all your customers?"

Cooper jerked, smacked his head on some big block-looking thing, and spewed an impressive stream of profanity before rising out of the machine. Rubbing his head, he looked as angry as Mabel the Charging Chicken until he realized who she was. Almost instantly, a goofy grin crossed his face. "Hey there, Hal." He stepped around the front of the car, looking intent on giving her a potentially greasy greeting.

"Whoa there, big boy," Haleigh said, holding up both hands to stop him. "Keep your nasty fluids to yourself."

Glancing down at his overalls, he said, "You deal with nastier fluids than this, remember?"

"We are not going to compare our dirty work. Maybe I should have called first."

"No," he assured her. "This is fine. Let me get out of these overalls and we can talk." Haleigh resisted the urge to help him undress. The smells of gasoline and exhaust fumes were great libido suppressants. "Come on into the office and I'll slip these off."

She followed him to a glass door at the end of the garage, but as they approached the exit, the burly greeter called to Cooper. "The sheriff's office is expecting that car fixed and ready by five today."

Grabbing a bottle of motor oil off the counter beside them, Cooper hurled it through the air. "Then you should stop standing around and get to work."

Haleigh couldn't decipher the mumbled response, but had no doubt it wasn't pleasant.

"Do all of your employees question you like that?" she asked.

"Don't mind Frankie. He's been here since Tanner owned the place. Cranky as a badger in a box, but he can fix a transmission with his eyes closed." Cooper nodded to the girl behind the tiny checkout counter before pointing Haleigh toward a back room that turned out to be a slightly cluttered but very professional-looking office. "Have we gotten a confirmation on that tire order?" he asked from the doorway.

"Ten minutes ago," the girl answered. "I put it on your desk."

"Thanks, Kelly."

Closing the door behind him, he unsnapped the grease-covered outfit and dragged it down his arms. The T-shirt he wore underneath clung to his abs like a second skin. Haleigh nearly swallowed her tongue. When he'd tugged the coveralls over both boots, he hung them on a hook on the back of the door without looking and walked her way.

"Now, let's try that hello again." In less than a second, Haleigh found herself pulled tight against Cooper's chest, staring up into eyes darkening to the shade of emeralds. "Hey, doc," he said. "I missed you."

And there was the kind word she needed. Feeling like a schoolgirl with her first crush, she gave her best smile in return. "How much did you miss me?" she flirted, unable to help herself.

"Telling you wouldn't really explain it," he quipped. "I'd better show you."

Cooper had turned kissing into an art form. He started slow and sweet, but didn't stay that way for long. Between his hands and his tongue and his powerful body, Haleigh couldn't decide which part of him she liked best. And then she remembered that there were parts she hadn't even explored yet. That thought turned her brain to mush.

When the backs of her thighs connected with something hard and unmoving, common sense kicked back in. She had a reason to be here that didn't involve getting naked on Cooper's desk, and though she wasn't eliminating that from the to-do list, they needed to conduct business first.

Breaking the kiss, she said, "We need to slow down here. I don't think we're at the sex-on-the-desktop phase yet."

"You're right," Cooper agreed, more readily than she liked. He could have protested at least a little. "When we do make love, it isn't going to be in this ratty old office."

The word *when* created a shiver of anticipation. Man, was she a goner.

"I really am happy to see you," he said.

"I noticed," she laughed. "I was afraid you'd be upset that I didn't call first."

Dropping a kiss on her nose, he said, "You never have to call first."

The gesture was beyond sappy, but Haleigh ate it up like a kitten with a bowl of warm milk. "That's nice to know." Not wanting to start out with *Hey, can I use your connections,* she said, "How has your day been?"

Cooper lost the playful expression. "I had another surprise visitor this morning."

"I hope you didn't give them the same greeting that I got," she said, unnerved by his sudden change in mood. "An unhappy customer?"

"An unhappy sister," he replied.

"Oh." Haleigh would have liked to come up with a better response, but she was too busy worrying about what might come next.

"Actually," he said, "it's good that you're here. This way we can clear the air right now."

"Clear the air?" Haleigh asked. "I didn't realize the air had gotten foggy." She should have known this was too good to be true.

Turning them around, Cooper propped on the edge of the desk and pulled her in between his legs. "Abby decided I should know certain things about you, about your history, before I got myself in too deep."

Pulling her hands from his, she said, "Did she, now?"

"I don't like the way she did it, but here's a chance to tell your side."

"So now I'm on trial?" This was not going to happen. Cooper was the one person who didn't treat her like a criminal, and now he wanted to play judge and jury while she pleaded her case? No thank you. "Let's just forget it."

"Hal, wait." Cooper caught her hand and refused to let go. "Why are you so mad?"

"You lied, Cooper. You said good or bad, and the minute you got the ugly truth, you spooked. Which is exactly what you said wouldn't happen."

"But I didn't—"

Too pissed to listen to anything he had to stay, Haleigh ripped her hand away and charged for the door.

∽

"Now wait a damn minute," Cooper said, catching Haleigh before she reached the door. "All I've done was offer you a chance to have your own say. If I'd believed Abby and told you to get lost the minute you walked in, then fine. You'd have every right to be pissed. But if you recall, I didn't do that."

"I shouldn't have to defend myself," she growled, madder than he'd ever seen her. "Not to you."

"Who said anything about defending yourself? Jesus, Hal. What do you think she told me? A few engagements and a drinking problem aren't exactly felony charges."

"Don't do that." Haleigh poked him in the chest. "Don't make light of who I am and pretend it doesn't bother you."

"And don't put words in my mouth," Cooper said, poking her in the arm. "If by *bother me* you mean am I annoyed by what you've been through? Yeah, I'm bothered. If you mean am I ticked that your best friend would betray you, yes, I'm bothered by that, too. But if you think for one minute that I'm going to run the other way because you've actively avoided marrying someone, or tried to drown yourself in a bottle once or twice, you're wrong."

Like a tire driven over a nail, Haleigh collapsed, her forehead dropping hard against his sternum. "I wish it was only once or twice."

"I admit," he said, rubbing her back, "I don't know what it's like to fight off the demons you carry around. But if you'll take some backup, I'm ready to fight with you."

Her head rolled from side to side. "No. No no no. *That's* why we shouldn't do this." A golden curl fell over her right eye as she looked up. "You shouldn't have to fight anything. You deserve an easy life with a simple girl. A girl who doesn't have enough skeletons in her closet to stock a Halloween store."

Tucking the wayward strand behind her ear, Cooper smiled. "Simple is overrated. And boring."

"Heartache and frustration are not an alternative to boring."

Seeing that she was determined to push him away, Cooper offered a compromise. "How about this. I take you to lunch. You tell me about these bozos you were smart enough not to marry, and if you want to talk about the other part, that's up to you. Either way, after I hear the ugly details, I'll decide if I'm in or out." He couldn't tell if she looked relieved or defeated, so he pulled her close and whispered, "But here's a spoiler. I'm in no matter what you tell me. Just so you know."

She didn't smile, but she came close. "Abby is so right. I do not deserve you."

"Then it's a good thing Abby doesn't get a vote." Cooper opened the door and allowed Haleigh to step through first. Before they reached the front counter, Ian stepped in from the garage. "Hey, cuz," Cooper said. "I'm taking Haleigh to lunch. You want me to bring you something back from Mamacita's?"

"Heck, yeah," Ian said. "Get me four tacos and an enchilada."

"Are you feeding a small army?" Haleigh asked.

"Nope," he said with a grin as he patted his stomach. "Just a growing boy."

"Boy is right," Cooper agreed. "Let Frankie know I'm leaving."

They didn't make it a step before Ian asked, "How's Jessi doing?"

Haleigh said, "She's good. Busy with the baby. Thankfully, Emma is starting to sleep longer and scream less."

"She didn't scream at all the night of the cookout. That's a good little baby," said Ian.

"What do you know about babies?" Cooper asked. Ian didn't have younger siblings, and he sure didn't have any kids of his own.

The youngster squirmed. "I know when one's being good," he defended. "Anyhow, Jessi gave me the number for Abby's place, since she doesn't have a cell phone, but I wasn't sure if I should call or not."

When Haleigh didn't answer right away, Cooper elbowed her. "That one's for you."

"Oh, right," she said. "I'd definitely say give her a call. Try around seven. That's when Emma's usually down for a good while."

Ian smiled and did his best impersonation of a bobblehead. "Great. Seven. I can do that." He continued to stand around, grinning like a lovesick fool. Cooper would have made fun of him, but he'd likely worn a similar expression in the last few days.

"Can we go now?" Cooper asked, gaining a confused look from his cousin. That earned the kid a flick in the forehead. "Get back to work, Ian. And don't forget to tell Frankie that I left."

"Dang," he said, rubbing his head. "You know I hate when you do that."

Haleigh passed through the outside door chuckling as Cooper yelled back, "Tell Frankie!"

Chapter 19

Haleigh had no idea where to start. They'd driven to the restaurant separately, since she'd need to go straight to the hospital from lunch. Luckily, the trip from the garage to the restaurant wasn't far enough for her to chicken out and ditch her lunch partner.

From the moment they met at the entrance, Cooper had been his typical gentleman self—opening doors, a hand on her back, letting her order first. Nothing in his behavior indicated the slightest concern over their impending conversation.

Once the waitress had taken their order and the drinks were on the table, she could prolong the inevitable no longer. As a habitually linear person, Haleigh opted to start at the beginning.

"I know you said I don't have to talk about the drinking."

"Up to you," Cooper said.

Shredding her straw wrapper, she said, "It's actually the easier part. Well," she corrected, "not easier, but without sharing that part, the rest won't make any sense."

Cooper nodded but held silent.

With a deep breath, she dove in. "As you know, the summer before college wasn't so great for me. But what you don't know is that the years before that weren't exactly peachy either. My parents didn't have the happiest marriage, and I became the pawn they used against each other. To this day, my mother blames me for every misery in her life." With a rueful grin, she added, "Needless to say, going off to college was like being liberated from a mental prison."

"I knew things weren't great at home," Cooper said, covering her hand with his. "Our bedroom walls were pretty thin. I heard a lot of what you told Abby."

"Then you really did know why I couldn't tell my mom about the pregnancy."

"That's not why I helped you, but yeah, I knew."

His empathy was all well and good, but they hadn't reached the tough part yet.

"Due to some financial arrangements Dad made before he was killed, coupled with the scholarships I'd earned, my first four years of college were paid for, including room and board. Unfortunately, Dad hadn't made arrangements that would take care of the family should something happen to him. This meant that I was set at college, but Mom was struggling back home. And, as was the pattern, I was to blame for that struggling.

"So there I was, embracing my newfound freedom, and every chance she got, Mom would call to remind me how hard things were at home. There was always some reason I needed to send money—new sports gear for my brother or new tires for the car. With each call, the guilt grew heavier and heavier until I just didn't want to feel it anymore. I remember the first time I got drunk at a party. It was like nothing could touch me. I was numb and it felt incredible. From that point on, that's how I coped. Until the beginning of junior year."

Haleigh ran her hands through her hair, struggling not to let the past get a grip on her psyche.

"You're good," Cooper said. "We can take a break."

If she took a break, Haleigh feared the rest would never come out. Shaking her head, she continued. "I was still functioning, but my grades started to suffer. There were mornings when I woke up and huge chunks of the night before were missing from my memory. I didn't know who I'd been with or what I'd done. And then a girl in my sorority fell out a window during a party in our house. Some said I was in the room with her at the time, but I didn't remember. I still don't."

She stared unseeing at her water glass, wishing it was vodka.

"Phoebe didn't survive to say whether I was there or not." Looking into Cooper's sympathetic eyes, she said, "I could have saved her. Or I could be the person who made her fall. Either way, I'll never know because I was too drunk to remember."

"That girl's death wasn't your fault," he assured her.

"You don't know that," she snapped. "No one does. But I live with the possibility every day."

"Listen to me. Torturing yourself isn't going to bring her back. Or give your mom a happier life. People make choices. If they don't like how things turn out, they can make new choices." Cooper laced his fingers with Haleigh's, tugging until she met his eyes. "If your mom was unhappy in her marriage, she had the power to get out, but she *chose* to stay. That is not on you, and you are not required to do penance for something you had no control over."

Sadly, Cooper's response wasn't anything Haleigh hadn't heard before. More than one therapist had tried to reprogram her faulty wiring. The problem was, no platitudes, no matter how rational, could change reality. If Haleigh had never been born, several lives might be better today. That was a fact, and the weight she carried.

"Up here," she said, tapping her temple, "I know that. And that's why the night at Brubaker's was the first time I've had a drink in four years. Mom just pushed the wrong button, and I let the craving win. I can't guarantee I'll never mess up again, but if I do, it won't be anytime soon. I hadn't lined up a counselor since returning to town, but I've rectified that and my first appointment is next month."

With unwavering faith, Cooper nodded. "I believe you."

He couldn't possibly know how much those words meant.

A waiter showed up with their food, sparing Haleigh the task of responding. Which was helpful, since she had no idea what to say.

"All right, folks, who gets the enchilada?" Cooper motioned for the dish and the waiter proceeded to set the other plate in front of Haleigh. "Everything look good? Can I get you all anything else?"

"This will do it, thanks." As the man walked away, Cooper tucked his napkin into his shirt collar. "Based on what you just told me, I'd say you turned out better than expected. Despite everything you've been through—"

"You mean everything I've done to myself."

"No," he stated. "You didn't choose the best coping mechanism, I won't argue with that, but the rest was inflicted by others. The fact that you still managed to become a successful doctor is damn impressive."

Shooting for full disclosure, Haleigh said, "You'd be surprised how many doctors are really screwed-up individuals."

He paused in the middle of slicing his food. "Really?"

"Well-intentioned and well-trained, but there's something about having the power to fix others when you can't fix yourself."

Cooper tilted his head and looked up. "That actually makes a lot of sense."

In mutual silence, they proceeded to eat their meals. Cooper had been right about the quesadilla, and Haleigh considered using the food to avoid the next part of her explanation. But a glance to her watch said she was running out of time. Her shift at the hospital started in less than forty minutes.

"I guess now we move on to the rest of my sins."

"Something tells me I'm not going to like this part," he said.

"Believe it or not, the engagements aren't nearly as complicated as what we've covered already."

"Good to know." Setting his silverware on each side of the plate, he dropped his hands beneath the table and said, "Let's hear it."

With a flutter in her gut, Haleigh reminded herself that the worst was over. Now she just had to figure out how *not* to sound like a fickle woman with commitment issues.

Cooper kept telling himself that nothing that had happened in Haleigh's past had anything to do with what might happen in their future, but he still needed to hear about these engagements. Being a good guy willing to give her the benefit of the doubt didn't mean he lacked self-preservation. Abby had been right in the fact that Cooper needed to know what he might be stepping into. Which sounded ridiculous considering they hadn't even been on an official date yet—a circumstance he planned to change real soon.

Twisting her fork in her guacamole, Haleigh said, "I'm not even sure the first engagement counts. It only lasted two weeks."

Stating a fact, he said, "That's two weeks longer than I've ever been engaged."

"This is not the time to remind me that you're perfect."

"As much as I'd like you to believe that, I'm far from perfect." In all fairness, Haleigh shouldn't be the only person dragging her history onto the lunch table. "The truth is that I can't imagine tying myself to one person for the rest of my life. Legally, anyway."

Haleigh stared unblinking. "You're going to have to repeat that because I'm sure I heard it wrong."

"You know the stats," Cooper said. "How many people get married believing they've found the perfect person only to find out down the road that they were wrong?" His mother had endured more than twenty years with a man who'd treated her and his kids like crap. That would not happen to him. "Getting married is like putting all your money on one roll of the dice in Vegas. I'd rather keep what I have and go about my business. So why did the first guy only last two weeks?"

"Oh, no. You don't get to drop a bomb like that and not follow it up. Are you saying you never want to have kids?"

This had always been the kink in his thinking. His mother had stayed for the sake of her children, and because in her generation, till death meant exactly that. Which meant Cooper knew from experience that staying only made things worse for the entire family.

"I'd love to have a couple munchkins, but that would make the whole thing imploding even worse." At her incredulous look, he said, "I'm not saying never, I would just have to be sure. Like, really, really sure."

Propping her chin on her hand, she said, "You want a guarantee that you'll live happily ever after."

Lifting his glass, Cooper said, "I'm cautious, not stupid. Nothing comes with a guarantee." After taking a drink he added, "Let me put it this way. If I buy a car, I know enough about that machine that, with a thorough inspection, I know what I'm getting. It's still a risk, as there's always a chance of a hidden problem, but I feel secure enough about my knowledge of the subject to commit to buy. You meet a woman you've never met and you're required to buy in, with a diamond, no less, practically sight-unseen. No manual. No clue what's lurking under the manifold. Put your money down and hope for the best." With a tap on the table, he said, "No, thank you."

With her hands on her cheeks, Haleigh said, "Who are you and what have you done with the guy I came in here with?"

"Still me, darling." Cooper picked up his fork. "And still single for a reason."

"Ha," she laughed. "And I thought *I* would sound like a commitment-phobe."

With a shake of his head, he said, "I'm not afraid to commit. I simply haven't found enough reason to do it." With a bite on the end of his fork, he pointed it Haleigh's way. "Now let's get back to why you're still single. Why three tries and no wedding?"

"That's easy. Danny was a musician. I was twenty and in full rebellion phase, looking for anything that would piss off my mother. We got engaged one week after meeting, and two weeks later I caught him with two women in the back of a club."

"What is it with women and musicians?" Cooper asked. "I've never gotten that."

"What is it with big boobs leaning over the hood of a muscle car?" she asked.

"You saw the calendar, huh?"

Haleigh nodded. "She was hard to miss."

Cooper surrendered. "We'll call that one a draw. Engagement number two."

"Phillip was a great guy. We met in recovery, and though it works for some, two addicts in one relationship was two too many for us."

"That does sound like a recipe for disaster." Growing up with one alcoholic parent had been enough to make Cooper's childhood miserable. He couldn't imagine growing up with two in the same household. Not that all drinkers were like his dad, obviously, but the possibilities were still more than he wanted to consider. "And lucky number three?"

"That would be Marcus." Haleigh's light tone vanished. "We broke up right before I moved back to Ardent Springs because Marcus didn't want to live in a dinky little town—his words. He's out in LA now, attempting to become the plastic surgeon to the stars."

The first two castoffs Cooper could handle. A recent breakup with a doctor knocked him off balance.

"Plastic surgeon?"

"A young, up-and-coming plastic surgeon is how Marcus Appleton refers to himself. He was the opposite of Danny in that instead of trying to tick Mom off, I went out of my way to find a man who would meet her standards." Lifting her glass before leaning back in her chair, Haleigh said, "And boy, was she pleased. Mother *loves* Marcus."

Not what he wanted to hear.

"Shouldn't that be *loved* him?"

"We broke up, but he's still alive." Haleigh chuckled. "She still calls him to *check in*, as she calls it, but I know she's trying to convince him to change his mind."

"And what if he does?" Cooper asked.

"No chance." Haleigh cut into a quesadilla. "Marcus will never agree to move here. He'd swallow his best scalpel before moving to the middle of nowhere."

"But would you take him back?"

"What?" She stopped mid cut. "Didn't you hear me? That's a moot point."

Not the right answer.

"It's a simple question, Haleigh Rae. Yes or no?"

As he waited for her response, a voice in Cooper's head taunted, *Maybe Abby was right.*

The look of insecurity in Cooper's eyes took Haleigh by surprise. Here was the guy who never got rattled. Who, by his own admission, preferred not to get too involved. Yet here he was, worried about her pompous, shallow ex-fiancé. She took the show of jealousy as a positive sign.

"Of all the things I've shared today, I never would have guessed that Marcus would cause the biggest issue."

Cooper's jaw twitched. "Still not an answer."

"Okay, big guy. Let me be clear. Marcus and I are done. In fact, I'm not only done with him, but guys like him."

"You mean doctors in general?" he asked. "Or young, up-and-coming plastic surgeons?"

"Whoa," she said. "Where is this coming from?"

Ripping the napkin from his collar, Cooper said, "I guess I'm trying to find out if I'm your version of downgrading. Or maybe you're back to rebelling and seeing me would be a great way to annoy your mom."

Was there another conversation going on that she wasn't privy to? Because nothing Cooper just said made any sense.

"By guys like him I meant jerks. Selfish, materialistic, pig-headed jerks who care more about their careers and social lives than about me. And guess what, Cooper? Those characteristics aren't limited to doctors. In fact, I know a mechanic who's doing an outstanding impersonation of a horse's ass right now."

The full boil on the other side of the table dropped to a simmer as Cooper said, "I can't compete with a doctor."

"Who said there was a competition?" She'd confessed to being an alcoholic who may have pushed a poor girl out a window and he latched onto a freaking occupation? "You're a better person than Marcus will ever be. Hell, than he even wants to be. You're definitely better than anything I deserve. If either of us should be reeling with insecurities, it's me. I'm the one who's screwed up, remember?"

"You aren't screwed up." Cooper tossed the napkin onto his plate. "You've got a few dings and dents, that's all."

Shaking her head, Haleigh said, "We're going to have to discuss this habit of comparing women to cars."

"You'd be surprised how much they have in common," he said with a half grin. "Did we just have our first fight?"

Amazed by how quickly the man went from angry to charming, she said, "I think we did."

Cooper chuckled. "That horse's ass bit was good."

"Well," Haleigh nodded, "when the saddle fits."

"Yeah, yeah. You've made your point." After waving for the check, he said, "Are you working Friday night?"

"I'm off at five thirty so long as no babies demand my attention, but I'm having dinner with my mother." The food soured in her stomach at the thought. "It's our first dinner since the night of my show-stopping performance at Brubaker's."

"Then it'll be the perfect night for what I have in mind."

His voice didn't carry a naughty tone, but Haleigh's brain still took the obvious route. "Am I going to like what you have in mind?"

Cooper waited until the waitress had dropped the check and walked off before answering. "You are." The grin was both panty-melting and mysterious. "Make sure you bring a pair of socks."

Pajamas she'd have understood. But socks? The guy wanted socks?

Sliding cash into the check folder, he said, "I can see that mind of yours churning a mile a minute." Rising, he pulled her out of her chair and dropped a quick kiss on her lips. "Just go with it." Pulling back, he added, "You never got around to why you came to see me in the first place."

The shelter. She'd forgotten all about it. "There's no rush. We can talk about it Friday."

"Are you sure?" Cooper asked as she walked in front of him to the door.

"I am. I have to get to work now anyway."

He walked her to her car, opening the door when she unlocked it from her key chain, and proceeded to kiss her senseless, seemingly indifferent to the fact that they were standing in a public parking lot.

When they finally came up for air, Cooper slid the windblown hair out of her eyes and said, "I've waited a long time to be able to do that."

Her brain only half working, she said, "A couple of weeks isn't all that long."

"No," he agreed. "But a couple of decades is."

Once again, she could not have heard him right. "Decades?" she said, swallowing hard.

Green eyes glowed down at her. Kind eyes. Patient eyes. She'd never known how patient.

"All this time—" she started, but Cooper pressed a hand over her mouth.

Echoing her words, he said, "We can talk about it Friday." As if she were a small child, he put her in the car, kissed her cheek, and closed the door.

As she watched him walk away, Haleigh repeated, "All this time."

Chapter 20

Cooper had believed that learning Haleigh's history wouldn't change how he felt. But he'd been wrong. After hearing the painful details of her past, he was more determined than ever to send her demons packing.

How to do that, he didn't have a clue. But being clueless had never stopped him before. And though he recognized the inherent insult in the thought, he couldn't deny the truth of it.

"Two weeks to go," Spencer said. "Are you ready for the final report?"

Though there would be a Ruby Restoration meeting the night before the fundraiser, the final summary, including the projected profit, was on the agenda for this evening.

"I'm ready," Cooper answered. "Buford has the handouts up front to pass out for review. By the time I get up there it'll be a matter of pointing out the bottom line numbers and projections. Shouldn't take long."

He hoped the entire meeting wouldn't take long. They were already getting a late start thanks to an untimely power outage at the restaurant earlier in the day. Though electricity had returned around five, the restaurant needed extra time for prep and didn't open again for service until nearly eight.

As Spencer and Cooper took their seats, Stallings called the meeting to order. The usual proceedings rolled along—approving the minutes from the last meeting, the reading of the treasurer's report, and the call for old business. Thankfully, no one wanted to rehash the car wash vs. movie night debate of the week before.

Harvey Brubaker, owner of the town grocery store and the dance hall that bore his name, had suggested a car wash fundraiser, which Jebediah rejected over water costs and possible flooding down Margin Street. Never mind that Margin Street had never flooded in the history of the town.

Jebediah had countered with a movie night, saying it made the most sense in relation to the theater and reminding folks why they were trying to save the building in the first place. Of course, the movie would run on weekend nights, cutting directly into Harvey's business at the club.

After a loud discussion that threatened to escalate into a brawl, both topics were tabled for a later date. Cooper thanked his lucky stars that date was not tonight.

Once Spencer updated the committee on the architectural plans and the next phase of the physical restoration, which could only progress at the rate at which monies flowed into the coffers, Cooper was called to the front. He summarized the handout passed around at the start of the meeting, explaining that though all available slots were not yet filled, registrations continued to come in daily and they were confident the lot would sell out before the event.

"I have a question about the For Sale section," Jebediah interrupted. Heaven forbid the man wait until questions had been invited. "According to this list, you have two of your own vehicles in that section."

"That's right," Cooper said. "What about it?"

"As the organizer, should you really be profiting from this event?"

"I'll only profit if the vehicles actually sell." Pointing to Buford, he added, "The committee is reimbursing the hardware store for the materials used for signage. And the local food vendors get to keep the money they make. What's the difference?"

"The difference is," Jebediah drawled, as if speaking to a child, "neither Buford nor the food vendors are organizing the rally. Also, how do we know other potential attendees, ones who would spend their dollars at several other local businesses, aren't being turned away because you've taken these spots?"

A hush fell over the room as Cooper struggled to check his temper. "As you'll see if you look at the handout, there are still three open spots in the For Sale section, which means no one is being turned away."

"That being said, don't you think it's a conflict of interest for you to cross the line from organizer to participant?" Winkle pressed.

Reaching his breaking point, Cooper said, "No, Mayor, I don't think it's a conflict of interest. Does anyone else?"

Twenty-three sets of eyes darted from face to face. If anyone agreed with the mayor, they kept their thoughts to themselves.

"I think that settles the issue." Buford smacked his gavel on the podium. "Thank you, Cooper, that should do it." Turning to the gathering, he asked, "Does anyone else have new business to discuss?" Not a hand went up. "Then this meeting is adjourned." Another smack of the gavel and the sound of scraping chairs filled the air.

"That was one hell of a comeback," Caleb said.

Lorelei hugged Cooper's arm. "I'd pay money for a picture of his face when no one backed him up."

Cooper shrugged, adrenaline still pumping. "He'll do anything to push back on this project." Glancing over his shoulder to see the mayor beat a hasty retreat, he added, "Winkle will get his comeuppance eventually. I just hope I'm there to see it." Cooper checked his watch. If he was going to reach Abby's house by nine, he needed to leave now. "I'll see y'all later."

"What?" Spencer asked. "You aren't coming to Brubaker's?"

"Nah," Cooper answered with a grin. "I've got a date."

Lorelei tucked her arm through Spencer's. "And who's the lucky girl?" she asked, knowing full well he meant Haleigh Rae.

"Just the prettiest girl in town," he said over his shoulder, laughing at the protests that echoed behind him.

In a ridiculous effort to start the night off on a positive note, Haleigh had made sure to change out of her scrubs, putting on a dress no less, and picked up an apple pie, her mother's favorite, on the way over. Instead of walking in as usual, she rang the doorbell and waited on the porch for her mother to answer. Allowing her mother to fulfill the hostess role, therefore being firmly in charge and somewhat bowed to, was sure to play in Haleigh's favor.

Or so she'd thought.

"Why did you ring the bell?" her mother said upon opening the door. No hello. No what do you have there? "I was finishing my makeup and you made me stop to open a door for which you have a key."

Strike one.

"I was showing respect that this is your home and not mine anymore," Haleigh answered in the most diplomatic and nonconfrontational tone she could manage. "I brought you a pie." She thrust the dessert forward after stepping into the foyer.

Ignoring the offering, her mother said, "Haleigh Rae, you grew up in this house. It will always be your home, and I'd prefer you not force me to open the door like some hired housekeeper."

Keeping her smile firmly in place, Haleigh thrust the treat forward again. "It's an apple pie."

"It's hard enough to keep my figure at this age without you bringing me pies."

Strike two.

"I can take home whatever we don't eat."

Taking the offering from her hands, she said, "If you planned to take it home, why did you bring it at all?"

And strike three. This had to be some kind of record.

The only thing that kept Haleigh from making an immediate exit was the knowledge that once this visit to hell ended, she'd spend the rest of the evening with Cooper. The man who now knew all of her grisly details and wanted her anyway. If that wasn't a bona fide miracle, Haleigh didn't know what was.

Not that she planned to tell her mother about this miracle. Then there would be judgment and insults and snobbery of epic proportions. None of which Haleigh wanted to deal with tonight.

She did, however, plan to share her other endeavor.

Once her mother had settled into her second glass of wine—she'd never felt the need to refrain while her daughter was around—Haleigh said, "I've been asked to take the lead on a new project just underway."

"Really?" her mother said with mild interest as she sliced her chicken cordon bleu courtesy of Lancelot's Restaurant. "Will it mean a promotion at the hospital?"

Slicing her own chicken, Haleigh replied, "This project isn't connected to the hospital."

Pausing mid-bite, her mom said, "I hope it won't interfere with your duties, or force you to cut back your hours."

Fewer hours would mean less pay, which would take money out of Meredith's pocket. So much for appealing to her mother's altruistic side.

"I don't plan to cut any hours at the hospital," she explained, not sure how she could work sixty-five hours a week once the shelter opened for operation, but that was months away, or more likely a year or more. "We're barely in the planning stages, but I'm excited about our prospects."

"You're being needlessly mysterious. Spit it out already."

Keeping her eyes on her plate, Haleigh said, "We're working to open a women's shelter."

As Haleigh shoved her green beans around her plate, her dinner partner held silent. Chancing a quick glance, she saw her mother staring while chewing intently, both her food and her daughter's announcement.

"Do you mean a place for homeless women?"

"Our purpose is to provide a safe place for women in harmful or dangerous situations."

"You mean women with abusive husbands?"

Haleigh nodded. "Exactly."

Her mother's next response served up the shock of the century. "This area could use a facility like that." As if she couldn't bear the taste of positivity on her tongue, she added, "So long as it doesn't steal focus from your career."

Feeling as if she'd received a blessing from the pope, Haleigh said, "Yes, ma'am," and proceeded to stuff three green beans in her mouth. If finally winning her mother's approval required giving up sleep, she considered it a small price to pay.

"You look happier than I expected," Cooper said after Haleigh offered a rather friendly greeting at the door. "Did the dinner with your mom go better than usual?"

"Way better," she said before waving a pair of socks in front of his nose. "Now why do I need these?"

"All will be revealed in due time," he replied, braving a look toward the living room. "Is Abby here?"

"She's working a twelve-hour shift until six in the morning. I'd have met you at the car otherwise."

He shook his head. "We aren't going to sneak around to appease my sister."

"No," Haleigh agreed, "but there's no need to stir the pot, either." Stepping back to the entrance to the living room, she said, "Jessi, we're heading out. Do you need anything?"

"I'm good," the teen said, never taking her eyes off the television as she kept Emma's bouncy chair moving with her foot. "See ya, Cooper."

"Bye, Jessi," he replied. On their way to the car, he said, "She seems content for a teenager spending a Friday night alone."

"Ah, but she won't be alone."

"I know she has Emma, but she isn't much of a talker."

Haleigh flashed a knowing smile. "I mean she'll have Ian. He should be here any minute, but I think he wanted to avoid running into you."

"Ian is coming here?" Cooper wasn't sure how he felt about this. "Does Abby know she's having a guy over?"

"No idea." Haleigh climbed into the passenger seat and reached over to lock her buckle.

Cooper considered the situation as he crossed to his side. The intention had been to let Jessi recover, and then send her back where she'd come from or on to her father. Another week had passed with no developments on the J.T. hunt. They were going to have to make a decision about what to do next, as Jessi couldn't live with Abby forever.

Whatever was decided, a budding relationship with Ian added one more layer to an already complicated problem.

"I'm not sure I like this," he said as his buckle clicked into place.

"Like what?"

"That," he said, nodding toward the house. "Jessi and Ian becoming an item."

"You sound like an overprotective father," she said with a husky laugh. "They aren't children. I think it's cute that she's found someone."

"Hal, we're going to have to tell her that this J.T. person doesn't exist. At that point, the girl needs to find an alternative to living with Abby, and Ian can't be that alternative."

"Why not?" she asked. "He's twenty-one. He has a good job and comes from a good family. Jessi is a good mom and determined to do her part to support herself and her little girl. I think they could have a shot."

She made it sound so simple. "They barely know each other. Ian can hardly take care of himself let alone a girl and her baby."

"You're selling your cousin short," she said. "He's here all the time and does great with Emma. Just because you're afraid of commitment doesn't mean everyone else is."

"I am not afraid of commitment," he corrected.

"Of course you aren't," she said with a pat on his arm. "Now," she said, turning in her seat. "Where are we going?"

Following her lead on the change of subject, he said, "You'll see when we get there."

"You really aren't going to tell me?" she said as he pulled onto the highway.

"Nope," he said. "But you'll see soon enough."

Refusing to give up, she said, "Are we going to eat? Because after having two pieces of apple pie at Mom's, I couldn't eat another bite."

Cooper checked his mirror. "This place serves food, but you don't have to eat if you don't want to."

They traveled half a mile in silence before Haleigh's hand drifted onto his thigh. The move was so unexpected, he revved the engine.

"You okay over there?" she asked, false innocence in her tone.

"I'm good." Cooper kept his eyes on the road, but every nerve in his body was focused on her touch. "Perfectly fine."

The tip of her finger drew circles on the inside of his thigh. "You sure you don't want to tell me?"

"You are devious," he said, taking her hand in his and holding it captive near his knee. "Keep that up and we'll be in a ditch before we get anywhere."

She shrugged. "It was worth a shot. I suppose blowing in your ear is out of the question?"

"Darling, you can blow on anything you want once I stop this truck."

"Hmmm . . ." she mumbled. "Good to know."

Resisting the urge to pull over in the next parking lot, Cooper couldn't help but grin at his good fortune. At this rate, he was in for one hell of a night.

Haleigh spotted the sign dead ahead and the truth dawned. Pink, gaudy, and covered in neon hearts, the place hadn't changed a bit in more than a decade.

"Lovers' Lanes?" she said in awe. "Are you kidding me?"

"Now you know why you needed the socks." Cooper hopped out and trotted around to Haleigh's side, while she continued to stare at the long flat building ahead.

Even the tilted pins painted on the front wall were the same.

As Cooper helped her down, she said, "I thought for sure this place would have been flattened and replaced with a strip mall by now."

"You should know better than that. Nothing changes in Ardent Springs. And we definitely don't do strip malls."

Looking up into Cooper's green eyes, she said, "I'm glad I came back."

His contented smile tugged at her heart. "So am I."

They lingered beside the truck, lost in their own little world of newfound happiness, until a car raced by, tossing gravel in its wake. Haleigh felt as if she'd been jerked from a dream.

"Are you ready for a butt-whupping?" he asked her.

Haleigh's competitive side sparked to life. "Bring it on, sweet cheeks." She dragged him toward the entrance. "And try not to cry when I shatter that giant ego of yours."

"You're talking to the league high-scorer three years in a row," he claimed.

Stopping short, Haleigh spun. "You bowl in a league?"

"Not for a couple years, but Spencer and I ruled these lanes. Bowlers feared us."

She tried to keep a straight face, but failed. "You're a total dork. A muscle-bound, tattooed dork."

With narrowed eyes, he said, "Is that good or bad?"

Tapping the dimple in his chin, she replied, "Oddly enough, I find it quite charming."

"Then dork it is," he said, sweeping her off her feet and charging toward the entrance.

Chapter 21

As they changed from the bowling shoes back to their own, Haleigh said, "The location is where you come in."

For more than an hour, his date had deployed every distraction tactic known to womankind, including actually blowing in Cooper's ear, which made it very hard to follow the current conversation. Especially while she was bent over to slip on her flats, giving him a clear view of the pink lace covering her perfect breasts.

"Are you listening?" she asked, snapping her fingers in front of his nose.

"The shelter," he said, forcing his eyes down to his boots. "Sounds good."

Haleigh laughed. "You didn't hear anything I said for the last two minutes."

"I'm a man, okay." Cooper finished tying his shoe and sat up. "The sight of perfect, lace-covered breasts shuts down ancillary systems like hearing and intelligent speech."

Gripping her shirt collar closed, she said, "Is this better?"

"*Better* isn't the word I'd use," he said with a grin, "but I can hear you now."

"Good. Carrie has found the perfect location, but the asking price is more than I think we'll be able to afford just starting out. I'm hoping, since you know everyone in town, that you might have an in with the owners. Do you know anything about JW Property Management?"

Based on her enthusiasm and the animation in her voice, Haleigh had found a passion and a purpose in spearheading this project. Which meant Cooper wanted nothing more than to help her in any way he could. Regrettably, she'd found the one situation in which he could be no help at all.

"I know about JW Properties, but I can't do you any favors there." He picked up both pairs of bowling shoes and motioned for her to step up in front of him.

"Oh, come on," she said, giving her best damsel in distress look. "One phone call. An introduction is all we need."

Dropping the shoes on the counter, Cooper said, "Thanks, Tony. See you next time."

"Don't be a stranger, Coop."

"So?" Haleigh said. "Please help."

Nodding to several locals on their way to the exit, Cooper said, "I'll explain once we're outside."

Confusion clouded her eyes, but Haleigh held her tongue until they reached the truck. "You're acting like this property company is run by the mob or something. What am I missing?"

Cooper sighed. If this was the only viable property, then he was about to impart some very bad news.

"JW Property Management is owned by the mayor."

"Mayor Winkle?"

"JW is Jebediah Winkle. He owns a couple of businesses, and the property company is one of them. The other is an estate auction business he picked up not long ago."

"Okay." Haleigh crossed her arms. "So as a fellow business owner, you must be friends."

"Not in the least." Cooper opened her door. "In fact, we don't like each other at all."

Haleigh allowed him to lift her onto the seat, then stared down in surprise. "That's crazy. Everyone loves you."

She made him sound like the town puppy. "Flattering, but no. In fact, Jebediah and I had a run-in earlier this evening at the Ruby meeting."

"The mayor is on the committee?"

Cooper nodded. "He is, but all he does is throw interference at anything that isn't his idea. He and I have butted heads for years, so when I agreed to plan the car rally fundraiser, he became the number one opponent of the event."

"What's wrong with a car rally? Not that I know what that is, but still."

"Hold on," Cooper said with a chuckle. "I'll explain in a second."

Closing her door, he crossed around the front of the truck and climbed in. Who might be able to help Haleigh deal with the mayor? No one came to mind.

As soon as he buckled his seat belt, she said, "So what exactly is a car rally fundraiser? And I'm sorry I snapped your head off the first time you mentioned it."

Her reference to the night they'd danced at Brubaker's reminded him how far they'd come in the last two weeks.

"You'd had a rough night, so don't worry about it," he said, running his fingers through a curl sitting across her shoulder. "The rally is pretty simple. A bunch of owners bring their classic cars to show off and talk shop with other enthusiasts. And those who wish they owned a classic car come to check out their dream machines. In some cases, they can even buy one. If all goes to plan, lots of folks come out, the theater raises a good chunk of change, and local businesses like hotels and restaurants benefit from the out-of-towners."

She twisted in her seat, sliding her fingers through his. "And how much does one of these dream machines cost?"

"That depends on the car. My '56 Ford pickup should pull about twenty grand, but others can go upwards of fifty thousand."

Haleigh's jaw landed in her lap. "Are you shittin' me?"

Cooper loved that her accent thickened the more she relaxed. "No, ma'am. I've seen some go for millions. Mostly Ferraris."

"I'm in the wrong business," she said with a whistle. "Wait. Did you say you have a truck worth twenty thousand dollars?"

"Yep," he said with pride. "I restored her over the winter so I could put her up for sale at the first rally."

With real interest, she said, "Can I see it?"

He hadn't planned anything beyond the bowling, assuming that's where the date would end, but he'd take any reason to keep her with him. That she actually wanted to see one of his cars was the second-best reason he could think of.

"Darling," he said, starting the engine, "it would be my pleasure."

Haleigh knew nothing about cars beyond what she needed to know to drive one. Like most people, she admired the look of a beautiful classic when one crossed her path, but beyond that, she was clueless.

She was also starting to feel rather clueless about Cooper.

Though she'd known him forever, Haleigh had never put much thought into what he did for a living. If memory served, Cooper started working on cars around the age of fourteen. The memory came clearly because that was the same year that her parents had insisted she abandon sports to focus all her energy on academics. Cooper had leapt into his passion against his father's wishes and Haleigh recalled being in awe of his open defiance, wishing she'd had the same courage.

From then on, Cooper had practically lived in a garage. Though his love for gears and motors drove him there, the desire to avoid his disapproving father had kept him there.

The Ridgeway patriarch had been a mean drunk who rarely had anything nice to say to either of his children, but especially not to Cooper. Abby had stood by Haleigh's side through the worst of her battle with alcohol, and she'd often wondered whether her friend's diligence had been because of her father or in spite of him. Like maybe saving Haleigh had been a way to make up for not being able to save the man who'd raised her.

Considering what Cooper had endured, and knowing that Haleigh carried the same affliction, it was a miracle he wanted anything to do with her.

"The truck is over in the garage," Cooper said, dragging Haleigh from her thoughts. She looked up to see that they'd arrived at his house while she'd been taking a walk down memory lane. Squeezing her hand, he said, "You'll have to walk past the coop, but I won't let Mabel get you."

She tried to make her laugh sound sincere, but it came out stiff and forced.

"What's wrong?" Cooper asked, sensing the growing tension in her body.

In a whisper, she said, "Your dad was an alcoholic and so am I. Why in the world would you want to be with me?"

Staring out the windshield, Cooper tapped the steering wheel but stayed quiet. He hesitated so long, Haleigh's nerves threatened to snap.

"I'm only going to say this once." He turned in his seat. "You are not like my father. You hear me? You're nothing like him, and you never will be. He was a coward and a failure and chose booze and misery over his family."

"He had a disease, Cooper. I have the same one. You can't refuse to see that."

"It isn't the disease that matters. It's how you deal with it. The fact that you beat it and make a choice every day not to reach for a bottle is proof that you're better than he ever was." Rubbing his thumb along her bottom lip, he added, "You were a good person before you took that first drink, Haleigh Rae. And you're still the same good person right now. I see it every time I look at you."

Grasping his wrist, she placed a kiss in his tender palm. "I'd give anything to see the girl that you describe staring back at me from the mirror."

"She's in there," he said, pressing his forehead to hers. "She's always been in there."

Wanting to believe him, Haleigh pressed closer as if the message might convey by osmosis. No matter what Cooper said, she couldn't change her past, but that past didn't have to define her future.

Pulling back, she took a deep breath. "Enough of that. This is supposed to be a date, not a therapy session. Now show me this fancy truck."

"Here she is," Cooper said as he lifted the garage door. The motion-activated light inside illuminated the space the minute the door started to move. He kept his eyes on Haleigh to catch her reaction.

"Holy blindness," Haleigh said, holding a hand in front of her eyes. "What the heck kind of wattage you got in here?"

"It's a one-hundred-fifty-watt floodlight. If anybody moves a thing in this garage, that baby lights up. It works as my visual security alarm—I can see it from my bedroom."

"Why not use a regular security system?"

"I'm afraid it would give the chickens a heart attack."

Haleigh shook her head. "Leave it to you to be more concerned about the chickens than having a prized car stolen." Once her eyes adjusted, she took in the truck in the middle of the space. With a puzzled expression, she said, "It's teal."

"Technically, it's Bahama Blue."

"Right," she agreed. "Teal." Her head tilted to the left as she said, "It's cute!"

Cooper groaned. "You don't call a 1956 F100 pickup truck *cute*."

"But it is," she argued. "All curves and circles. Look at the front. He looks like he's smiling."

"She," Cooper corrected.

With raised brows, Haleigh said, "Unless you specifically installed a vagina during the makeover process, I can call it any gender I want. And I say *he* is cute."

"You're killing me, woman." Cooper waved her forward. "It's called a restoration, not a makeover. Come closer and have a look." Reaching through the open driver's side window, he popped the hood. "I gave her a two-hundred-twenty-three-cubic-inch, six-cylinder engine. Runs like she came off the factory floor last week."

"I have no idea what that means, but it sounds very exciting."

"Let's just say there is serious power under the hood."

She leaned over the grille. "It's so clean. Like a giant toy instead of a real truck."

"It's both. A toy that will get noticed and make the guy who buys it feel like a badass going down the road."

"Ah, I get it," she said. "Boys and their toys."

"You buy expensive purses. We buy expensive toys."

"Wrong girl," Haleigh said, trailing a fingertip along the fender on her way to peer through the passenger door. "I can't afford cheap purses, let alone expensive ones. Why is the dashboard so plain?"

"Not much need for bells and whistles back in the fifties." Cooper preferred to talk about her other statement. "I don't want to pry into your business, but shouldn't you be able to buy any purse you want?"

He watched her shrug from where he leaned on the driver's side door. "Maybe someday. When my student loans are paid off. Or if my mother's house is ever paid for."

The first part made sense. Med school couldn't be cheap. But surely her mother wasn't still demanding money.

"Haleigh, tell me you aren't supporting your mother."

Moving along the truck, she answered, "Afraid so. Wow. The bottom of this truck bed looks like a hardwood floor."

Meeting her at the tailgate, Cooper forced her to look at him. "Is this why you live with Abby?"

"Trust me. I'd get my own place if I could afford it, but if Abby ever throws me out, the only place I have left to go is back home. And I'd rather stick a set of forceps up my nose than live with my mother."

Cooper didn't blame her, but the unquestioning acceptance of her fate bothered him.

"How much are we talking in student loans?"

Brown eyes stared up to the ceiling as she said, "I think I'm down to one hundred forty-five thousand."

"*Down* to that?" Not going to college hadn't been such a loss after all. "Haleigh, that's a mortgage."

"Oh no, my naive friend. A mortgage would have a better interest rate."

Quick calculations ran through Cooper's brain. If he sold the truck and the '55 Fairlane, he'd still only have a third of what she needed. But if he did the '57 Corvette up right, he could sell it for a hefty chunk of the balance. Unfortunately, that project was still months from completion.

"I have two cars up for sale in the rally. If they sell, we can put some of the profits toward the loans."

Staring as if he'd suggested they use Mabel as a basketball, she said, "You're serious, aren't you?"

"Dead serious." Haleigh's life-sucking mother was a problem Cooper couldn't do anything about. But he'd be damned if Haleigh would live in poverty on the generosity of others while he had the means to help. "I can't guarantee we'll get top dollar, but they should each pull a significant amount. And if they don't go this month, I'll put them in the next rally in June."

Stepping forward, Haleigh slid her arms around Cooper's neck. "You're an incredibly generous man, Cooper Daniel Ridgeway. Completely and thoroughly out of your mind, but generous nonetheless."

"Let me do this for you," he said, pulling her close. "Take the offer."

Haleigh slowly shook her head. "There's only one offer I'd take right now," she said, dropping a kiss on the dimple in his chin before rising onto her toes to nip his bottom lip between her teeth. "Do you know what that might be?"

Ideas were coming to him, but the blood rushed from his brain too fast for him to catch them. In lieu of answering, Cooper shook his head.

Rubbing her thigh between his, she pulled his head lower to whisper in his ear. "Offer to show me your bedroom, Cooper. I promise, I won't turn you down."

Chapter 22

When Cooper froze, Haleigh feared she'd crossed the line too early. This *was* their first date after all. Not that they hadn't been dancing around this for more than two weeks. And according to Cooper, he'd wanted her a lot longer than that.

"Or not," she said, trying to hide her embarrassment. "Forget I said that."

Lifting her chin, he asked, "Are you serious?"

"Well," she hedged. "I was, but since you aren't dragging me to the house, I'm guessing I've read this all wrong."

"Do you think I brought you here because I intended to get you into bed?"

"No," she answered. "Coming here was my idea, remember? Look," she said, stepping away, "I've ruined a really good night, so let's pretend the last couple minutes didn't happen and you can take me home."

"The last thing I want to do is take you home," he said, running a hand through his hair. "You just took me by surprise is all."

"Like I said, I screwed up." Mortification threatened to choke her. "You aren't there yet. That's fine. Really. We have plenty of time." Unable to look Cooper in the eye, Haleigh bolted for the driveway.

She'd nearly reached the entrance to the garage when he caught up to her.

"Hal, I'm there," he said, stepping in front of her. "I'm all the way there. Hell, I've imagined *there* for longer than I'm willing to admit." Taking her hand, he grinned like a guy who'd just been offered his dream machine. "And if you'd like to come up to my bedroom, we can make a good night even better."

The look on his face banished her insecurities, while the warmth of his hand reignited the spark she thought she'd smothered. Feeling oddly bashful, she nodded. "I'd like that very much."

They crossed the yard in silence, exchanging heated glances filled with longing and anticipation. By the time they stepped through the back door into the kitchen, Haleigh felt like a teenager sneaking off to have sex for the first time.

Though this felt nothing like the first time had. No doubt or fear. No feeling pressured or guilty. Tonight was about enjoying a man who believed her to be truly beautiful, inside and out. And maybe by morning, she might believe a little bit, too.

By the glow of the stove light, they crossed the kitchen still hand in hand and Cooper led Haleigh up a creaking wooden staircase to a spacious room at the top. The bedroom ran the length of the house and featured a window at each end, one presumably looking over the front porch, and the large one to her right providing a view of the back of the property. From her vantage point, she could see the garage they'd just visited, as well as the scene of their first kiss illuminated by the light of the moon.

"When I bought the place, this second floor wasn't finished," Cooper said, walking her to the window. "I turned it into a master bedroom and had the large windows installed so I could see out over the property."

"You did the work?" she asked, wondering if there was anything the man couldn't do. The space was simple, but well-furnished in a sleek, masculine style, with hints of country charm.

"I hired out stuff like plumbing and electrical, but with help from Spencer and Ian, we knocked this out over a few weeks' time." With a gleam in his eyes, he tugged her toward the monstrosity in the center of the room. "The bed is really comfortable."

"Is it now?" she asked with a smirk. "I should try it myself to be sure."

"Yes," he said, dropping onto the mattress. "Yes, you should."

Strong hands dug into her hips as Haleigh grasped powerful shoulders and closed the space between them. Her clothes felt restrictive as she straddled his lap, impatient to feel him against her. Cooper's eyes darkened as he stared into hers, and nothing in the world mattered in that moment but the man beneath her and what they were about to do.

Sliding a hand behind her neck, Cooper took her mouth in a kiss filled with fire and possession, longing and raw desire. Her hands tangled in his hair, and with every lick and suck Haleigh lost a little more control.

When they came up for air, her hands dropped to the buttons on his shirt. "This needs to come off," she panted. "I need to touch you."

"Whatever you want, baby," he said, holding her in place while she opened his shirt. "I'm all yours."

God, that sounded good. Haleigh would take Cooper over a pile of money any day. As soon as the last button surrendered, she slid her hands along his broad shoulders, dragging the shirt over perfectly defined biceps to trap his arms against his sides. "You're so gorgeous," she breathed, unable to keep the awe from her voice.

This was what a body was meant to be. Every muscle primed and sculpted. Every inch of skin taut and firm, made for a woman's touch. She explored each dip and curve, aroused by his heat and the way his body responded beneath her touch. A quick flinch or jolt that said he liked what she was doing.

"I need to touch you, too," he said, the words rough with need.

"Not yet," she replied, trailing her tongue down his throat—the taste of salt and man a heady combination. "I've had dreams about this body." Her teeth grazed his collarbone. "Vivid dreams. Lucky for me, the real thing is even better."

Straining against the shirt, he rasped, "You're driving me crazy."

"That is the idea," she said, tracing the outline of his lips. "I want to make you cry out my name."

Reaching behind him, Cooper ripped the shirt off the rest of the way and drove his hands into her hair.

"Is that a challenge?" he asked, nipping her earlobe. "Because I definitely want to make you scream."

Dropping her jacket to the floor, Haleigh offered a seductive glare. "I'm looking forward to it."

Her shirt joined the jacket on the floor with little effort, revealing the strips of pink lace he'd only glimpsed earlier in the evening. Cooper fought the urge to rush. The fear that he was dreaming added an urgency to taste and touch as much as possible before he woke alone and dazed.

But this wasn't a dream. And he definitely wasn't alone.

With reverence, Cooper ran his unworthy hands up slender arms, over pale shoulders, and into moonlit waves of gold. "So soft," he mumbled, leaning forward to drop a kiss at the base of her neck. Before he could taste her lips again, Haleigh reached down between them to undo the button on his jeans.

"I need more," she said, backing off his lap to stand before him. "I need it all off."

Happy to oblige, Cooper untied his boots in record time and kicked them off to the side. He would have stood to drop the jeans, but Haleigh had other ideas. With one finger on his chest, she shoved him down to the bed.

"Allow me," she said, and Cooper lifted enough for her to drag the denim over his hips. Skipping the extra steps, she removed his boxer briefs and socks along with the pants. "I am one lucky girl," she said, admiring him with her eyes. He grew harder under her gaze. "Very lucky."

Cooper would have returned the compliment, but the ability to speak fled when her hands trailed up his thighs. When she blew across the tip of his dick, his brain ceased functioning altogether.

"Time to taste," she whispered, leaning over him. His body became a six-foot-four-inch tension rod as anticipation rocketed through him. The second her lips closed around him, he nearly imploded from the impact.

Haleigh sucked and teased, stopping a second before explosion to trail her tongue down his shaft. While working her way back up, she gripped him tight, massaging with her thumb, and licked his cum from the tip. Cooper's lungs burned for air as he gasped and bucked, near death and ready for the final release.

Seemingly finished with the warm-up, Haleigh took him deep, cupping his balls as the pace increased. A growl escaped as he struggled to hold on, the pressure building higher with each lick and suck. Within seconds, Cooper lost control, yelling her name as his hands shoved into her hair, his body bucking wildly as sensations shot through his extremities. Body burning, his muscles twitched, and his brain floated somewhere in the clouds.

As if he'd run a marathon with an engine block chained to his waist, Cooper panted, riding the adrenaline high sluicing through his blood. He'd never imagined he could feel this good.

"You're awesome," he said when he could once again form words.

Dropping hot, wet kisses across his abs, Haleigh worked her way up his body. "And you're a mouthful," she said, straddling his torso. With a lick of her lips, she added, "Not that I'm complaining."

"Does that mean I pass inspection?" he asked, toying with one pink bra strap.

Rubbing against him, she flashed the smile of a woman with plans. "I should really take a full ride before passing judgment."

"Then by all means, darling," he said, tipping the strap off her shoulder, "let me show you what I can do."

Haleigh gasped when he kissed her nipple through the lace of her bra. As her body focused on that one hardening peak, a moan echoed from deep in her chest. When his tongue dipped behind the material, she arched against him.

"So hot," he murmured against her sensitive flesh. "So beautiful."

Cooper unclasped her bra with one hand as he rose to a sitting position, never breaking contact with her breast. Haleigh wrapped her arms around his neck, reeling in sensations. Heat pooled between her legs and her movements grew frantic.

"Slow down, darling," he drawled, taking her face in his hands. "We've got all night."

Her mind rebelled as he pushed her feet to the floor and she dug her nails into his shoulders.

Undoing the button on her pants, he said, "It's my turn to look at you."

Modesty temporarily smothered desire as Haleigh feared what Cooper would think of her. She'd been running on coffee and little else for so long, her body had devolved into a series of hard angles and sharp edges, lacking the curves that most men preferred.

"Maybe we should close the curtains," she said, crossing her arms over her chest. The moonlight looked beautiful on Cooper, but would have a lesser effect on her pale skin.

Sitting on the edge of the bed, he held her eyes captive as he pulled her arms gently to her sides. "You're beautiful in every way, Haleigh Rae. Sexy and delicate," he said, running a finger down her cleavage. "Elegant and graceful." Callused hands cupped her breasts as his thumbs grazed her nipples, making her shiver with need. "Let me show you." Sliding his fingers behind her waistband, he kept his eyes locked on hers. "Let me see you."

With a nod, Haleigh braced her hands on his shoulders as he slid the cotton down her legs and over each foot. When the garment had been tossed to the side, he placed a kiss inches below her navel, along the elastic band of her pink lace panties.

Glancing up with a seductive smile, he said, "This is by far the best present I've ever unwrapped."

"It's all for you," she said, words she'd never spoken to any man before. "I'm all yours, Cooper."

"I've waited a lifetime to hear that."

Passion flared between them like gasoline thrown on a fire. Cooper pulled Haleigh onto the bed to cover her body with his. She'd known skin to skin would be a heady rush, but the power of the connection threatened to overload her system. His mouth worshiped her breasts as his knee pressed hard between her legs.

She ground against him as the pressure built, moaning breathlessly for more. When his talented tongue traced down her stomach, Haleigh grasped the dark blankets in a death grip as her body arched up of its own volition.

Cooper kissed her clit through the narrow strip of satin, and Haleigh sighed, "Oh God, do that again."

Answering the plea, he kissed her harder as his hands grasped the sides of the panties. When Haleigh lifted herself again, the underwear went flying, and so did she.

Her knees drew up as Cooper settled between her legs. Firm hands latched onto her cheeks and lifted her for better access. When his tongue dove inside, she pulled hard on the blankets as her head thrashed from side to side. The tremors started at her core and vibrated through her body. Haleigh feared she couldn't take any more when first one finger and then another pressed deep as his mouth closed over her clit, his tongue drawing circles that sent her racing over the finish line.

Not only did Haleigh scream his name, she repeated it over and over as the waves hit one after another. Cooper stayed with her through them all, sending her soaring beyond anything she'd ever experienced. Her body shook with the force of the orgasm, and she would have sworn the zing reached the ends of her hair.

With tingling teeth, she panted for breath as her body relaxed into a puddle of sheer bliss.

As if he hadn't just tried to kill her, Cooper kissed his way up her body to nestle against her, and with a leg thrown over hers, he said, "Not bad to get us started."

Haleigh tried to laugh, but a strained croak escaped instead. "Pretty sure my vital signs say that was more than getting started. If what's to come is better than that, I may not make it through the night."

"You can't give up now," he said, nuzzling her ear. "We haven't gotten to the best part."

Arousal sparked anew. "You've set the bar pretty high if you plan to top that," she said, wrapping her hand around the appendage currently poking her in the hip. His breathing thinned as she worked him up and down. "But I'm willing to let you try."

Moving fast for a man his size, Cooper shifted her beneath him, holding most of his weight on his elbows as his pulsing heat pressed against her core.

"Trust me," he drawled. "You won't be disappointed."

Eyes the color of aged whiskey looked up with anticipation as the smile softened from flirtation to open invitation.

Pressing an index finger against his lips, she said, "You could never disappoint me, Cooper. Ever."

Unable to find the words to respond, he answered with actions. Cupping her breast, he worshiped her nipple until she arched in offering, moaning in satisfaction. Slick and hot, her body responded to every lick and tug, pinch and bite, until Cooper was certain she'd reached the edge. He pulled back and received a cry of protest.

"Don't stop. Please, don't stop."

"There's no need to rush," he said, transitioning to the other breast and repeating the process.

The moans grew louder and her nails dug into his back. When her knees came up to cradle him between her thighs, Cooper teased her entrance, testing the limits of his control. Taking her mouth, his tongue drove deep and Haleigh demanded more, wrapping her arms around his neck and bucking against him.

"I need to be inside you," he said, reaching for the nightstand. "I can't wait."

"Yes," she purred, her fingers digging into his ass. "Now. Right now."

Ripping the condom open with his teeth, he rolled to the side to sheathe himself and then pulled her with him, giving her the top position. With a gasp, she braced her hands against his chest and lowered her hips, taking him in until they were fully joined.

"God, that feels good," he growled, unable to resist driving up hard against her.

Haleigh sighed in agreement, taking each thrust deeper. Setting a steady rhythm, her body bowed forward while damp curls danced across her breasts. Cooper cupped her breasts with both hands. She leaned into his touch, her skin flushed with arousal.

"So close," she panted, throwing her head back.

As her hands locked on his thighs, Cooper slid a hand down between them to rub his thumb against her clit. Within seconds, Haleigh tensed as she hit the peak, clenching tight around him and sending Cooper flying with her. They trembled together until Haleigh collapsed on his chest, golden locks draping his shoulders.

Silent and struggling to catch his breath, Cooper held tight to the woman sprawled on top of him. If he never saw the light of day again, he'd had one night of perfection.

Chapter 23

"You better not be sleeping," Haleigh mumbled against Cooper's chest. She'd have looked up to check on his state of consciousness, but every muscle in her body remained useless. For all she knew, she'd dissolved into a puddle on the bed.

"Mmmm . . ." Cooper hummed, the vibration stirring her weakened limbs. "I was thinking about it."

Resting her chin on his sternum, she tweaked one of his nipples. "Then I hope it's only a cat nap to recharge, because we definitely need to do that again."

His bark of laughter threatened to dislodge Haleigh, but she held on, averse to surrendering her cozy position.

"Now who is trying to kill who?"

"I think it should be whom."

"Thank you, Mrs. Featherstone," he replied, referring to their former English teacher. "Either way, you're going to be the death of me."

Twirling a finger through the fine hair on his pecs, she said, "At least we'll go together."

Pulling her up his body until they were face-to-face, Cooper lifted Haleigh's hair out of her eyes and said, "If that's the case, then I'll die a happy man. How about you?"

Haleigh struggled to put her feelings into words. To say she was happy would be the understatement of her life. Cooper did more than make her happy, he made her feel cherished and protected, lighthearted and optimistic. He fed her spirit and drove away the voices of doubt and denigration. Most of all, he made her feel wanted. Not for what she could do, but for who she was.

Cooper was the first person in her life who had glimpsed all her dark corners, and found the light even she didn't believe was there. A voice in the back of her mind pointed out that all of those feelings could be summed up in one word. A word that scared Haleigh to the tips of her toes.

"Yes," she said lamely. "I'd definitely go with a smile on my face."

As he ran his fingers through her hair, one corner of his mouth curled up in a sensual grin. "Does that mean you found the main event acceptable?"

"That means," she said, pausing for a mind-melting kiss that ended with them both breathless and aroused, "I liked it so much, I demand an encore performance."

Powerful hands locked on her bottom as he ground against her. "I do aim to please," he said, before rolling to pin her beneath him. When her head settled on the pillow, he grew serious, his green eyes locked intently on hers. "I can make you happy, Haleigh Rae. Just give me the chance."

Thankful for the fading light, Haleigh ignored the tear that rolled down her temple. "I'm not going anywhere," she said, her voice heavy with emotion.

"That's all I needed to hear," he said, before proceeding to make Haleigh happy enough to scream his name many more times.

By Tuesday morning, Cooper still couldn't believe the turn his life had taken. Haleigh Rae had spent every night since Friday sleeping beside him until just before dawn, when she raced home to arrive before Abby pulled in from work. He'd argued that they were adults and Haleigh shouldn't have to hit some early-morning curfew to placate his sister, but their friendship meant a lot to Haleigh, and she hoped that Abby's feelings would change before she and Cooper revealed how far they'd taken their relationship.

Of course, the fact that he was *in* a relationship at all with Haleigh still blew Cooper's mind.

"It's good to see that you aren't dead," Spencer said as he stepped up to the car that Cooper was working on. "I don't suppose you've checked your messages lately?"

Between keeping up with repair jobs and spending all his free time with Haleigh, Cooper hadn't been paying much attention to his phone.

"By your tone, I'm guessing I missed something?"

"Lorelei had a question about a vendor for the fundraiser. She needed you to provide the answer."

"What's the question?" he said, tugging a stained rag from his back pocket to wipe his hands.

Spencer shook his head. "Too late. When she couldn't give them an answer yesterday, they backed out. That means we're down one food truck, thanks to you."

Where the hell was the dickish attitude coming from?

"I don't appreciate your tone," Cooper said, stepping away from the car. "I didn't ignore the message on purpose, so don't give me shit because your girlfriend is annoyed."

"This isn't about my girlfriend," Spencer hissed. "This is about you shirking your responsibility because Haleigh Rae Mitchner is finally giving you the time of day."

"Look," Cooper said, widening his stance. "Missing one phone call isn't a criminal offense. So we're down one truck. We still have two others."

"Based on the projected turnout, we were already stretching it thin with three."

"And that projected turnout is only happening because I've busted my ass for months to *make* it happen." Cooper would be damned if he'd let anyone dismiss the work he'd put into this fundraiser. Not even Spencer. "I didn't harass you during football season when you went trailing after Lorelei, shopping down in Nashville, instead of watching the games like we always have. And I've never said a word about her tagging along on pool nights, or insisting we include her and Snow on poker night. But now that I have someone, you're going to give *me* shit?" Shoving the rag into his pocket, he said, "I don't think so."

"We have less than two weeks to go," Spencer said, undeterred by Cooper's speech. "You want to blow us off after that, go ahead. But until then, answer your goddamn messages." Before he turned to leave, Spencer landed a parting shot. "And if you don't want my fiancée around, find yourself a new friend."

"Dammit," Cooper yelled. "Spencer, wait."

His oldest friend didn't so much as slow down. Knowing they'd both crossed a line, Cooper charged out of the garage.

"I said wait up." Cooper reached the silver Dodge before the shorter man could open his door. "Since when is it such a hassle for me to have a life?" he asked, blocking the vehicle.

"You can have whatever life you want, Cooper. Now get the hell out of my way."

"We both know that I can kick your ass," he answered. "And we both know that I won't do it, so back up and listen. When you got back together with Lorelei, I was happy for you. I could have told you that you were being an idiot and might get your ass handed to you, but I didn't. Because that's not what friends do."

"Your support is overwhelming. What's your point?"

"It's my turn, man. Haleigh is my Lorelei. She's the one, and I'm not going to apologize for spending as much time with her as I can." Pointing at his friend, Cooper added, "You, of all people, should understand that."

Spencer continued to fume before shaking his head. "This just isn't you, Coop. You don't drop stuff like this."

"This *is* me," Cooper defended. "It's just me with a new priority. But I'm as committed to this rally as ever. I'll find another vendor, okay?"

Relaxing his stance, Spencer said, "I don't know how you plan to do that with such short notice, but if you do pull off a miracle, let Lor know so she can keep everything on the food side straight."

"Will do," Cooper said, stepping to the side.

After opening the door, Spencer hesitated before climbing in. "Do you really think Haleigh Rae is the one for you?" he asked.

Considering that Spencer knew better than anyone how long Cooper had wanted this, the question took him by surprise.

"I do," he answered. "I always have."

"Does she feel the same about you?"

They'd only been together for four nights, and no one had thrown around the L-word yet, but the way Haleigh responded, the way she gave as much as he did, made Cooper confident that she'd get there. Eventually. Considering the alternative made him want to punch a hole in Spencer's truck.

"She hasn't said as much, but I think we're heading in the same direction."

Stepping into the driver's seat, Spencer said, "I hope you're right, buddy. But if you hit a snag, you've got friends, okay?"

"No snags in sight," Cooper said, more for his own benefit than Spencer's. "But that's good to know."

⌒◡⌒

For all intents and purposes, Haleigh should have been a walking zombie considering how little sleep she'd had in the last few days. Instead, she'd never felt so awake in her life.

Each night, they talked about their day while making small meals in Cooper's kitchen. Another benefit from the high-energy sex was a return of Haleigh's appetite, and her new lover was more than happy to feed her, body and soul. Never much of a domestic goddess, she'd been surprised to feel so comfortable in Cooper's kitchen. She made sandwiches while he mixed sweet tea. Or he flipped the grilled cheese while Haleigh stirred the tomato soup.

What they were doing didn't seem to matter as much as that they were doing it together. And heaven help her, Haleigh wanted to keep doing everything with Cooper for a very long time.

Not that she'd admitted as much, at least not aloud. To say Cooper had gotten a head start on this relationship was like saying the sun was kind of far away. For Haleigh, this was all brand-new. Shiny and bright and possibly misleading. What did she know about healthy relationships? She still didn't even like herself all that much, though the more Cooper preached of her awesomeness, the more she grew to believe him.

That fact was, each day she spent with him, the happier she got. And the happier she got, the greater the fear of messing up.

"You just couldn't stay away from him, could you?" asked a voice behind her.

Haleigh jumped, splashing coffee onto her hand. "Hot hot hot," she said, shaking the steaming liquid off her skin. "Warn a girl before you scare her half to death, Abby," Haleigh mumbled as she reached for a napkin.

Since Abby's shift had ended hours ago, encountering her in the cafeteria at ten in the morning was unexpected. And based on her opening line, her sentiments regarding Haleigh dating her brother hadn't altered in the last two weeks.

"I talked to Jessi this morning," her roommate said, ignoring the sarcastic comment. "She's exhausted. It seems Emma still isn't sleeping and there hasn't been anyone else around to help during the night." Tilting her head, she added, "I've been at work. What's your excuse?"

Abby must have caught Jessi in a weak moment. She never would have squealed otherwise.

"It's obvious that you know where I've been, so excuse me if I refuse to play your interrogation game." As much as she loved her best friend, Haleigh was creeping extremely close to her limit where this attitude was concerned. So she didn't have a great track record. Big effing deal. Everybody deserved a second chance.

Haleigh moved to step away from the coffee counter, but Abby blocked her path. "You promised."

"I promised not to hurt him," Haleigh clarified. "I never said I wouldn't see him."

"We both know that one always leads to the other," Abby insisted.

Taking a deep breath, Haleigh battled with the desire to tell her best friend exactly where she could stick it. Instead she said, "What did I do, Abby? What unforgivable sin did I commit to bring this on? Every relationship I've had didn't end with a man going down in flames. Have they all been healthy? No. Was I always the worst person in the pairing? Absolutely not. I admit that I have issues. Everyone does. But I'm doing my best to make a change, and I am not going to continue being unhappy because you and my mother believe I haven't yet paid my penance."

Once the words were out, Haleigh felt a weight lift off her shoulders. She was not a villain, and she would no longer accept being treated like one. Since Abby didn't respond, she said, "Now if you'll excuse me, I'm going back to work."

Unfortunately, Abby wasn't finished. "I want you out," she said, jerking Haleigh to a stop with her words. "You have thirty days."

Open-mouthed, Haleigh watched the dark-haired stranger walk away. No way in hell was this all about Cooper, but whatever the source, Abby had officially pulled the plug on their friendship. Haleigh fought down the bile collecting at the back of her throat.

Twenty-three years and Abby tossed her away without showing a hint of regret. As if cutting Haleigh out of her life was as simple as taking out the trash. Feeling empty, she waited for the urge to hit. The desire for a drink that would tip her off the wagon once more.

But Haleigh didn't want a rum and Coke. She wanted Cooper. Which sparked the question—was she trading one diversion for another? Was she using Cooper because he made her feel good? Made her forget who she was? *What* she was?

Doubts pummeled her from every direction. Her old reliable friends, worthlessness and regret, whispered in her ears. Some distant voice told her to fight, but what was the point? Abby had made her feelings clear. The thought of moving in with her mother stirred a wave of panic. There had to be another answer.

As Haleigh's mind raced, the cell phone in her pocket went off, signaling a call from the maternity ward. In the end, Haleigh was good at only one thing—her job. At everything else she was a roaring failure.

Chapter 24

Disappointed that Haleigh had to stay over at work, Cooper found himself wandering aimlessly around the house, as if he'd forgotten how to spend an evening alone. Ever since the visit from Spencer, he'd been playing back every conversation with Haleigh over the last four days. They'd discussed their day, their pasts, and everything from music to movies, but neither had brought up the future.

Except on that first night. His request for a chance to make her happy had been answered with the simple statement that Haleigh wasn't going anywhere. Not exactly a vow of forever. He'd taken the answer in a positive light, but then they'd been in the middle of sex and his brain hadn't been as fully engaged as the rest of him.

So had Cooper only heard what he wanted to hear? Did Haleigh see this situation as nothing more than two adults enjoying each other until they grew bored and moved on? And if she did, was he prepared to let her go?

Annoyed by the direction of his thoughts, Cooper hit the workout room to burn off some energy. On his second set of twenty pull-ups, he placed the blame for his doubts squarely where it belonged.

On Spencer.

Why had he stirred this crap up? Why couldn't he let Cooper be happy living in his own illusions, if that's what they were? Only an idiot would sit a woman down four days in and say, "Where do you see this going?" and Cooper was not going to be that idiot. Or that needy.

But damn, he wanted the answer.

By ten o'clock, he'd completed double his normal reps on every exercise in his routine. The harder he pushed, the more his mind raced in the wrong direction, and the faster he pumped to shut down his mind. Which meant when Haleigh showed up at his door at ten fifteen, she found a dripping wet Cooper looking like a man who'd just run a marathon through a downpour.

"Is there a water leak somewhere?" Haleigh asked when he greeted her at the door.

"Doubled up the workout," Cooper replied, still breathing heavy from the sit-ups he'd been doing when she rang the bell. "I meant to shower before you got here, but I lost track of time."

"I'm sorry," she said, lingering on the threshold. "Maybe I should go home."

"No," Cooper said, pulling her into the house. "Don't be crazy. I'm glad you're here."

Haleigh did not return the sentiment. "It's been a really long day," she said, staring at her shoes. "I shouldn't be invading your life every night."

The waver in her voice caught his ear. Bending to see her face, Cooper said, "Darling, are you crying?" She shook her head quickly but the sniffle gave her away. "Hey now," he said, pulling her chin up, "you *are* crying."

"I know," she said. "I feel like an idiot."

Knowing she'd stayed late for a difficult delivery, he feared she might have lost a patient. "Come sit down and tell me what happened." Due to a lack of tissues, he handed her his discarded T-shirt off the back of a chair. "I'm afraid this is the best I can do."

Wiping her nose, she said, "It's fine," before jerking the cotton away. "Whoa, that smells."

"Yeah, sorry." Searching for another solution, he said, "Let me grab a paper towel." After a quick run to the kitchen, he handed her a full roll.

She blinked up at him. "A bit excessive, don't you think?"

"I'm not good with crying women. Just take what you need."

Ripping one off the roll, she blew her nose. "This is so stupid. I really should go home."

As if he'd let that happen. "I'm not letting you go anywhere until I know what brought on these tears."

Struggling to even out her breathing, she said, "Abby found me at work today. She knows that I've been staying over here."

"We knew she'd find out eventually. What did she say?" Of all the people who could come between him and Haleigh, Cooper never thought his sister would be the biggest obstacle.

Haleigh swiped at the tear running down her cheek. "She's kicking me out."

"She what?" Cooper said, rising to his feet.

Staring at her hands, Haleigh added, "At least she's giving me thirty days."

"To hell with that," he raged. "She is not kicking you out because of me."

"Of course she isn't," Haleigh corrected. "She's kicking me out because of *me*. Because I'm a worthless human being who is more than likely going to ruin your life. And if that's the case, I'm going to have to do it while living in my car."

"No," he said, dropping back down beside her. "You are not worthless and you are not going to ruin my life. Abby is angry over losing

Kyle and she's taking it out on you. On us. Whatever the reason, it doesn't matter."

"It does matter," Haleigh cried. "She's been my best friend since we were nine years old. We've gone through everything together. She knows every horrible thing my mother has ever said to me. She didn't abandon me when I couldn't get my nose out of a bottle, and then once I got out and kept falling back in, she was never more than a phone call away. Through it all, Abby has been there, and now she's so sure that this is a mistake, she's willing to throw me out of her house to save you."

Cooper's hands curled into fists. He'd never wanted to throttle his sister as much as he did in that moment. Why would she take this away from him? Why would she get in the way of the happiness of two people she claimed to love?

"I don't care how far she's willing to go," he said, "she's wrong."

"I don't think she is," Haleigh said, her voice crumbling. "What if all I'm doing is switching out one addiction for another?"

"What's that supposed to mean?"

"I drank to drown out the voices. To numb the pain and feel good, even if that good wasn't real. What if I'm doing the same thing with you?"

"I'm not a drink, I'm a person, Haleigh Rae. There's nothing wrong with two people making each other feel good. And there is nothing fake about what's going on here."

Brown eyes stared up at the ceiling. "You don't know that. I don't know if I'm here because this is real or because when I'm with you all the bad stuff goes away. You're as much a drug for me as a bottle of whiskey ever was. I don't want to use you like that."

Dropping to his knees in front of her, Cooper cupped Haleigh's face, forcing her to look him in the eye.

"Do not believe for one second that this isn't real. What happens in that bedroom upstairs is something I've never had with another woman. When you're working beside me in the kitchen, I can't imagine a day when you won't be there. After you leave in the morning, I smell your scent on my pillow and think about the next time I'll get to touch you. Nothing has ever been this real for me, and I know you feel it, too. I know it every time you arch against me, every time you smile at me over your coffee, and every damn second that we're apart. If I'm your drug, then you're mine, and I refuse to give you up."

Taking one of his hands, she placed a kiss in his palm, "That's the best thing anyone has ever said to me. But that's why I have to protect you. Because you won't protect yourself."

"Protect me from what?" he said, frustration pulsing through him.

"From me! I came within inches of diving straight into a bottle instead of coming here. Tonight, I controlled it, but what happens when I screw up and give in? When I reach for a drink instead of you?" she asked.

"It isn't *when* but *if*, Haleigh. And if that ever happens, I'll be there to take you home and hold your hair back and help you find the strength to say no the next time."

Haleigh shook her hands in front of his face. "You make it sound so simple."

"It is simple. I'm here. I'm not going anywhere."

"And what happens when I push you too far?" she asked. "What happens when we have a fight and I say horrible things?"

"Exactly what's happening right now," he answered, realizing for the first time ever that he'd found someone he was willing to fight with. And fight for. "I know what you've been through. And I know that you've been strong enough to overcome it all. I won't be another person who let you down, Haleigh. You can lash out and throw things for all I care, but when you're done, I'll be here. Ready for another round or a good cry or a night of make-up sex. Whatever you throw my way, I am not giving up."

Falling into his arms, Haleigh pressed her face into Cooper's neck. "I don't want to give you up, either."

Relief shuddered through him, echoed by the knowledge that he'd just crossed a line in his own mind. The chance of losing the woman in his arms had been the push he needed. Cooper had found the one. Haleigh had always been the one.

"It's about time you came around," he said, speaking to himself as much as to her. Placing a kiss on her hair, he remembered his sweaty condition. "I'm sorry I smell like a locker room. You're a brave woman to get this close."

Lifting her head, she caressed his whiskered cheek with her knuckles. "Didn't you say something about taking a shower?" she asked, a sexy look in her damp eyes. "I'd be happy to help with all the hard-to-reach places."

Rising to his feet, Cooper took her with him, cradling her in his arms. "I'm really sweaty," he said as she wrapped her arms around his neck. "We might need to do a full scrub at least twice."

Circling his earlobe with her tongue, she murmured, "I'm willing to go for three if you are."

Cooper took the stairs two at a time, with Haleigh laughing against him all the way.

Haleigh really, *really* wanted to believe every word that Cooper had said. And she knew without a doubt that he believed them with complete conviction. But no matter how hard she tried, the what-ifs still lingered in the back of her mind. He'd made some bold statements that implied this was more than a fling on his part. Not that she wanted a love 'em and leave 'em affair, but Haleigh hadn't been thinking in terms of forever. At least not for more than a few scary seconds before chasing the thoughts away.

As Abby had so kindly made known, Haleigh already had three strikes under her belt when it came to marriage. Well, engagements.

But not one of her exes was half as amazing as the man who'd just given her a knee-buckling orgasm in the shower. Cooper was far and away the best man that Haleigh would ever find. And he wanted her. Till death do they part from the sound of things.

If—and that was a big *if*—Haleigh committed to becoming the woman that Cooper believed her to be, there were still two problems standing in her way. The first being her lack of a home come thirty days from now. Cooper would likely insist that she move in with him. In the past, she'd have taken that easy answer, but not now. If they were going to make this work, Haleigh needed to come to him on equal ground, which meant taking control of her financial and domestic circumstances.

Both of which led straight into problem number two—her mother. She'd need to play this carefully. Do some research on smaller homes in the area for sale, but also on refinancing the existing mortgage to possibly lower the payments. They'd bought the house on Rebel Circle when Haleigh was eight. If her parents signed a thirty-year mortgage, the balance should be almost nothing compared to a full loan. Of course, there was the second mortgage, and who knew what that looked like.

Multiple requests to see the paperwork had resulted in a string of guilt trips about respecting her mother's privacy and not treating her only living parent like a senile old woman. Per their arrangement, Haleigh forked over a set amount each month while living on a shoe-string budget and paying next to nothing to rent a bedroom from Abby. An option no longer on the table, leaving Haleigh potentially homeless.

"This is a long shot, but do you know of any food vendors in town who might be willing to serve food at the rally?" Cooper asked, walking out of the bathroom with a towel slung low around his hips and drying his hair with another. "Thanks to my screw-up, we had one drop out, and I need to find a replacement."

"How did you screw up a food vendor?" Haleigh asked, allowing the mouth-watering scenery to distract from her conundrum.

"Good question," he said with one brow raised. "One of them had a question Lorelei needed me to answer, but I didn't check my messages, so I didn't get back to her in time. I still don't know what the question was."

Feeling defensive of her man, Haleigh asked, "Then how do you know Lorelei couldn't answer it without you?"

"Because Spencer said she couldn't when he reamed my ass today."

Haleigh hopped up to her knees, pulling the sheet over her naked breasts. "He shouldn't be blaming you for Lorelei's mistakes."

Settling on the bed next to her, he said, "I appreciate your support, but I'm the guy in charge, and if they need me, I need to be available. Not that I regret how I was distracted." Cooper ran a finger along the top of the sheet. "You know I've seen what's behind there, right?"

Shivering in response to his touch, her eyes dropped to his full lips. "And I've seen what's behind that towel, but you still wore it out of the bathroom."

Green eyes darkened with desire. "Would you like to see it again?" he asked, leaning close.

"I'd like to do a lot more than see it." Haleigh fell back to the pillow, tugging him with her, but just as their lips met, the cell phone on his nightstand went off.

"Dammit," he mumbled against her mouth.

"Ignore it," she ordered, locking her arms around his neck.

Cooper pulled free. "I can't. That's the business phone."

Leaning on her side, she watched him answer the call, take down a location, and say he'd be there in a half hour.

"Do you really have to go?" she asked once the cell was back on the table.

He dropped a quick kiss on her lips. "I really do. That was Dale Lambdon with the sheriff's office. A couple high schoolers buried a Mustang in a ditch out on Highway 76. I need to tow them out and see how much damage they've done."

"Send Frankie or Ian. We were just getting started." How was she supposed to put off thinking about her crappy situation if he left her there alone?

"Ian doesn't run the tow truck, and Frankie handled calls all weekend. It's my turn."

"There aren't any other tow services in the county?" she pressed.

Cooper rose to his feet. "If you got a call from the hospital, you'd have to go, right?"

"Come on," she replied. "Pulling a car out of a ditch isn't the same as delivering a baby." The minute the words hit the air, Haleigh smacked a hand over her mouth as Cooper's face went hard. "Oh my God," she said. "My mother's voice just came out of my mouth."

"Unless she's a long-distance ventriloquist, that was you." Draping the loose towel around his neck, Cooper said, "I know the difference between what we are, doc. You don't need to remind me."

Haleigh leapt from the bed to chase him to his dresser. "Cooper, I'm so sorry. That isn't what I meant. What you do is important."

"But not life and death. And I didn't have to go to school for nearly a decade to learn how to do it." With clean clothes in hand, he charged back into the bathroom.

"Please, Cooper," she begged, trailing behind. "This is the perfect example of what I was talking about earlier. I say stupid things. Things I don't mean."

"Let it go," he said. "It's fine."

"It isn't fine," she argued. "That was a horrible thing to say. I don't know where it came from." After buttoning his jeans, Cooper reached for the deodorant, pretending she wasn't there. "Dammit, look at me!" she yelled. "I love you and I would never say anything to make you feel inferior because I've known that feeling my whole life and you don't do that to someone you care about."

The Speed Stick hit the counter. "What did you say?"

Now that he actually was looking at her, Haleigh realized she was standing in the middle of his bathroom stark naked and raving like a mad woman. Snatching a towel off the bar to her left, she wrapped it around herself. "I said I'm sorry. I didn't mean to hurt you."

Unblinking, he said, "You said you love me."

"I did?" Replaying the heartfelt speech in her mind, Haleigh heard the words play back. "I did say that," she whispered, as surprised as Cooper looked. "I shouldn't have said that."

"But you did," he said, crossing the distance between them. "Did you mean it?"

"Well, yeah," she hedged, unable to lie when he was staring at her so intently. "But you don't have to say it back. That's not why I said it. I just needed you to know that I didn't mean what I said. Originally."

"I love you, too," he said, a smile splitting his handsome face. "I can't believe you said it." Sweeping her off her feet, Cooper spun them around with a bark of laughter. "I love you, Haleigh Rae Mitchner."

"Who's the overachiever now?" she asked, clinging to his shoulders. "That's twice now and I've only said it once."

Looking like a big kid with a ticket to Disney World, he said, "Then say it again."

Toying with the damp curls behind his ear, she fulfilled his request. "I love you, Cooper Daniel Ridgeway."

The whoop of joy took her by surprise, and Haleigh buried her nose in his pine-scented neck, unsure how they'd gone so quickly from her blatant blunder to proclamations of love.

"I still have to go," he said, dropping her to her feet. "But this will be the fastest tow Dale has ever seen. And then I'm coming back to make love to you for the rest of the night."

Feeling the blush crawl up her neck, Haleigh smiled into the most beautiful green eyes she'd ever seen. "I would like that very much, Mr. Ridgeway."

Chapter 25

Haleigh had ordered him not to do this, but Cooper wasn't about to sit back and let Abby throw away a more than twenty-year friendship without an explanation. Besides, Haleigh was still at work and what she didn't know wouldn't hurt him.

To Cooper's surprise, Ian answered Abby's front door.

"What the hell are you doing here?" Cooper asked.

"I'm moonlighting as a butler," the smart-ass replied. "Nice to see you, too, cuz. Come on in. We were just finishing up dinner."

"*We?*" Cooper echoed. "You make it sound like you live here."

"Not yet," Ian said with a grin. To his boss's scowl, he added, "I'm kidding. Damn. What's up your butt?"

Stepping into the foyer, Cooper glanced toward the living room. "I need to talk to Abby."

"Good luck with that," Ian whispered. "She's been walking around like a ticking time bomb for days."

"That's why I'm here." Elbowing the younger man, he said, "Take Jessi out back or something. I don't want an audience for this."

Ian nodded. "I can do that." Walking ahead of Cooper, he stepped into the living room and said, "Hey, Jes. Let's take Emma out back and sit on the patio."

"Why?" she said, spinning to look over the back of the couch. When she spotted Cooper, she grabbed the baby's blanket from beside her. "Good idea." With Emma on her shoulder, she mouthed *good luck* in Cooper's direction.

He responded with a nod as Abby walked in from the kitchen and abruptly stopped. "When did you get here?"

"Just now," he answered. "We need to talk."

"I'm not interested." She turned tail and marched back through the arched doorway.

Determined, Cooper followed. "Get interested," he said. "Why are you doing this?"

"Doing what?" she asked, stacking cups in the top of the dishwasher.

"You know what, Abby. Why are you so against me and Haleigh being together? And why are you throwing your best friend away like a piece of garbage?"

Keeping her back to him, she said, "I told you. She's wrong for you."

"Actually, she's perfect for me," he said, walking around the island to stand beside her at the sink. "We make each other happy, and I'd expect you to be supportive of that."

"Then you expect wrong."

"Look at me, Abby," he ordered, spinning her to face him. "You're breaking her heart, dammit. She's your oldest friend."

"Which means I know what she's capable of," she argued, slamming the tea towel onto the counter. "I know the damage she can do firsthand."

"Why do you make her sound like a monster?"

"Leave it alone, Cooper. Just get out while you can."

"There's something you're not telling me, Abbs." Grabbing her hand, he said, "Why have you turned on her like this?"

His sister snatched her hand away and yelled, "Because Haleigh Rae is the reason that the last words I ever said to my husband were in anger! Thanks to her, my husband died in the sand on the other side of the planet and I didn't tell him I loved him."

Before Cooper could respond, Haleigh stepped into the kitchen and said, "Cooper, would you leave us alone, please?"

"I—" he started, but she held up a hand to silence him.

"It's okay," she said. "Let me take it from here."

Recognizing the calm assurance in Haleigh's eyes, he backed away, stopping beside her. "I'll be out back if you need me."

"I appreciate that," she said.

Turning back to see Abby staring out the window over the sink, Cooper left the two women alone.

"Why didn't you tell me?" Haleigh asked, patience and understanding replacing the hurt and confusion of the last few days.

Shaking her head, Abby replied, "Because there was nothing you could do to fix it."

Taking a guess, Haleigh said, "Kyle didn't want me to move in here, did he?"

A nod yes was her only reply. Words weren't really necessary.

"You should have told me."

"Why?" Abby spun. "What difference would it have made? Was I supposed to tell my oldest friend that my husband didn't want a drunk living under our roof?"

She was being deliberately mean, but Haleigh didn't blame her. This wasn't Abby talking. It was the hurt. The loss. The anger.

"I would never have expected you to go against your husband's wishes."

"You've gotten so good at playing the martyr, haven't you? Is that how you've blinded Cooper? Played up the Mommy Dearest story so he believes that your addiction isn't your fault? That you can't be blamed for all your bad decisions?"

"I've taken responsibility for all of my mistakes, but unlike some people, Cooper doesn't hold them against me. He doesn't consider me damaged goods because I've made some bad choices. And though you can lay a lot of things at my feet, Abby, I didn't kill your husband."

The grieving woman clung to the countertop until her knuckles were white. "He was so mad that I refused to tell you no. That I had the nerve to defy him. When he got mad, Kyle couldn't sit still. That's why he volunteered for that extra duty. He wasn't even supposed to be out on the road, Haleigh Rae. But he went because I'd made him mad. Over you."

"He was in a war zone, Abby." Haleigh moved slowly around the island. "The same thing could have happened the next day when he was scheduled to be out there. You making him mad didn't get him killed. You didn't kill Kyle any more than I did."

"No." Abby shook her head and turned to face the window. "I should have agreed with him. I shouldn't have been so angry that he wanted me to turn you away. I should have been a better wife. If I'd just done what he wanted, he'd still be here." Shaking, she cracked. "It's my fault."

Haleigh wrapped her arms around her friend. "You're wrong, honey. None of it's your fault."

After a brief struggle, Abby surrendered, spinning to return the hug. "I loved him so much, Haleigh Rae," she sobbed. "I want him back."

"I know you do," she said, stroking Abby's hair. "I wish I could do that for you."

Haleigh's shoulder grew damp with warm tears as the sobs racked the slender woman's body. She couldn't help but shed some of her own. When the crying subsided, Haleigh reached for the towel to dab at Abby's cheeks.

"Why did you let me move in anyway?" she asked. "I'd have understood if you'd told me the truth."

Abby's breath hitched. "You didn't have any place else to go, and I didn't want to be alone. But then I started to feel like I'd betrayed him, like I chose you over him, and I got angry. Angry that Kyle took that patrol that wasn't his. Angry that you were here and he wasn't."

"You have every right to be angry about all of that."

"But I shouldn't have taken it out on you," Abby said, the tears coming again. "I don't know what happened. I saw you and Cooper getting closer and the idea of you being happy made me even madder until I couldn't see straight. Cooper is right, I've made you out to be a monster when I've been the awful one. God, when I think of the horrible things I've said."

"Forget about it," Haleigh said, relieved to have her friend back. "A lot of what you said was true, but I want you to know that I'm really trying to do better. I'm going to make you proud of me, Abby."

"I've always been proud of you, Haleigh Rae. Always. You're the reason I became a nurse."

"I am?"

Abby shared a watery smile. "I knew I didn't have what it took to be a doctor, but I still wanted to be like you, so I settled for nursing school."

"Oh, hon," Haleigh said, squeezing Abby's shoulders. "You'd make a fabulous doctor."

"Are you kidding?" Abby said with a harsh laugh. "Nurses really run the show. I wouldn't trade my RN for an MD any day."

Relief and love filled Haleigh's chest. "I love your guts, Abby Lou."

"I love your guts, too, Haleigh Rae. I'm so sorry. For everything."

"I'm the one who's sorry. I shouldn't have dropped my mess of a life on your doorstep."

Taking her hands, Abby said, "Your mother put you in a tough situation, and I'm glad I could be here for you. What you said is true. The same thing could have happened to Kyle any moment that he was there. But I can't help knowing that if he hadn't taken that duty, he might have come home. And then I get angry all over again."

"I know what it's like to lose someone because they were in the wrong place at the wrong time," Haleigh said, remembering how she'd cried on Abby's shoulder for weeks after her dad had been killed. "You helped me through it, and I'm here to return the favor, okay?"

Abby nodded. "Okay." After several more sniffles and an extended hug, her friend pulled back to ask, "Do you really love my brother?"

Unable to suppress the sappy grin, Haleigh said, "Yes, I do. Very much."

"Good. Because he's loved you for years."

The grin slid into a full smile. "That's what I hear. How did I miss that?"

"You were too busy believing that no one could love you, I guess. If you don't believe something is possible, you don't see when it's staring you in the face."

The truth of Abby's statement struck like a blow. Other than her brother and Abby, Haleigh never imagined anyone would ever really love her. Not when her own parents hadn't been able to do it.

"Then it's a good thing that your brother is a determined man," she said.

"Yes," Abby agreed. "Yes, it is. And if you decide to live with him, I'll understand, but you're welcome to stay here as long as you need."

Grateful to have such an amazing person in her life, Haleigh brushed a stray lock out of Abby's eyes and said, "I won't be moving in with Cooper anytime soon, but I won't be staying here much longer either. It's about time I start acting like a grown-up and get my own place."

"But I thought you couldn't afford to do that while paying your mom's bills."

"I'll figure something out," she answered, not sure how yet, but determined to stand on her own. "Now I think this night calls for hot fudge sundaes. What do you say?"

Flashing a smile so much like her twin's, Abby said, "I'll get the bowls. You go get the others."

By Monday morning, Cooper had pulled off two miracles.

The first being the preservation of Haleigh and Abby's friendship, which he didn't really have all that much to do with, but he'd enjoyed taking credit for the save all weekend. The second was the reason he'd stopped by Snow's Curiosity Shop.

"I hear I owe you an apology," he said, stepping up to the coffee counter at the back of the store.

Lorelei glanced up from arranging cookies in the glass display. "Don't apologize to me. I'm not the one who'll have to explain why there isn't enough food to go around on Saturday."

"Ah, but we'll have plenty of food. I've lined up not one but two new vendors."

She stopped with a stack of treats in her hand. "The event is this weekend. You found food vendors willing to commit on such short notice?"

Cooper nodded.

Dropping the cookies on the tray, Lorelei propped her hands on her hips. "This better not be Girl Scouts running a lemonade stand."

"Oh, ye of little faith," he said. "I found a barbecue joint in Gallatin that runs a food truck on the weekends. Lucky for us, they had an opening for this Saturday. *And* the owner has a friend who runs a taco truck in Hendersonville. She had a cancellation, so I signed her up as well."

"That's amazing, Coop." Lorelei barreled around the end of the counter to poke him in the chest. "I can't believe you did it."

He pulled a sheet of paper from his back pocket. "Here's the info on both with contact names and numbers. I've also given them your info in case they have any questions."

Staring at the sheet in her hand, Lorelei shook her head. "You've had us all fooled, Cooper Ridgeway. You're a lot more than a good ol' boy with a toolbox and a penchant for flirting."

Slightly insulted, he said, "Believe it or not, there's a brain between these big ears."

"Oh, no," Lorelei said. "I didn't mean—"

"I know what you meant." With another tip of his hat, he said, "I'll let you get back to the counter."

"Wait." A delicate hand wrapped around his wrist. "Really. I'm sorry I said that. I've always known you're a smart guy, Cooper. You wouldn't be running such a successful business if you weren't."

Mollified, he let her off the hook. "I appreciate you saying so."

"Um . . ." She looked around as if making sure no one could overhear. "Spencer told me what you said last week. About Haleigh being your Lorelei. Did you mean that?"

"Haleigh means a lot to me, yeah."

"No, I mean, do you really see me as a good thing for Spencer? I know that you get annoyed with me tagging along and butting into your guy stuff."

Why did Spencer have to be the most honest guy on the planet?

"I was mad that day Spencer tore into me. I didn't mean the stuff I said. You're fun to have around, Lorelei." Tilting his head from side to side, he added, "I do think you should let Spence watch football instead of going shopping, but the rest I don't mind."

With a sly smile, she said, "I guess I can find another shopping buddy in the fall."

"I appreciate your willingness to compromise."

Lorelei laughed. "Anyway, I'm happy for you. It's about time Haleigh Rae came around to what a great guy you are."

"She took some convincing, but I finally won her over."

"I never doubted you for a minute." Lorelei leaned his way. "If you want, I could pack some cookies up to go. My treat."

"You don't have to ask me twice." No way would he turn down Lorelei's cookies. "I'll pay for a few extra for Ian or he'll eat all of mine."

"That reminds me. Your cousin and that Jessi girl were in here over the weekend."

"I'm not surprised. They're practically connected at the hip."

"Have you noticed that she looks a lot like Becky Winkle did in high school?"

Cooper tried to picture it. "Maybe a little."

Lorelei dropped half a dozen cookies into a Lulu's Home Bakery bag. "I didn't see it at the cookout, probably because Jessi doesn't have her nose in the air like Becky does, but when she looked at me over this counter, I almost did a double take. The hair is different, obviously, but they could be long-lost cousins or something."

It had been a full month since Jessi had come to town on that rainy Monday night, and though she continued to believe that she would someday find her father, they'd all agreed that if he'd ever lived in Ardent Springs, he hadn't been there long. Ian had joined the hunt with the rest of them, asking extended family if they'd ever heard of a J.T. and going so far as to check county records, but with no luck.

Considering Lorelei's observation, he asked, "Jebediah has a brother, doesn't he?"

"He does, but as far as I know he hasn't lived in this area for years." Lorelei filled another bag. "I don't know how much alike they are, but

I can't imagine having more than one disapproving Winkle driving us all nuts."

After so much digging, Cooper's first instinct was to dismiss Lorelei's claim. Two women looking somewhat alike didn't mean they were related. And the possibility of Jessi being a Winkle was not good news. He highly doubted they'd welcome her with open arms.

Even so, he asked, "Do you remember the brother's name?"

Handing over the cookies, she said, "I'm thinking Samuel, but I'd have to ask Granny to be sure."

So much for the lead.

"How much do I owe you?"

She waved the question away. "Consider it payment for all those football games you had to endure alone."

"Fair enough," Cooper said. "Let me know if you have any trouble with those vendors."

Lorelei gave him a thumbs-up as she turned to deal with another customer. Strolling through the store, he speculated on the Winkle connection. Maybe Lorelei had been wrong about the brother's name. Or maybe Jebediah had another relative to consider. Though for Jessi to look as much like Becky as Lorelei claimed, the connection would have to be close.

Or maybe Lorelei was seeing things and Jessi wasn't a Winkle at all. Cooper hadn't noticed a resemblance between the two women, and he wasn't about to get Jessi's hopes up on such a slim chance. The girl had been through enough already.

He'd share Lorelei's observation with Haleigh, do a little research on the Winkle family, and see what turned up. If they found concrete proof that Jessi really was a long-lost cousin, they'd fill her in. But not before.

Chapter 26

"Why are we here?" Haleigh's mother asked as the Mamacita's hostess showed them to their table.

"We're here for lunch, Mother," she answered, preferring to keep the real reason to herself until the time was right. After rehearsing her speech all weekend long, Haleigh had opted to have this conversation in a public place in the hopes of saving them both a painful scene. Telling Meredith Mitchner that her money train would no longer be making regular deposits required tact and diplomacy.

And a potential audience to minimize the blowup.

Dusting off the booth seat, Meredith scowled. "You know I don't like ethnic food."

"Your favorite dish is lasagna."

"Oh, please," the older woman replied. "That's as American as meatloaf and potatoes."

Placing her napkin in her lap, Haleigh said, "Actually, it isn't, Mom. Not even close."

Holding the menu with the tips of her fingers, she said, "What am I supposed to eat?"

"You could be adventurous and try the fajitas. They're really good. Or you can order a steak. They have those, too."

Her mother closed the menu. "I don't like the description of the fajitas. The steak will be fine." Linking her hands on the table, she asked, "Why aren't you at work?"

"I'm working nights this week. Doctors don't really keep business hours, remember?"

"No need to talk to me like I'm a child."

The waitress saved Haleigh from having to respond to that quip. Once their orders had been taken and the waitress departed, they fell into an awkward silence. Any effort to butter her mother up with small talk would be a waste, so Haleigh breeched the subject at hand.

"Have you thought any more about selling the house?"

With a pained expression, Meredith said, "I've told you before, I'm not selling my house."

"Do you know how much is left on the mortgage?"

Narrow shoulders shrugged. "Not off the top of my head."

"How about the second mortgage?"

"Haleigh Rae, what is this about?"

Time to rip off the Band-Aid. "Mom, I can't afford to pay your bills anymore."

"Did they cut your hours?" she asked.

"No. I simply need to get my own place, and I can't do that and keep paying your bills. So we need to figure out something with the house. Maybe you could refinance to a lower payment."

"Is that why you dragged me out here?" she hissed. "So you could pull the rug out from under me where I wouldn't make a scene?"

The woman was astute, Haleigh had to give her that. Shrewd and astute.

"No one is pulling anything. We're both adults and there's no reason we can't find a solution that works for both of us."

"You mean one that gets me off your back." Lips pursed, her mother said, "After all I've done for you. I gave up my whole life to raise you kids. And this is what I get in return."

Prepared for the old standby, Haleigh said, "I never asked you to give up anything, and I can't spend the rest of my life paying you back for raising me. At least not monetarily."

"So what? You'll drive me to my doctor appointments when I can't see anymore? And come visit me in the home you seem determined to put me in?"

That one she hadn't expected. "Who said anything about a home?"

"Why else would you want me to sell the house?"

"I want you to sell the house so you can buy something smaller that you can afford. Don't you get tired of having to clean that huge place?"

"Now I'm supposed to live in a hovel."

This was going nowhere. Reverting to plan B, Haleigh asked, "Have you ever considered getting a job?"

"Ha!" her mother chirped, followed by an unladylike snort. "Who is going to hire a fifty-four-year-old woman who hasn't held a job in thirty years?"

A valid question. "What did you do before you had kids?"

"I have a degree in social work." To Haleigh's surprised stare, she added, "Contrary to what your father would have people believe, you aren't the only intelligent female in this family."

"Why didn't you ever tell me that?"

"Why would I?" Slender hands toyed with her silverware. "You never asked until now."

Recognizing insecurity in her mother's expression, Haleigh ignored the insinuation that her ignorance about her mother's past was entirely her fault.

"Social workers are hard to find," she said. "Especially in rural areas. I'm sure you could find a position."

Clearing her throat, Meredith's eyes darted around the room. "I've tried. No one wants me."

This lunch was one revelation after the next. "There has to be something."

For the first time in her life, Haleigh witnessed her mother truly humble. Regardless of how she'd treated her, Meredith was still the only mother Haleigh would ever have. Which spurred an idea.

"I could hire you."

Familiar brown eyes glanced up in surprise. "What?"

"The shelter," Haleigh said. "Someone will need to run the place, and I can't do it while fulfilling my duties at the hospital."

Still defiant, Meredith said, "You'd do that? Wouldn't it have to be approved by someone?"

Haleigh laughed. "I have no idea. I haven't gotten that far yet. But if you're involved from the very beginning, I don't see why you couldn't step into the role when the time comes." For the sake of full disclosure, she added, "*If* the time comes. Right now there's an issue concerning the shelter location, but I'm hoping we can overcome that."

"What's the problem?" her mother asked.

"We're looking at the old band camp, but it's currently owned by JW Properties and I doubt we could meet their current asking price." Tapping the table, she said, "I also doubt the place is worth the price they've put on it."

"That's Jebediah's business."

"Yes, it is. And according to . . ." Haleigh had yet to tell her mother about the new man in her life, and considering how far they'd come today, this was not the time to broach the subject. "According to a friend, the mayor is unlikely to negotiate."

Crossing her arms, Meredith said, "I'll handle Jebediah."

"Excuse me?"

"I said I'll handle him." She flashed the arriving waitress an uncharacteristically friendly smile. "Now let's eat."

"She said she'd handle him?" Cooper asked from the pantry.

Since Haleigh had worked the night shift, they were having this conversation over breakfast.

"That's exactly what she said. She even smiled at the waitress." Haleigh blew across the top of her coffee. "It was creepy."

"Let me get this straight," he said, pouring cereal into a bowl. "Your mother is now going to be involved in launching this women's shelter, and you're good with that?"

"Crazy as it sounds, it was my idea," she admitted. "Turns out she has a degree in social work. She hasn't used it in thirty years, and I didn't even know she had it, but she admitted that she's tried to find a job and no one will hire her."

Cooper was unaccustomed to hearing about positive encounters between Haleigh and her mom. The change gave him hope that his potential mother-in-law might actually stop torturing the woman he planned to marry.

Pouring the milk, he said, "I can't imagine trying to find work after thirty years out of a field."

"I have no doubt she's brilliant," Haleigh assured him. "With Meredith Mitchner at the helm, we'd have the most efficient and well-run shelter in the state."

The sudden praise seemed misplaced. Or at the least, unearned.

"Playing devil's advocate here," he said, "wouldn't working with her drive you crazy?"

"Oh, I have no intention of working with her."

"You just said she's going to help you start the shelter. How is that not working together?"

Lifting one delicate brow, she said, "You underestimate me, my hunky boy toy. Once Mother gets her hooks in, I'm out and she's all Carrie's problem."

"That's just mean," he laughed. Poor Carrie. She had no idea what was coming. "But how does this solve the money issue?"

"Right." Haleigh dropped into a kitchen chair. "I didn't quite resolve that one. We made more progress during this lunch than has been accomplished in the last fifteen years. Riding the high of unexpected approval, I decided not to push my luck."

Secretly relieved there would be no immediate apartment hunting, Cooper said, "Half your clothes are here already. I could have the rest moved in before you get off work tomorrow morning."

Setting the coffee mug on the table, she sighed. "You know that I love you. And we both know I'll move in here eventually. However, I need to stand on my own. At least for a while. If for nothing else, to prove to myself that I can do it."

Not completely what he wanted to hear, but the *eventually* part helped.

"Okay, darling. Let me know when you figure it out, and I'll have the truck ready and standing by." After dropping a kiss on the top of her head, he asked, "Do you want me to go with you the next time? When she amps the manipulation, you might want backup."

"No," Haleigh said a little too quickly. "I mean, no, thank you. Sweet of you to offer, though."

Sweet had not been his intention. The woman was the source of nearly all Haleigh's triggers. She shouldn't be charging into that battle on her own. Plus, at some point, they needed to have an official meet-the-parent dinner. Not that he and Mrs. Mitchner didn't know each other, but they'd certainly never met as potential relatives.

"I'm here if you need me. You know that, right?"

"I do." She nodded. "Which is a big reason I'm able to do this now."

Amazed at the turn his life had taken, Cooper couldn't help but smile at the beautiful woman sitting in his kitchen. That she was his boggled the mind.

"My cereal is getting soggy, and you need to sleep." He bent to give her a quick kiss, lingering longer than intended. Pressing his forehead to hers, he said, "I love you, Haleigh Rae."

"I love you, too, Cooper."

In all his days, he would never get tired of hearing that.

"Oh," he said around the bite of Cheerios in his mouth. "Hold on." Swallowing the cereal, he said, "This is a weird question, but do you think Jessi looks anything like Becky Winkle?"

Haleigh frowned. "I'm not sure. Why?"

Cooper shook his head. "Lorelei said she looks like Becky did in high school and made the comment that they could be long-lost cousins."

The implication wasn't lost on Haleigh. "Jebediah could be the J in J.T."

"I highly doubt it. Winkle is a self-righteous jerk, but I can't imagine him crossing the line into infidelity. Lorelei says he has a brother, but thinks his name is Samuel."

"Well, crap," she muttered. "I thought we had a clue there for a minute." Running a finger around the rim of her mug, she said, "Whoever her father is, he either lied about his name or he never lived here."

Sitting down at the table, Cooper said, "I really wanted to help her find this guy. At least her coming here wasn't a complete bust. She might not have found her father, but she found Ian. He talks about her constantly at work."

"She's also found a job," Haleigh informed him. "Started at the bookstore yesterday. Your mom got her boyfriend to give her part-time work. Against my medical advice, I might add. She needs to wait two more weeks, but she was so excited I didn't put up too much of a fuss. Though I did insist on no lifting anything over ten pounds. Not even that if she can avoid it."

He'd stopped listening at the word *boyfriend.* "Do we have to call him Mom's boyfriend? Really?"

Stealing a Cheerio, she said, "That's what he is. You might as well get used to it."

Cooper didn't want to get used to anything where his mom and Bruce Clemens were concerned. "Who's watching Emma?"

"Linda. I think she got Jessi the job with the sole purpose of having Emma all to herself several hours a week." Haleigh unfolded out of her chair. "In spite of this coffee, I'm struggling to keep my eyes open." She placed a kiss on his cheek and said, "Have a good day. I'm off to la-la land."

"Sweet dreams," he said, watching her walk away. She gave a wave before disappearing up the stairs, leaving Cooper alone with his soggy breakfast. He considered following her. What was the point of being your own boss if you couldn't play hooky whenever you wanted?

Then again, she wouldn't get that much-needed sleep if he stayed home. Carrying the bowl to the sink, he dumped what was left down the disposal. At least now he had an excuse to stop for doughnuts on the way to the garage.

By Friday afternoon, Haleigh had reached new levels of exhaustion, stress, and guilt. Thanks to their crossed schedules, she hadn't seen much of Cooper since Tuesday morning. He'd offered two more times over text to be there when she told her mother the money was going away for real. Since she had yet to even mention Cooper's name to her mom in any context other than as her best friend's brother, explaining why he was tagging along for such an important conversation would be a bit complicated.

It wasn't that she didn't *want* to tell. Haleigh simply hadn't found the right moment to say, "Oh, by the way, I'm in love with the town mechanic and I'm probably going to marry him, can you pass the butter?" Maybe she could enlighten her mother after the fact. When it was too late for her shrewish ways to chase Cooper off.

And so the guilt mounted. Her inexcusable cowardice reeked of shame, but Haleigh pushed that thought aside. She was not ashamed of Cooper or what he did for a living. She'd love him no matter what profession he chose. Her mother's prejudice was the problem. Heck, her own daughter had become a doctor and that rarely impressed the snobby woman. Expecting her to graciously accept a son-in-law with grease-stained hands was like asking a politician to take a lie-detector test.

Neither scenario would end with positive results.

Speaking of politicians, Haleigh checked her phone for the third time since arriving at the steps to city hall. Her mother had lined up a meeting with the mayor for two o'clock. As instructed, Haleigh had arrived promptly at one forty-five, professionally dressed, shelter plans in hand, and ready to let the elder Mitchner do the talking.

Oddly, the elder Mitchner had yet to arrive. Confused and concerned, Haleigh took a seat on a bench near the building entrance.

"Don't slouch like that once we get inside," her mother said, sneaking up behind her like the evil ninja that she was. "Do you have the file?" Haleigh waved the manila folder in the air. "Good. We won't show him, of course, but it's good to have the documents with us."

"We won't—"

"I wish you'd worn your hair up," Meredith interrupted. "Clearly you and I don't agree on the meaning of the word *professional.*"

Haleigh ground her teeth to keep the angry rebuttal from escaping.

"At least you're wearing heels. That's something." When they reached the check-in desk in the city hall lobby, Meredith informed the security guard behind the counter who they were there to see, taking charge to the point of printing Haleigh's name in the visitor log as if she couldn't do so herself. On their way to the elevator, her mother said, "Having Elmer Culpepper as a security guard is as worthless as letting newborn kittens defend the White House. Whoever gave him that job should be fired."

Rethinking their plan of allowing her mother to do the talking, Haleigh said, "I do hope your first question for the mayor will not be an inquiry into the hiring of Mr. Culpepper."

As they stepped off the elevator, the older woman pulled a compact from her purse, checked her hair and her teeth, and returned the mirror without missing a stride. "Don't be ridiculous, Haleigh Rae." Stopping before the mayor's office, she said, "Keep your head up, shoulders back, and smile without appearing simpering or intimidated. Understand?"

An army drill sergeant had nothing on Meredith Mitchner. Without a word, Haleigh gave a brisk nod, tucked the folder beneath her arm, and attempted the look her mother described. Apparently failing.

"Never mind," her mother mumbled with an exasperated eye roll. "Before we go in, I have a surprise for you after the meeting."

Certain she'd heard wrong, Haleigh said, "A surprise?"

"Yes. Which is another reason I wanted you to look nice."

Haleigh's mother did not do surprises. In fact, she hated surprises and once threw the fit of the century when Haleigh's father had surprised the family with a puppy. Who didn't want a puppy?

Coldhearted Meredith Mitchner, that's who.

Suspicious, Haleigh said, "What is it?"

Another eye roll. "If I told you then it wouldn't be a surprise. Now remember what I said." Her mother made the universal sign for locking her lips. "No talking." Before Haleigh could reply, the office door was halfway open. "Here we go."

Chapter 27

Four days without Haleigh in his bed made Cooper a moody mechanic.

"Cooper!" yelled Ian from the front of the garage, causing his boss to bust his knuckle for the third time in the last hour.

"Son of a bitch," Cooper barked. "What the hell is it now?"

"Chill out, dude. There's someone here to see you."

"Unless they can get this fucking oil filter off, I'm not interested."

"Try wrapping sandpaper around it and using a band wrench," Caleb said. "Better friction that way."

Pulling his hands out of the under body floating above his head, Cooper said, "So you're the pro now?"

Glancing around, Caleb said, "Do you know where Cooper Ridgeway is? He should be around here somewhere."

Taking the hint, Cooper tossed the filter wrench into the open toolbox drawer. "I've been working this thing for nearly an hour and it's kicking my ass."

"Sounds like the perfect time for a break. How about we talk in your office?"

The suggestion of privacy piqued Cooper's interest. "Is this about the rally?" he asked. The fundraiser started in less than twenty-four hours. Whatever went wrong now would have to stay wrong.

Caleb shook his head. "Not the rally. Your friend Jessi. I have news."

"Ian, I'll be in my office," he said, leading Caleb through the garage and into the counter area. "Kelly, call Ronnie Ottwell and tell him his car won't be ready until tomorrow."

"Will do, boss," she replied as the two men stepped into the office and closed the door.

"What's the word?" Cooper asked

"You aren't going to believe this." Caleb leaned his weight on the back of a heavy metal chair. "Gerald is finally back from his California trip, so I asked about your J.T. character, expecting the same answer we've gotten everywhere—that he'd never heard of him. But I should have known better."

Excitement mounted. "So he knows who it is?"

"Gerald says there's only one person in this town who has those initials, but he's never actually gone by them, which is probably why no one else thought of him."

"Come on, man. Who is it?"

With a satisfied smirk, Caleb said, "Jebediah Thomas Winkle."

Cooper couldn't believe his ears. The answer had been obvious after all. "And he's sure there's no one else?"

"He's sure. And here's the clincher. Back in the day, youth ministers from Ardent Springs Baptist Church used to go on extended retreats." Pausing for effect, he added, "To Bowling Green, Kentucky. Guess who used to be a youth minister?"

"Holy shit. He *is* her father."

"He'll demand a DNA test to prove it, but I'd bet money he's your sperm donor."

Processing what he'd just heard, Cooper walked around his desk and took a seat. "You think our self-righteous mayor could bear the scandal of a paternity suit and proof of infidelity?"

Caleb dropped into the chair he'd been leaning on. "Hell no, but are you willing to bring him down like that?"

Was he? Political scandals happened on prime-time dramas or in big cities back east. Nothing like this ever happened in Ardent Springs.

"I agreed to help her find the answer, but it's up to Jessi what to do with it." Cooper leaned back in his chair. "If she wants to go public, I'll support her, but I won't tell her what to do one way or the other."

"That's a lot of power," Caleb pointed out.

"Whatever happens, he brought it on himself. He took advantage of a young girl, got her pregnant, and then left her with nothing. If he burns for it, I won't shed a tear."

"You won't hear me defending him." Caleb got to his feet. "I have one request. If she does go public, give the paper first dibs on an interview."

Cooper stood to show his friend out. "Like I said, it's up to her how she wants to handle things, but I'll make the case for the paper if it comes to that."

"Needless to say, I didn't tell Gerald exactly why I was asking. That means you and I are the only ones who know right now."

Which reminded Cooper that he had a phone call to make. Checking the clock on his office wall, he realized Haleigh was in the scumbag's office at that very moment, trying to negotiate a better price on the band camp property. After seeing Caleb off, he sent a text saying to call him as soon as she was free and that he had big news.

When this mystery had landed in his lap more than a month ago, Cooper never pictured it ending this way. Though he supposed this was just the beginning. He didn't know Jessi well enough to guess what she'd do with the information, but if she did make it known that she was the illegitimate daughter of Mayor Jebediah Winkle, Ardent Springs was about to get a lot more interesting.

Thirty minutes into the meeting Haleigh realized she had no idea why she was there. Her mother hadn't let her speak a single word, nor had she mentioned the file in Haleigh's lap. They'd started the meeting with the typical niceties, asking about family and exchanging observations on the local happenings. Within minutes Haleigh had sussed out that Meredith hadn't given the mayor a reason for their visit when setting the meeting. At least not a truthful one.

Unless Jebediah possessed award-winning acting skills, the subject of the available property took him by complete surprise.

He'd attempted a bob and weave, explaining that he couldn't discuss personal business matters in the civil office. Meredith ignored the excuse and barreled on. The discussion moved to a debate on area property values and the square footage of the camp, which Winkle exaggerated and Meredith corrected. The woman had a memory like a steel trap. Haleigh had only given her the information the day before, so she must have studied the paperwork thoroughly.

When it appeared that Meredith would pull out the victory, Haleigh zoned out as she stared at the degrees hung in neat frames behind Jebediah's head. Degrees that revealed his full name—Jebediah Thomas Winkle.

Lorelei had said that Becky Winkle and Jessi could be long-lost cousins. Or maybe . . . sisters.

"Mayor Winkle?" Haleigh cut in, earning a reproachful look from her mother. "Have you ever been to Bowling Green, Kentucky?"

The other two participants in the meeting looked confused, but the mayor answered, "I have, but it's been a long time. Why?"

Haleigh scrambled for a plausible response. "There's a shelter up there I'm considering going to see. For research purposes. I wasn't sure how similar that area is to ours to make it worth going." She quickly added, "How long is a long time?"

With a strained smile, he replied, "Nearly twenty years, I guess. I'm afraid I don't know how much the area has grown in the last couple decades."

Haleigh fidgeted in her seat, anxious to end the meeting so she could call Cooper. Thankfully, Winkle agreed to set up another meeting that would include his business partners and be conducted away from city facilities. He'd also agreed that they should be able to find a common ground on the asking price. Too excited about the paternity revelation, Haleigh put off celebrating her mother's triumph until after her call to Cooper.

The moment they reached the bottom step in front of the building, she opened her phone.

"What are you doing?" her mother asked.

"Please, Mom. I just have to make this quick phone call. Give me two minutes." Not waiting for approval, she walked several feet away and placed the call.

Cooper picked up on the second ring. "You are not going to believe what I found out," he said in way of greeting.

"Whatever it is, I can top it."

"I don't think so," he said.

Haleigh made sure her mother was out of earshot. "Cooper, I know who Jessi's father is."

"I know," Cooper said. "It's freaking Jebediah Winkle."

Totally let down, she hissed, "How do you know that when I just figured it out myself?"

"Caleb found out that Winkle has those initials and that back when he was a youth minister, he made trips for the church up to Bowling

Green. The time frame fits perfectly." As if just realizing what Haleigh had said, he paused. "Wait. How do you know?"

Now he asked about her mad sleuth skills. "While sitting in his office, I noticed his full name on his degrees—Jebediah Thomas. Remembering Lorelei's observation about Jessi and Becky looking alike, I asked if he'd ever been to Bowling Green."

"Just like that?" Cooper asked. "Didn't that seem weird?"

"I didn't say I was smooth at this. It's not like I solve mysteries every day," Haleigh huffed. "Anyway, he said he's been there but not for nearly twenty years. Again, the time frame fits."

"Haleigh, you need to get off the phone," her mother said.

"One more second, Mom." Stepping farther away, she said, "Now what do we do?"

"Tell Jessi," he answered. "Your shift starts at six, right?"

"That's right."

"Then let's meet at Abby's place at five and we'll tell her then."

"Haleigh Rae, you're ruining your surprise," her mother snapped.

Spinning to ask for another minute, she saw the surprise strolling her way. "Oh, mother of God, you didn't."

"What's happening?" Cooper asked through the phone, but Haleigh was too busy dealing with her mother's diabolically poor timing.

"Mother, what did you do?"

"What you should have done months ago," the older woman replied. "Now get off that phone."

"Cooper, I need to go," she said, eager to end the call before the wrong person was overheard. "I'll call you later."

The second she broke the connection, Marcus said, "Hey there, beautiful."

"What are you doing here?" she asked, too shocked to be civil.

"For you," he said, as if the answer was obvious. "I told you. I miss you."

"Isn't it sweet of him to come all the way from Los Angeles to see you?" her mother asked.

"*Sweet* is not the word that comes to mind," Haleigh said. Asinine was more like it. Unnecessary. Unwanted. "I'm sorry that you came all this way, Marcus, but we have nothing to say to each other."

"Don't be ridiculous," her mother cut in, the pleasant cordiality of a moment ago gone. "Marcus came all this way and the least you can do is spend some time with him. Now you two go eat. Talk. Have a nice evening."

Waving toward his rented Mercedes, he said, "Come on, babe. Give me a chance."

Standing smack-dab in the middle of the town square—which was actually a circle—Haleigh felt blindsided and on the verge of panic. Assessing the situation, she weighed her options. Option one, telling her mother that she didn't want Marcus because she had Cooper, held little appeal considering the scene that would follow. A scene that would no doubt play out in front of the entire town. On the other hand, she had two hours until she needed to meet Cooper at Abby's. Surely she could get rid of her ex-fiancé in two hours.

Haleigh climbed into the rental car, and as her mother waved them off from the sidewalk, she said, "I agree to one quick meal and then you're gone. Where are we going?"

"I found this great Italian place," Marcus said, resting his hand on her thigh.

Haleigh put the hand back on the gear shift. "You mean Main Street Pizzeria?" She wouldn't call the little pizza joint great Italian, but there wasn't anything else in Ardent Springs that might fit the description.

"Of course not," he said, pointing the Mercedes toward the interstate. "We're going down to Nashville."

⌒

Haleigh didn't show up at Abby's at five. She didn't show up at five thirty either. At five forty-five, she finally answered one of his multiple texts to say she was fine and would explain everything when she saw him. At seven he received a text from Abby saying Haleigh wasn't at work. Buford Stallings had just called the Ruby Restoration meeting to order when the message came through.

"I need to go," Cooper whispered to Spencer.

"What?" his friend answered. "The meeting just started. You need to give an update on the rally and make sure the volunteers know where to be in the morning."

Cooper shook his head. "I don't care about the rally right now. Haleigh Rae is missing."

"She's what?" Lorelei cut in, drawing attention from the rest of the room.

Before Cooper could respond, his business cell rang. "Let me see what this is," he said, leaving his chair to step out of the room. The call was from a rental car company regarding one of their vehicles broken down just off the interstate not far from his garage. Thanks to Frankie being at a show down in Nashville, there was no one else to run the truck.

Cooper fired off two quick texts. The first to Spencer saying he wouldn't be returning to the meeting, and the second to Abby telling her to contact Haleigh's mom to see if she might know where to find her.

That he'd heard from her little more than an hour before was the only reason he was taking the tow call. With luck, she'd call him before he finished the job so he could stop worrying. Otherwise, he planned to drive his tow truck straight to the Mitchner front door.

Whatever happened to dependable German engineering?

"Are you sure you didn't run out of gas?" she asked for the third time as they stood helpless on the side of the road staring at the non-functioning luxury car.

"The gauge read more than half a tank," Marcus defended. "I don't know what's wrong with the damn thing." Kicking a tire, he added, "I should have taken the BMW instead."

Haleigh wanted to kick something herself, but it wasn't the car. "What did the rental company say?"

He shrugged. "They're sending someone. I assume from Nashville, so we could be out here for a while."

"Marcus, I'm already late for work. I told them I'd be there by now."

"What do you want me to do?" he asked, throwing his hands up. "I didn't get us stranded out here on purpose."

"If it weren't for you, I wouldn't be out here at all!" she yelled, angry at herself for getting sucked into this mess. Frustrated that she couldn't let Cooper know where she was because her stupid phone was dead. Not like she could ask Marcus to let her call her boyfriend since her ex would run straight to her mother with the news. Bad enough she hadn't mustered up the guts to tell her yet. Hearing the fact from someone else would send her mother into even more of a tizzy.

Propping his linen-clad butt on the fender of the car, Marcus said, "I don't remember you being this bitchy."

They'd determined over dinner, during which Haleigh had repeatedly demanded to be taken home, that they were no longer a match. Meredith had apparently convinced Marcus that the aging country music elite would clamor for his services if he were to set up practice in Music City. Then he and Haleigh could live in Ardent Springs with a simple commute to the big city and everyone would live happily ever after.

By the time their entrées had arrived, the futility in that plan was apparent even to Marcus. Simply put, Haleigh no longer tolerated his crap. His condescension, his arrogance, and his false endearments made her want to drown him in his Italian wedding soup, a sentiment she loudly and quite colorfully shared.

"Funny," she replied with an empty smile. "I remember you being exactly this annoying."

As Marcus silently pouted, a set of headlights cut the darkness from Haleigh's left. When the tow truck slowed and pulled off the highway in front of the Mercedes and then backed up toward them, her stomach dropped to her knees. This clearly was not her night. Silently reciting prayers she hadn't rattled off in several years, Haleigh held her breath hoping to see Frankie's cranky bearlike figure step out of the cab.

And as had been the case when she was a child, Haleigh's prayers went unanswered as Cooper walked toward them.

Chapter 28

Cooper had never been so relieved in his life as when he laid eyes on Haleigh Rae standing on the side of that highway. The guy blocking his path nearly found himself planted in the trees until Haleigh made a slashing motion across her throat and mouthed the words *don't say anything*. What the hell? And who was this prissy asshole?

"Are you here from the rental company?" he asked. Which seemed like a stupid question from Cooper's point of view.

"I'm the one they called to come and get you, yeah," he said, humoring the guy. "Haleigh Rae, what's going on?"

"You know this guy?" Fancy Pants asked her.

"Uh . . . yes. Of course. Cooper is my best friend's twin brother." She rolled on her heels. "We go way back."

"I'm your best friend's twin brother?" Cooper said, more than a little confused that this was the connection she'd go with. "I'm also—"

"The best mechanic in town," she finished for him, shooting a pleading look over the pretty boy's shoulder. "This is Marcus," she said in way of an incomplete introduction, though the name rang a bell.

After half a second, he said, "The plastic surgeon?"

The guy said, "You told him about me?"

"She said you were a—"

"Long way away," Haleigh finished for him once again, which wasn't remotely what he'd been about to say. "Marcus came in for a short visit, and the sooner we get off the side of this road, the sooner he can head home. So, can we move this along?"

Stepping to the side, Marcus pulled Haleigh with him onto the grass saying, "Be careful when you load her up. I don't plan to pay for any scratches that I didn't put on it."

Haleigh cringed but held silent. Suppressing the urge to plant his fist in Pretty Boy's face, Cooper spoke through gritted teeth. "I'll do my best."

Cooper lifted the Mercedes onto the flatbed and secured the chains that would keep it there. Pulling off his gloves, he said, "Y'all can climb in now," as he opened the passenger door on the tow truck.

Hustling over, Haleigh climbed up and shifted into the middle of the seat, but Pretty Boy hesitated. "When was the last time this truck was cleaned?"

"Shut up and get in, Marcus," Haleigh ordered, saving Cooper from having to respond.

Ignoring the temptation to rub the frilly doc's face in the gravel, Cooper walked around to his own side, assuming Mr. Clean could get in and shut the door on his own. On the way around the truck, he reined in his temper by convincing himself that Haleigh must have a good reason for playing off their relationship. Though short of Fancy Pants being insane and homicidal to a new rival, Cooper couldn't come up with a plausible explanation.

The short ride to the garage passed in awkward silence as Marcus tried not to touch anything, and Haleigh gnawed at a fingernail, ignoring Cooper's sideways glances. Her nerves were so potent they put Cooper even more on edge. By the time they arrived at their destination, his jaw hurt from forcibly keeping it clamped shut. Thankfully, Jerk Boy leapt from the truck as soon as Cooper pulled to a stop and stepped several feet away with his phone to his ear.

As he lifted Haleigh out the driver's side, Cooper said, "Where have you been and why are you acting like we aren't together?"

"I don't have time to tell the whole story right now," she said, checking to see if Marcus could hear them. "Marcus dragged me down to Nashville for dinner, and since I didn't know we were going that far until I was already in the car, I didn't take a charger. Needless to say," she added, holding up her phone, "my cell is dead."

Cooper didn't give two shits about her phone. "Why did you get in the car with him in the first place?"

Crossing her arms, she said, "My mother insisted I at least eat with him. She set this up. I went to make her happy, believing I could get rid of him before I had to be at Abby's. Did you tell Jessi?"

"No," he answered. "If your mom knows that we're together, why would she bring your ex-fiancé all the way here?"

"About that . . ." she started the same time Marcus rejoined them.

"The rental company will send a truck up for the car tomorrow." Assessing his surroundings with a critical eye, he added, "This obviously isn't the kind of place equipped to deal with a Mercedes."

The only thing that kept the asshole from getting his head knocked off was Haleigh's hand on Cooper's chest.

Flashing a pleading look for patience, she said, "Marcus, do us both a favor and stop talking. Seriously."

"What?" he asked, clueless to his own sanctimonious attitude. "Your mother should be here to pick us up any minute."

"I'll take Haleigh home," Cooper said. To hell if he was going to let her out of his sight again tonight.

"You don't have to do that," she said, taking him by surprise.

"Yeah," he answered. "I do."

Meredith Mitchner pulled in beside the tow truck, cutting off the conversation when she rolled down the passenger side window and said, "Are you two all right?"

"We're fine, Mother." Haleigh stepped away from Cooper to open the passenger door. As Marcus climbed into the back, she said, "I'll call you later."

Just like that, she was gone.

Watching their taillights disappear into the night, one thing was abundantly clear. Meredith Mitchner had no idea that her daughter was in a relationship with Cooper Ridgeway. And Haleigh seemed determined to keep her in the dark. His heart demanded an explanation, but his brain knew the answer. He wasn't good enough for the woman's daughter. If Haleigh didn't agree with her mother, wasn't ashamed to be dating a lowly mechanic, then why go through so much trouble to keep him a secret?

Nothing opened a man's eyes faster than being proven a fool. No matter what Haleigh claimed, her actions told Cooper everything he needed to know. There would be no happy ending for them. She'd told him once that her motivation had always been to reach for the brass ring in order to please her mother. There wasn't anything about Cooper that would impress her mother, and there never would be.

Shaking his head, he ignored the pain ripping through his chest as he said, "I should have known it was too good to be true."

As soon as Haleigh's mother had dropped her at her car parked off the town square, she'd raced to work, arriving nearly three hours late, which meant working until nine in the morning instead of six. She'd tried to call Cooper several times before midnight with no answer. Her texts after that weren't returned either.

This was not good. Haleigh had royally screwed up, but was certain that if he'd simply let her explain, Cooper would understand the situation and see that things had gotten out of her control. If she'd even hinted to Marcus that she was seeing Cooper, he'd have told her mother. And if her mother found out, the small bit of progress they'd made in the last week would all be for nothing. The judgment and disapproval would reach new heights, and who knew what horrible things she'd say to Cooper?

Better to protect them both for a while longer. Once the shelter project was in full swing, her mother was completely immersed, and they'd securely reached new ground in their relationship, Haleigh could ease into the revelation. Until then, they needed to be patient. There was no reason they couldn't continue as they were. They were happy in private, and that's really all that mattered right now.

With the mission of convincing Cooper of the same, she scanned the crowd at the car rally looking for him. The packed Ruby parking lot made finding anyone difficult. She'd spotted Lorelei and tried to squeeze through a group of people to reach her, but by the time Haleigh stepped into open air, the blonde had disappeared. Passing a row of food trucks near the back wall of the theater, she ran into the last person she expected to see at the event.

"Mother? What are you doing here?"

"This is a community event, Haleigh Rae," Meredith responded. "Last time I checked, I'm still part of this community."

"Of course," Haleigh said. "But you never mentioned that you were coming to this."

"Neither did you," her mother pointed out. "After working all night, I'd expect you to be home sleeping right now."

Over her mother's right shoulder, Haleigh spotted Cooper standing next to the old pickup he'd showed her. "I have something I need to do," she said in way of explanation. "If you'll excuse me."

Grabbing her arm, her mother said, "What did you do to Marcus?"

Frustrated by the delay and the subject, Haleigh said, "I didn't do anything to Marcus except be honest with him. He should never have come here."

"Heaven forbid a man care enough about you to fly more than halfway across the country to see you."

"Mother, you don't know Marcus. He doesn't care about anyone as much as he cares about himself."

Looking stricken, Meredith put a hand to her chest. "I don't know how you can say that about such a sweet man."

"Marcus puts on a good act, but trust me, he isn't sweet." She couldn't tell her mother about Cooper, but Haleigh was determined to make her see the real Marcus. "He's selfish and shallow and if we'd have married he would have insisted I stop giving you money. Does that sound sweet to you?"

Stubborn beyond belief, her mother said, "That isn't at all the impression I get."

"Trust me," Haleigh said. "Your impression is what he wants you to see. Not the real person."

Unable to openly admit she might be wrong, the older woman said, "I suppose it doesn't matter since he flew back to Los Angeles today."

"Good," Haleigh said, relieved that at least one problem had been solved. Turning toward the row of vehicles for sale, she saw that Cooper no longer lingered beside his truck. "Now I really do have something to take care of." Her mother called her name as she walked away, but Haleigh picked up the pace, pretending not to hear her.

The calls had stopped before midnight, and the texts sometime around four in the morning. Cooper knew the moment the last message arrived because he'd been wide awake, pondering his own stupidity. The itch to continue the farce proved him weak *and* foolish. Haleigh had admitted up front that she wasn't a good person, but he'd been too lovestruck to listen. Too blinded by a boyhood crush to recognize the truth in her words.

At least he had the comfort of knowing he'd been right about one thing—a doctor and a grease monkey did not mix.

Through the ache in his chest and the heavy weight of exhaustion, Cooper struggled to enjoy his success. All registered cars had been in place before the gates opened, the food trucks were up and running with nonstop lines, and the crowd had grown thick enough to make navigating the parking lot difficult. Though no one seemed to mind the crush.

His personal life may have crashed and burned, but the fundraiser was well on the way to surpassing expectations. Rubbing the victory in Winkle's face would be a lackluster consolation, but Cooper would take what he could get after the shit storm of the last twenty-four hours.

"There you are," said a familiar voice behind him. "I've been looking all over for you."

Steeling himself, Cooper turned around. "I'm busy." Haleigh reached for his hand, so he stuck them in his pockets. "What do you want?"

"What do you mean, what do I want?" she asked. "I want to explain about last night."

"There's no need," he said. "I got the message loud and clear."

"Please don't shut me out, Cooper. I know I screwed up, but if you'll just hear me out—"

"I'm not interested, Haleigh Rae."

"But—"

For clarity's sake, he asked, "Does or doesn't your mother know that we were together?"

Shaking her head, Haleigh pleaded, "Don't say it in the past tense like that. We *are* together."

"Does or doesn't she?" he asked again.

"Not yet. I need a little more time to bring her around."

"Around to what?" Cooper focused on the anger to drown out the hurt. Neither of which hindered his need to touch her.

So pathetic.

Haleigh ran a hand through her hair. "Working together on this shelter project has built some sort of bridge between us, but it's still fragile. She believes in something I'm doing and we have a shared goal. I don't want to mess that up."

The implication cut like a knife. Still, he forced her to elaborate. Might as well take the full blow.

"And how would us being involved mess things up?"

"She's just . . ." As Haleigh struggled to find the words, Cooper braced himself. "You know my mother. She has these ridiculous standards and ideas about who I should be with."

"And an uneducated mechanic with grease under his nails doesn't meet those standards," Cooper clarified for her. His father's taunts echoed through his brain.

You'll never amount to anything. You're worthless. You'll never be good enough.

"I'll make her come around," Haleigh promised again, as if her willingness to make her mother accept her less-than boyfriend would solve everything.

"Don't bother," he said, letting his anger boil over. "All your life you've fought for that woman to approve of you. To accept you for who you are. And it's never happened. But you know who has always accepted you? Who was ready to love you unconditionally no matter what? Me, Haleigh Rae," he said, pounding his chest. "The man standing right here, with grease-stained hands who drives a dirty tow truck. I believed that you were more than your past. I believed that what I was didn't matter to you. I was wrong. Don't give me that bullshit about your mother not approving. *You're* the one who doesn't approve. You're the coward who can't see that what's inside matters more than what a person does or how much money he has. Because if you did, you wouldn't have made a fool of me last night, and you sure as hell wouldn't be asking me to be patient while you work up the nerve to tell Mommy that you've sunk below her standards."

Faintly aware that they'd drawn an audience, Cooper lowered his voice. "Consider yourself off the hook, because I'm done playing the hapless, lovesick idiot. You were right when you said I needed to protect myself. That kicks in now." Before walking away, he growled, "Thank you for opening my eyes to the real you before it was too late."

Desperate to plant his fist into something solid, something that would shift the pain ripping through his gut into a dull throb in his knuckles, Cooper charged through the crowd without looking back. Haleigh may have turned him into a pitiful sap, but she was not going to ruin the rest of his life. He had a rally to run, and by damn, he would see this through.

Chapter 29

Haleigh ignored the onlookers who'd just borne witness to her humiliation and heartbreak. Every word Cooper uttered rang true. Why did she do it? Why had she fought her entire life for something she would never have? And most of all, didn't need? If Meredith Mitchner didn't want a real relationship with her daughter, then that was her loss, not Haleigh's.

After all this time, it had taken falling for Cooper to make her years of therapy finally sink in. The gurus were right. She couldn't love someone else until she loved herself. And that would require forgiving herself. Something she'd never been able to do.

But by not holding the past against her, Cooper had proven how easy forgiveness could be. Her mistakes did not define her. Her addiction did not make her a bad person. And her worth did not depend on a bitter woman's approval.

Against all odds, Cooper had given her peace and love and genuine acceptance. And she'd thrown them all back in his face.

For nothing.

In stunned disbelief, she made her way to the edge of the crowd and dropped onto a curb at the back of the parking lot. What was she supposed to do now? Her heart demanded she not give up, but Haleigh didn't know how to repair the damage she'd done. Marcus had humiliated Cooper, yet she'd stood silent, asking the man she loved to be patient. To take the abuse, pretend that what they had didn't exist.

She'd poured her disease and self-loathing in his lap and he'd embraced it all. Loved her no matter what, and would have fought beside her to the end. Now he could barely stand the sight of her, and Haleigh didn't blame him one bit.

With her face in her hands, she rocked back and forth, swallowing the tears she had no right to shed. Cooper was the victim in this twisted web she'd spun. Like the tornado he never saw coming, Haleigh had ripped through yet another life. Collected another casualty.

"That was pretty tough back there," Lorelei said. Haleigh felt her drop to the curb beside her. "The last I heard, you'd gone missing last night. I'm going to guess Cooper found you?"

Keeping her head down, Haleigh nodded.

"Did you cheat on him?"

Haleigh's head shot up. "No! I would never do that to Cooper."

Lorelei didn't flinch at the outburst. "I had to ask," she said, as if they were talking about the weather. "Do you remember that painting I sold you for your bedroom?"

Wrapping her arms around her knees, Haleigh replied, "I'm not in the mood to talk home decor right now."

Ignoring the rebuttal, Lorelei pressed on. "You said that the woman in the painting looked as if she wanted the man to get up off his knees." Bumping Haleigh with her shoulder, Lorelei said, "He's up. Now what are you going to do?"

"I don't deserve him, Lorelei."

"Maybe not right now," she agreed. "But that doesn't mean you give up. I've never deserved Spencer a day in my life, but I wake up every morning determined to get there. To earn his love." Lorelei stared into the distance. "I know what it's like to be a work in progress. Finding a man willing to see past your faults and take you as you are is a gift, Haleigh Rae. A gift that's worth fighting for."

Listening to her instincts, Haleigh said, "I want to fight."

"Good." Lorelei shared a genuine smile as she rose to her feet. "I'll be rooting for you. For both of you."

With a silent salute, her old classmate dissolved into the mass of car enthusiasts, leaving Haleigh to formulate a plan of attack on her own. Somehow she needed to get Cooper's attention. To make him hear everything in her heart. As country music filled the air, an idea took hold.

"I'm so proud of you," Linda Ridgeway said, likely resisting the urge to pinch her son's cheeks. "You've done an amazing job on this rally. I bet this one event will bring in more money than the festival did last fall. If not by itself, then all the rallies combined by the end of the summer."

Determined to be a part of her son's success, Cooper's mom had volunteered to help with the fundraiser and was currently running the sign table. When vehicles in the For Sale section found a buyer, she provided the owners with a Sold sign for the car window. She'd also printed up description signs for all attending vehicles and distributed them as the cars had arrived so that guests could read the details of each without having to inquire with the owners.

"I didn't do it alone, Mama. Caleb made sure the word got out far and wide, and as you know, we have a ton of volunteers making sure things go off without a hitch."

With hands planted on her substantial hips, his mother said, "Cooper Daniel, you are the leader on this project and you carried the bulk of the responsibility. You had the connections and many of these car owners are only here because you're involved. Now stop acting like none of that matters and take the dang credit already."

He should have known better than to argue with his mom. "Fine," he said. "It's all me. I'm awesome. Now have there been any inquiries on my cars?"

"Not yet, but we have hours to go."

Until the events of the previous evening, Cooper had every intention of giving Haleigh the proceeds should either or both his vehicles sell. At some point during the night, he'd changed his mind and decided to donate the money to the women's shelter project. Anonymously, of course.

"Linda, hon," Bruce Clemens said as he joined them, "the ladies over at the main entry table asked that I send you their way. They need your opinion on something."

Ignoring the term of endearment that tested his already strained patience, Cooper wondered why the entry table would need his mother instead of him, but assumed the question likely had more to do with the town knitters than the car rally.

"Someone will need to watch my table," she said, sliding around the side.

"We'll take care of it," Bruce assured her. Once his mother drifted into the crowd, the bookstore owner attempted a conversation with Cooper. "How's your day going so far?"

In no mood to play friendly with his mother's new beau, Cooper said, "Busy. So if you'll excuse me . . ."

"Do you not like me as a person, or simply disapprove of me dating your mother?"

"I don't know you as a person," he said, making the latter the obvious answer. "Mama isn't sitting on a mound of cash, if that's what you're after."

With a half-smile, Bruce changed the subject. "I saw the scene with Haleigh Rae earlier."

Refusing to discuss his private life, Cooper said, "That's none of your business."

"I got the impression that a member of Haleigh's family doesn't approve of your relationship."

Cooper's jaw ticked as he kept his eyes on the activity in front of them. "There is no relationship. Not anymore."

"As we just established, you don't approve of me either, but I don't blame your mother for that."

"Leave it alone, Clemens."

"And I know she didn't tell you right away that we were spending time together. Which was her choice, and I respected that."

Heat danced up Cooper's neck as his hands balled into fists. "Not the same thing. You don't know shit about my situation."

Bruce shrugged. "Maybe not the details, but I know you love the young lady. Or so your mother tells me." Toying with a Sharpie, he added, "After that speech you gave, I have my doubts."

"I've loved Haleigh Rae for more than half my life and I'll love her until the day I die."

The older man nodded with a knowing grin. "Then it would be a shame to live without her, wouldn't it?"

"You're not my father, old man," Cooper said, too angry to admit that Clemens had a point.

Bruce smiled. "No, I'm not. And if I was anything like him, your mom wouldn't be giving me the time of day. Linda is a smart woman, Cooper. And she raised a couple of smart, capable kids. She wants nothing more than to see you happy. If you being happy makes her happy, then that's what I want to give her. So I'm telling you, as a man who's made the same mistake, don't let pride stand in the way of what you want."

Deflecting, Cooper said, "Is this where you tell me your sob story about the one that got away?"

"She only got away for a few decades." With the face of a happy man, Bruce said, "I have her back now, and I don't intend to make the same mistake twice."

Speaking of the woman he had now, Cooper's mom returned to the table saying, "Bruce, who asked you to send me over? No one at the entry table knew why I was there."

Bruce shared a conspiratorial grin with Cooper. "I'm not sure who it was now. Maybe they changed their mind." Dropping a kiss on her cheek, he added, "I'd better get back to work. Wouldn't want the man in charge to see me slacking off."

Mama watched Bruce shuffle between two Buicks. "I hope you were nice to him while I was gone. He really likes you, you know. If you'd give him a chance, I think you'd like him, too."

Coming to the same conclusion, Cooper said, "You're right, Mama. Maybe it's time I gave Bruce Clemens a chance."

"Really?" she asked, eyes wide.

"Yes, ma'am." Cooper placed a kiss on the top of his mother's head. "Exactly how long have you two known each other?"

Her round face softened. "Bruce and I went to school together. He took me to prom and we dated the whole summer before he went off to college. When I refused to move with him, he broke it off. I never thought I'd see him again, so you can imagine my surprise when he moved back to town a couple years ago." With a tilt of her head, she asked, "Did you know that he never married? In all that time." She shook her head. "Hard to believe."

Recognizing the pattern, Cooper said, "Not so hard. A smart man waits for the right woman."

"Are you a smart man, Cooper Daniel? Is that why you're still waiting?"

He chuckled. "I'm not feeling very smart today, Mama, but it's time I wised up. If you'll excuse me, there's someone I need to find."

Desperate times called for desperate measures, and Haleigh had passed desperate an hour ago. She'd been lingering near the tent she needed, biding her time until Cooper showed up in the area at the same time as the perfect opening presented itself.

"What are you doing skulking around the edge of the grass like this?" her mother asked, putting her ninja skills to work once again.

"I'm waiting for the right opportunity," Haleigh answered, keeping her eyes on the passersby. "I have to time this just right."

"Time what? You're dancing around like some wild animal. Have you been drinking?"

Ever the faithful and supportive parent. "I haven't had a drink, and I don't plan to have one ever again."

Her mother dropped her voice. "You've been saying that for years. And yet . . ."

And yet she'd slipped a time or two. But now she had a better reason to stay sober. The best reason.

Running the words over and over again in her mind, Haleigh spared her mother a brief glance. "I'm glad you're here, actually. You need to hear this."

"Did you make a request with the DJ?" Meredith asked. "You know country music is not my favorite."

She'd spoken to Zac Harwick but not about a song. Thank heaven the DJ proved to be a romantic at heart.

"There he is," Haleigh said, stepping onto the asphalt and signaling to the woman with the microphone, who held up a hand with all five fingers spread out. Five seconds to go. Haleigh's heart hovered somewhere around her knees as her palms slicked with sweat. She'd once embraced the concept of go big or go home. Today would be the epitome of that philosophy.

"What in the world are you doing?" her mother asked as Zac welcomed his listeners back to the live broadcast from the Ruby Restoration Committee's Rally for the Ruby.

"Just shut up and listen, Mother. I'm about to either make a fool of myself, or pull off the greatest save ever. Let's hope it's the latter."

"Now we have a special surprise for you folks," Zac was saying. "We need the man responsible for pulling this event together to step up to the booth. Cooper Ridgeway, would you join us over here?"

Haleigh couldn't feel her feet, and hyperactive butterflies filled her stomach. She was really going to do this. Good Lord, was she really going to do this?

As Cooper approached, Haleigh stayed hidden around the side of the radio tent. He looked perplexed, but less angry than the last time she'd seen him. When he'd basically told her to go to hell and that he was done with her.

The butterflies doubled and her lungs burned. Whatever happened, Cooper was worth the humiliation. If this didn't constitute fighting for her man, Haleigh didn't know what did.

"Mr. Ridgeway," Zac said. "I have someone who'd like to say something to you."

On cue, Haleigh stepped off the curb and accepted the microphone the DJ thrust into her hand. It was heavier than she'd expected, and Haleigh nearly dropped it.

"What's going on?" Cooper asked under his breath.

Diving ahead, she spoke into the microphone. "My name is Haleigh Rae Mitchner, and I'm in love with Cooper Ridgeway."

A collective gasp echoed from the crowd while her mother said, "You're what?!"

Ignoring her parent, Haleigh charged on. "Cooper, I know that I screwed things up. And I know that I don't deserve you. But I want to.

I want to be the woman that you see when you look at me. Because you make me want to be a better person. You're the most generous, caring, beautiful man that I've ever met, and you gave me your heart without hesitation, knowing that I was damaged goods."

"Haleigh—" he started, but she kept going.

"Of all the stupid things I've done, hurting you is the worst. And while I can't undo what I did, I vow to wake up every morning for the rest of my life determined to make it up to you. If you'll just give me a second chance, I swear that you won't regret it. Not for a moment."

A hush fell over the crowd as Haleigh finished pouring her heart out. Even her mother held silent. A miracle if there ever was one. But when Cooper too stayed quiet, Haleigh began to shake. This was it. She'd given it her all and it didn't work.

Cooper wasn't going to forgive her.

When the silence had carried for what felt like minutes, Haleigh's knees threatened to buckle. Fight-or-flight kicked in, and she was about to drop the microphone and take off running when Cooper finally said something.

"Haleigh Rae, I've loved you for as long as I can remember." He closed the distance between them, passing the microphone back to Zac without breaking eye contact. "And there is nothing you could ever do that would change that. Not now. Not ever." Cupping her face, he leaned close. "You're mine, Haleigh Rae. My one and only. And I'm never letting you go again."

The moment their lips touched, the crowd erupted in applause, but Haleigh couldn't hear them over the echo of Cooper's words in her ears and the beat of his heart beneath her hand. If she lived another hundred years, nothing would ever top this moment. This *was* the real thing. The best thing that would ever happen to her.

Chapter 30

Contrary to his mother's prediction, the car rally did not top the festival of the fall before for most money raised in the Ruby project, but the total came close and more than half the slots for the next month's rally were booked and paid for by the end of the day. To declare the event a success would be an understatement, but the real win for Cooper had been Haleigh. He still couldn't believe she'd put her heart on the line in front of such a huge gathering, never mind the entire KARD listening area.

And, of course, her mother. Meredith Mitchner had stared pinch-faced as her daughter clung to Cooper's arm, beaming with love and pride, immune to the older woman's blatant disapproval. The conversation that followed had been one of the oddest of Cooper's life.

"I love him, Mother," Haleigh had stated. "I don't want to lose you over this, but I won't bow and scrape to win your approval anymore.

And I won't give Cooper up for anything, so it's up to you what happens between us."

Staring daggers through his skull, Mrs. Mitchner had said, "Do you expect her to give up being a doctor to stay home and churn out children?"

Stunned by the question, Cooper had answered, "I don't expect Haleigh Rae to give up anything. If she wants to stay home someday when we have kids, that's up to her, but I'd never demand it."

His future mother-in-law had given a curt nod of approval. "Good. I don't understand why such a public scene was necessary, but if you're happy, Haleigh Rae, then that's all that matters."

"Who are you and what have you done with my mother?" Haleigh had asked.

"For heaven's sake. You act like I'm a monster," she'd said, rolling her eyes. "Now I suggest you go home and take a shower. You look like you slept in those clothes and your hair is a mess."

Haleigh had laughed as her mother walked away. "She's never going to like me, but that went better than expected."

"I like you," Cooper had said, pulling her tight against his side. "I like you very much."

Turning into his arms, she'd said, "And that makes me the luckiest girl in the world."

Two days later, Cooper felt like the lucky one as he witnessed yet another side to the woman he loved. Standing outside the entrance to JW Property Management, Jessi paced the sidewalk, on the verge of an impending meltdown.

"You don't have to do this if you don't want to," Haleigh calmly assured her. "You wanted to know who your father is and now you know. No reason you can't leave it at that."

"I came here to *meet* my father," Jessi corrected. "I had no idea he'd turn out to be the freaking mayor."

There was no reason to believe this meeting would go well. That Jebediah would welcome her with open arms as the long-lost daughter he'd abandoned before she'd even been born. Yet, Jessi had insisted on seeing him face-to-face. To see his expression when she announced their connection.

Haleigh took both Jessi's hands in her own. "Breathe, Jessi. Nothing that happens inside this office is going to change who you are. You're a brilliant and creative young woman and the mother of a beautiful little girl. If Jebediah turns you away, he'll be losing out on knowing someone very special. You already have a family that you helped create," she added, smiling Cooper's way. "We're right here no matter what. You aren't in this alone, okay?"

Cooper could not have loved her more in that moment. To Jessi's questioning gaze, he said, "She's right. You're one of us regardless of what happens today."

The anxious teenager blew out her breath as she nodded. "I can do this," she said, staring at the office door. "If he wants to stay nothing more than a sperm donor, so be it. At least I'll know I tried."

Together, they entered the building and gave their names to the receptionist at the tiny front desk. Oddly enough, Haleigh had recruited her mother to set up the meeting, and Cooper had no idea what the woman had given as a reason. He only knew that Jebediah Winkle had no idea what was about to hit him.

Haleigh held tight to Jessi's hand as they entered Jebediah's office, a space diametrically opposed to the one he occupied at city hall. While the civil office had been stark and sterile, Jebediah's degrees and a few awards hanging on the wall serving as the only decoration, this office was almost warm by comparison.

Tall bookshelves flanked the window behind the desk, each thick with books and family photographs. Haleigh recognized some dating back to their days in school. Becky in her cheerleading uniform and another of her and her parents on graduation day. Plants lined a table along the right side wall while two overstuffed chairs offered comfortable seats for visitors.

On the corner of the desk rested an ornate picture frame encompassing the image of three smiling faces along with two fluffy dogs. The picture ignited a flicker of hope in Haleigh's chest. This cold and often contrary man loved his family. Maybe he could extend that love to Jessi.

"Come in," Jebediah said, rising from his chair. At the sight of Cooper, he visibly tensed. "I didn't know you would be here, Ridgeway."

"I'm just here for support," Cooper answered, lingering near the door.

With a perplexed expression, the mayor passed over the bright-haired teen and asked, "Haleigh Rae, where's your mother?"

"She won't be joining us today," Haleigh answered, then gestured toward the chairs. "Should we sit?"

"Y . . . Yes," he stuttered, clearly off balance. "I'm curious what this is about." Dark eyes darted back to Jessi several times. The young woman had yet to speak.

They hadn't rehearsed how this would go, so, following her instincts, Haleigh took the lead. "Mayor Winkle, this is Jessi Rogers. She arrived in Ardent Springs a month ago on a mission. That mission has led us here today."

"To me?" he asked.

"You're my father," Jessi blurted, putting an end to Haleigh's diplomatic approach.

Winkle paled. "I'm your what?"

"You were in Bowling Green, Kentucky, in 1995, weren't you?" the child asked, a strong mixture of hope and accusation in her tone.

Jebediah seemed to be searching for an answer when Cooper said, "Don't lie to her, Winkle. We know you made regular visits up that way as a youth minister."

Sinking into his chair, the older man said, "Yes, I was there in 1995."

"And you met my mother, Gloria Rogers. Though her name would have been Gloria Watkins back then."

Aging before their eyes, Jebediah said, "You're Gloria's girl?"

"Gloria's *and* yours," Cooper corrected. "Take off the makeup and change the hair and she looks exactly like Becky did in high school."

The mayor's reaction took them all by surprise. "I can see it," he said, eyes locked on Jessi's face. "I had no idea."

"You didn't know that the young woman you took advantage of was pregnant when you left town?" Cooper asked.

Haleigh understood that Cooper's innate sense of justice and responsibility drove his anger on Jessi's behalf. His stalwart belief in doing the right thing made him the man he was, and she wouldn't change him for the world. However, in this instance, a less aggressive approach might yield more positive results.

"Jessi's mother gave her the impression that you knew about the baby," Haleigh clarified.

Narrowing his eyes at Cooper, Jebediah said, "I realize that some people in this town don't think very highly of me, but I assure you, I would never abandon a child that was mine. Not knowingly."

"But you *were* married, right?" Jessi asked. "Mama said you had a family already when you met her."

Shame filled his eyes, but he held his newfound daughter's gaze. "I did. And I have no excuse for my behavior. It was a moment of weakness on my part. One I guess I'm about to pay for."

Jessi bounded out of her chair. "I didn't come here for money."

"Sit down, child. That's not what I meant." Jebediah shifted his attention back to the menacing presence at the back of the room. "How much time do I have before this hits the paper?"

"That isn't up to me," Cooper said. "Ask your daughter."

"Wait. What?" Haleigh said, turning in her chair. "Who said anything about putting this in the paper?" Making this news public had never been discussed. This had been about Jessi finding her father, not ruining a man's life.

"I'm a public figure," the mayor stated. "This is proof of infidelity on my part. Bigger politicians have been brought down by less."

Cooper stepped forward to lean on the back of Haleigh's chair. "Jessi, what do you want to come out of this?"

Looking as if she'd been handed a weight too heavy for her to carry, she said, "I don't want to bring down anyone. I just wanted to meet my father."

"And you've met him," Cooper continued. "Do you want to have a relationship with him? If you spend time together, people will wonder how you know each other. This is a small town and secrets aren't easy to keep."

Turning to the man behind the desk, Jessi said, "Do you want to get to know me and Emma?"

Hesitant, Jebediah said, "Emma?"

"She's my little girl. I only had her a month ago."

Face lighting up like an airport runway, he said, "I have a granddaughter?"

Jessi nodded.

"Yes. I would definitely like to meet her."

Whoever Jebediah Winkle pretended to be outside this office, Haleigh knew in that moment that, in the end, he was a man with a heart. A heart much bigger than anyone would have guessed.

"I don't see any reason to get the newspapers involved," Jessi said to Cooper. "We'll figure something out." Looking back to her father, she said, "But what about your wife? What will she say?"

"Let me worry about that." Jebediah stood and rounded the desk. "I'll need a couple days to straighten things out, but if you'll let me know where I can find you, I'll be in touch." With the beginnings of a smile, he added, "I'd very much like to meet my granddaughter."

After jotting Abby's phone number on a sheet of notepaper, Jessi said, "Can I hug you before I leave?"

Tears sprang to Haleigh's eyes as father and daughter touched for the first time. As she dabbed at her cheeks, Cooper whispered, "I did not see that coming," drawing a laugh of relief and total agreement.

When the three of them were back in Cooper's truck, Jessi said, "Holy cheese balls. I have a dad."

And for the second time in a matter of days, Haleigh marveled at the unexpected turns life could take. No matter what happened next, she would never again doubt the power of love.

If she didn't have a heart attack before they reached the front door, Haleigh might actually survive the night.

"Aren't you going to ring the bell?" Cooper asked as she reached for the doorknob.

"That would be mistake number one," she answered. "Trust me, I've learned the hard way."

This would be their first family dinner as a couple. She'd offered Cooper several chances to back out, but the poor sap had refused, insisting on stepping into the fray beside her. Such a valiant knight. Stubborn and naive, but valiant.

As they stepped into the foyer, familiar childhood smells assailed her. Lasagna. As in, the one dish her mother actually cooked with her own two hands.

"Mom?" she yelled toward the stairs. "We're here."

"There's no need to yell," Meredith said from the kitchen doorway. "I'm standing right here."

Haleigh blinked at the sight before her. "You're wearing an apron."

"I didn't want to get sauce on my good blouse." As if this wasn't the most uncharacteristic thing the older woman could have said, she casually turned to Cooper and asked, "Would you like a beer before dinner? I asked the young man at the grocery store for a recommendation and he insisted on an IPA, whatever that stands for. I believe it's called Cutaway, though that seems like an odd name for a beer."

Looking as dumbfounded as Haleigh felt, Cooper glanced from mother to daughter and said, "Soda is fine."

"Tell me I didn't buy this beer for nothing," Meredith said, brows riding high.

Haleigh had tried to warn him of the minefield that was dinner with Mama Mitchner.

"He'll have the beer," Haleigh answered for him, giving Cooper a *don't argue* look.

"Good." Their hostess turned on her heel and strolled back into the kitchen. "Haleigh Rae, I made you a pot of coffee."

Caught off guard by the almost genial welcome, at least by her mother's standards, Haleigh lingered in the foyer.

"Shouldn't we follow her?" Cooper whispered.

"She made me coffee," Haleigh mumbled. "She never does that."

"What are you two waiting for?" her mother asked from the stove. "We aren't eating in the front hall."

"Coming, ma'am," Cooper said, shoving Haleigh in front of him. So much for the valiant knight leading the way.

Minutes later, the three were seated in the dining room. Per the plan, Haleigh breached the subject of the shelter as soon as the meal began. Her mother rattled off several suggestions for how to proceed with the project, requiring little more than the occasional nod of agreement from her guests. When the conversation lulled, Cooper gave Haleigh a hard look, motioning for her to launch the next topic. But before she could do so, Meredith revealed yet another surprise.

"I'm selling the house."

Haleigh dropped her fork. "You're what?"

"This is my good tablecloth, Haleigh Rae. Please be more careful."

Ignoring the admonition, Haleigh held her breath, certain she'd heard her mother wrong. "Did you say you're selling the house?"

"Yes. I talked to Ryland and he suggested I downsize. This house is really too much for just me. And it's a bear to keep clean."

Pointing out that she'd made these same arguments countless times would serve no purpose, but Haleigh nearly exploded with the need to scream into the wind. Meredith continued, oblivious to the frustration churning through her daughter.

"I talked to Ronnie Ottwell and he's showing me two options tomorrow. Fortunately, this house is nearly paid off, so I should make enough in the sale to put a large down payment on a smaller place and still have money in the bank to live on until I start earning a salary from the shelter."

Haleigh's brain struggled to process the unspoken implication in her mother's revelation. It sounded as if her mother intended to support herself going forward, but one could never make an assumption with Meredith. Haleigh needed clarification.

"When you say money to live on, do you mean you intend to support yourself? Fully? Without outside help?"

"I'm perfectly capable of taking care of myself," her mother replied, as if Haleigh's question were insulting. As if she hadn't spent years insisting quite the opposite. "Now, who wants dessert? I made Grandma

Mitchner's pecan pie today. Cooper, I'm counting on you to eat at least half of it."

Without awaiting an answer from either guest, her mother disappeared into the kitchen.

Haleigh stared at her water glass, certain she would wake any minute from whatever crazy dream she was having.

"I think she's really sorry," Cooper said.

"That's generous," Haleigh replied. "I think she's insane."

"Whatever she is, your problem is solved. And without the ugly scene you've been dreading."

This was true, but she knew her mother too well. The house wouldn't sell tomorrow. Meredith would require funds until it did. The truth of the matter sunk in.

"She's taking money from Ryland."

"She's what?" Cooper asked. "Didn't you hear what your mother said? She can take care of herself."

"No." Haleigh shook her head. "She's replacing my money with Ryland's. I'm sure of it."

"Then that's Ryland's problem." Rubbing his stomach, he said, "I'm not sure I can eat half a pie after two helpings of lasagna."

How could Cooper think about pie at a time like this? "Would you focus? What are we going to do?"

"Haleigh Rae, your brother is a grown man. If he wants to give your mother money, that's up to him. And you don't even know for sure if he is." Checking the doorway, he lowered his voice. "As far as I can tell, your mom is making amends. She cooked this meal. She hasn't insulted your outfit. And she's giving you your life back. This is a good thing."

Cooper had a point. A gracious apology wasn't Meredith's style, but neither was baking pies. Yet in she walked accompanied by the smell of fresh pecan pie. Being single and in the military meant Ryland didn't have many expenses and could likely afford to send money home. Who was Haleigh to interfere? Her baby brother wasn't a baby anymore.

Determined to let her misgivings go, Haleigh enjoyed the rest of the meal, watching her mother guilt Cooper into one more piece of pie, and then marveling in wonder as the man she loved drew relaxed laughter from a woman who rarely smiled.

As they drove home, Haleigh held two large containers of leftovers on her lap and clung to Cooper's hand. "You pulled off a miracle tonight," she said. "I hope you realize that."

"I didn't do anything," he answered, as she knew he would.

Instead of arguing the point, she laid her head on his shoulder and smiled. "I love you, Cooper. More than I can ever say."

Putting his arm around her shoulders, Cooper pulled her in close. "Then you'll just have to show me," he said, kissing the top of her head. "Every day for the rest of our lives."

Turning to see his happy grin, she said, "I like the sound of that."

"Good." He squeezed her tight. "Because I plan to do the same."

How had she ever gotten so lucky?

With a full heart and contented sigh, Haleigh cuddled against Cooper's side while giving thanks that the one and only man for her, the one who had been right there all those years, had loved her enough to wait.

About the Author

Photo © 2012 Crystal Huffman

Born in the Ohio Valley, Amazon and *Wall Street Journal* bestselling author Terri Osburn spent her childhood between the covers of her favorite books. Her love of the romance genre began in her teens and never faded. Just five years after she penned her first romance novel, she was named a 2012 finalist for Romance Writers of America's Golden Heart Award for *Meant to Be*, which went on to become her debut release. She resides in Virginia with her tolerant teenager, pampered pets, and beloved books.